SPICE & WOLF

VOL. 1

BY ISUNA HASEKURA
ILLUSTRATED BY JYUU AYAKURA

"Mm. 'Tis a good moon.
Have you any wine?"
— The God of the Harvest,
    Holo the Wolf

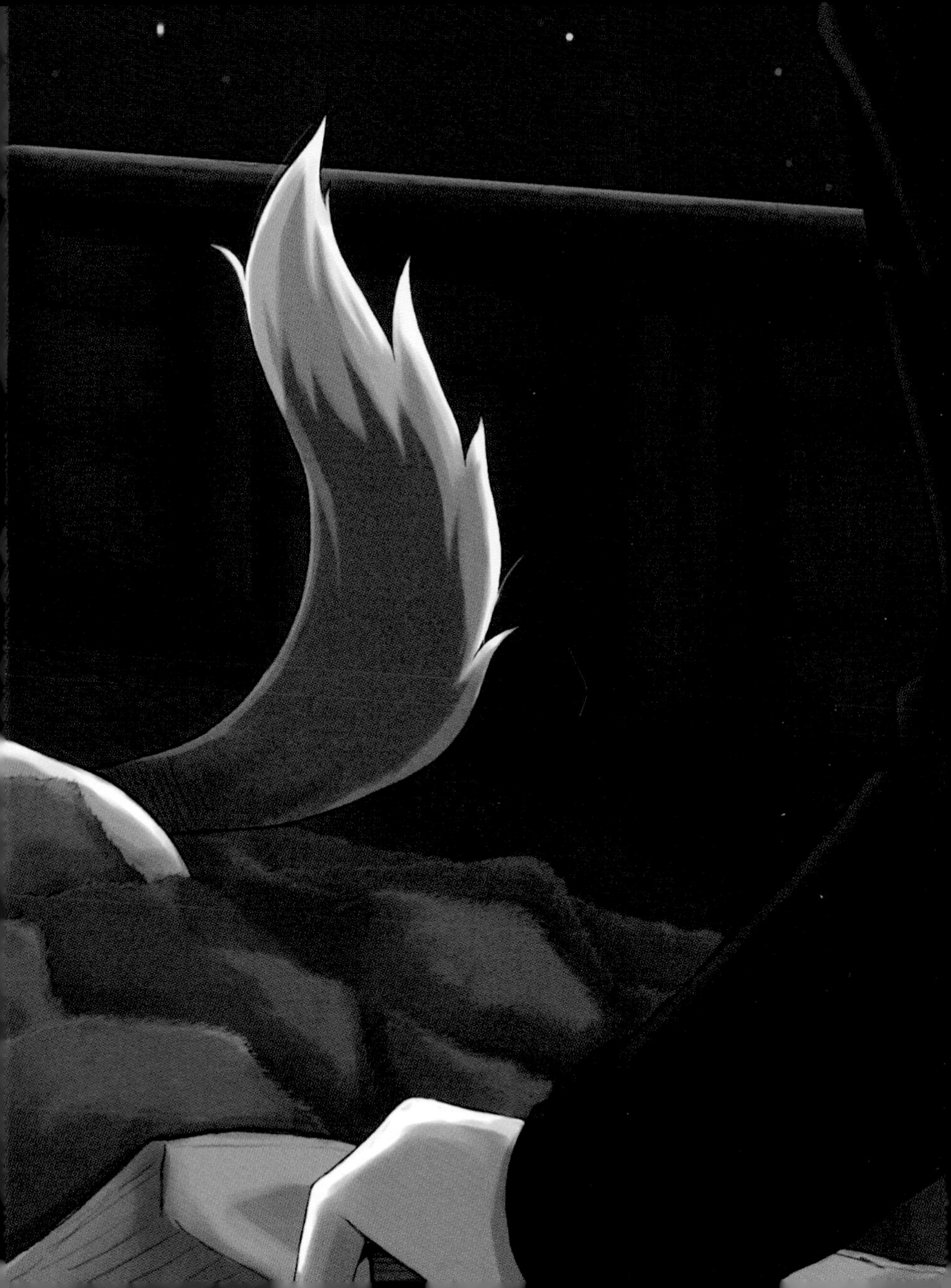

— LAWRENCE, THE TRAVELING MERCHANT

"HEH-HEH, YOU'RE QUITE SOMETHING!"
— ZHEREN, THE MYSTERIOUS MERCHANT

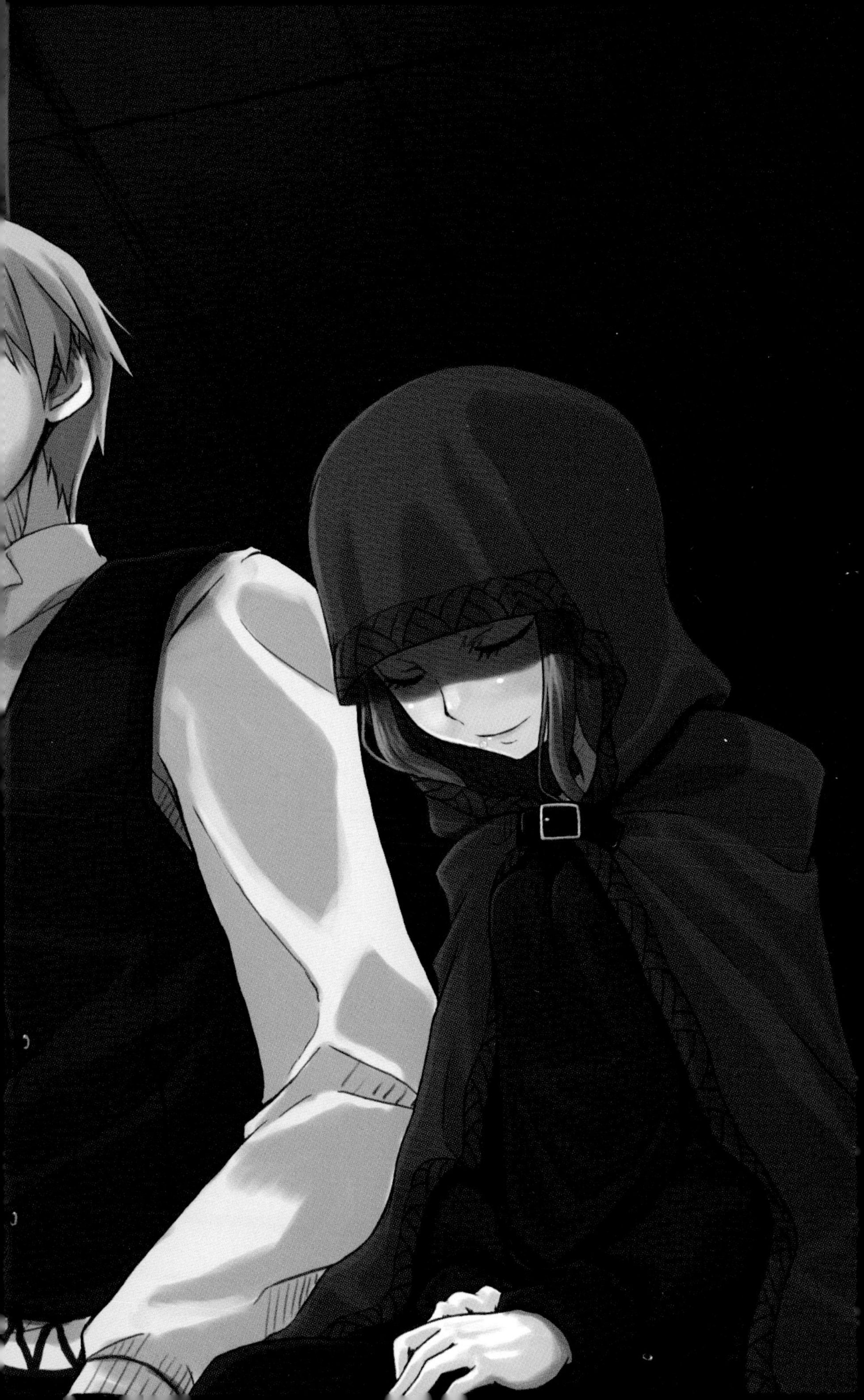

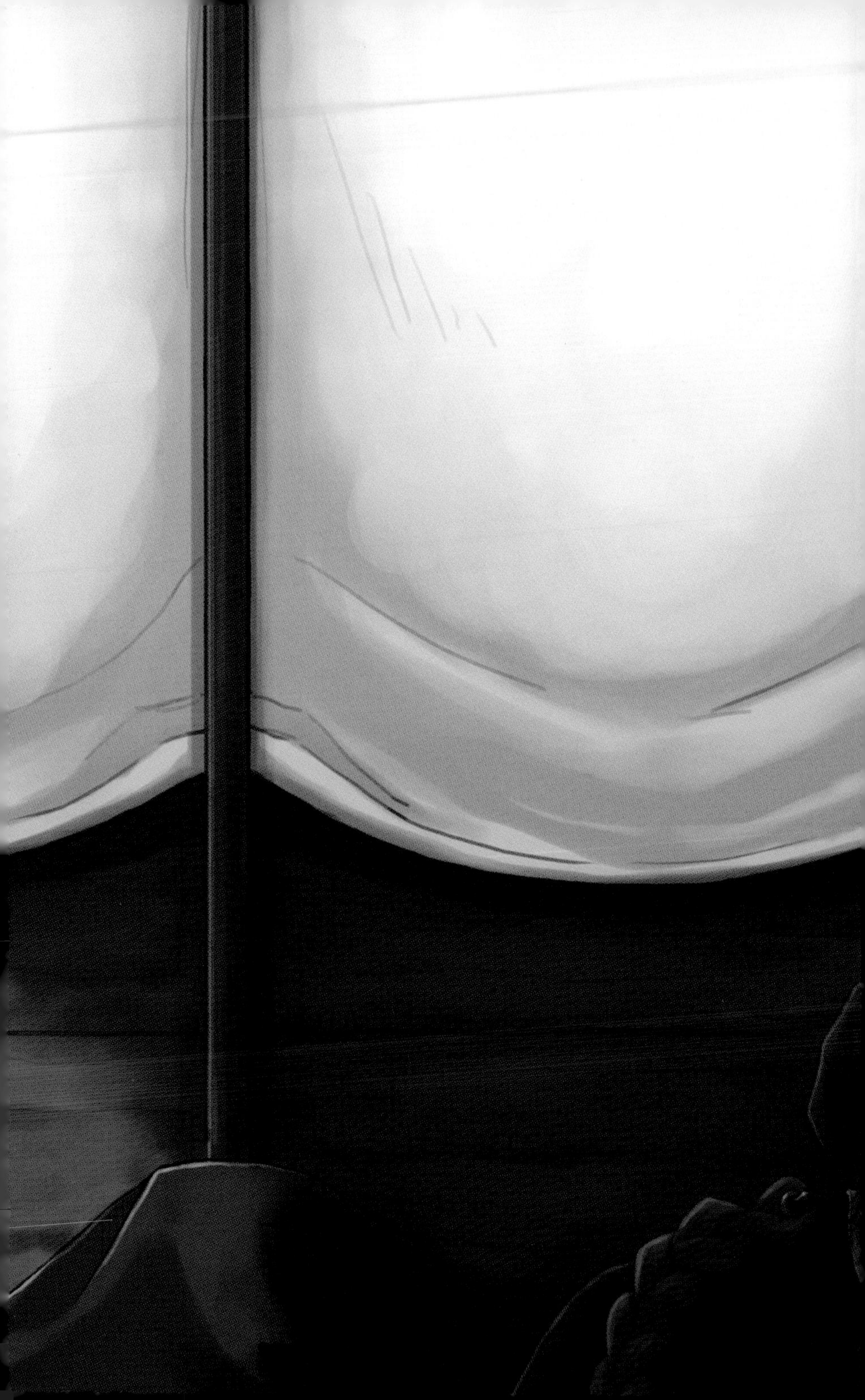

"I'M GLAD YOU'RE ALL RIGHT."
"SO LONG AS YOU CARRY THAT
WHEAT WITH YOU, I'LL NOT DIE."

Contents

SPICE & WOLF

ISUNA HASEKURA

Yen Press

NEW YORK

SPICE AND WOLF, Volume 1
ISUNA HASEKURA

Translation: Paul Starr

OOKAMI TO KOUSHINRYO © Isuna Hasekura / ASCII
MEDIA WORKS Inc. 2006. All rights reserved. First pub-
lished in Japan in 2006 by MEDIA WORKS INC., Tokyo.
English translation rights in USA, Canada, and UK arranged
with ASCII MEDIA WORKS INC. through Tuttle-Mori
Agency, Inc., Tokyo.

English translation © 2009 by Hachette Book Group, Inc.

The characters and events in this book are fictitious. Any
similarity to real persons, living or dead, is coincidental and
not intended by the author.

Jacket & Book Design by Kirk Benshoff

Yen Press
Hachette Book Group
237 Park Avenue, New York, NY 10017

Visit our websites at www.HachetteBookGroup.com and
www.YenPress.com.

Yen Press is an imprint of Hachette Book Group, Inc.
The Yen Press name and logo are trademarks of Hachette
Book Group, Inc.

First Yen Press Edition: December 2009

ISBN: 978-0-7595-3104-8

10 9 8 7 6 5 4 3 2

RRD-C

Printed in the United States of America

SPICE & WOLF

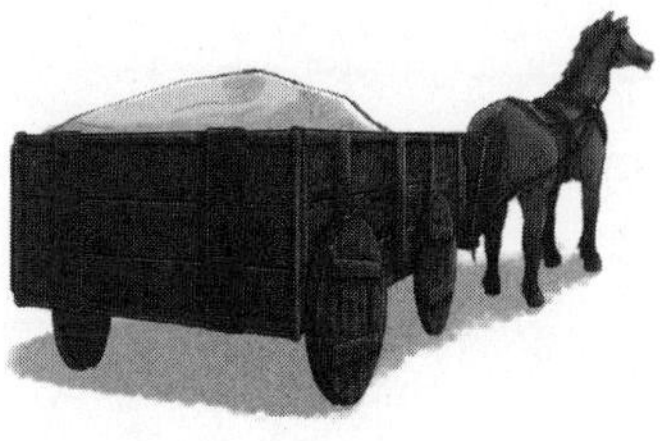

PROLOGUE

In this village, when the ripened ears of wheat sway in the breeze, it is said that a wolf runs through them.

This is because one can make out the form of a running wolf in the shifting stalks of the wheat fields.

When the wind is too strong and the stalks are blown over, it is said that the wolf has trampled them. When the harvest is poor, it is said that the wolf has eaten it.

It was a nice turn of phrase, but it had a troublesome aspect that flawed it, she felt.

Still, lately it was a popular sort of expression, and there were few remaining who wielded it with the sort of familiarity or awe it had held in the past.

Although the autumn sky that was visible between the swaying stalks of wheat had not changed in hundreds of years, conditions below that sky had indeed changed.

The villagers who tended the wheat as the years passed lived for seventy years at the most.

Perhaps it would be worse for them to go centuries without changing.

Maybe that is why there is no need for them to honor the ancient agreement, *she thought.*

In any case, she knew she no longer had a place here.

The mountains that rose in the east caused the clouds over the village to drift mostly north.

She thought of her homeland beyond those drifting clouds and sighed.

Returning her gaze from the sky to the fields, her eyes fell upon her magnificent tail, which twitched just past her nose.

With nothing better to do, she set to grooming it.

The autumn sky was high and clear.

Harvest time had come again.

Many wolves were running through the wheat fields.

CHAPTER ONE

"So that's the last, then?"

"Hm, looks like . . . seventy pelts, on the nose. Always a pleasure."

"Hey, anytime. You're the only one who'll come this far into the mountains, Lawrence. I should be thanking *you*."

"Ah, but for my trouble I get truly fine pelts. I'll come again."

The usual pleasantries concluded, Lawrence managed to leave the village just around five o'clock. The sun was just beginning its climb when he left, and it was midday by the time he descended from the mountains and entered the plains.

The weather was good; there was no wind. It was a perfect day for dozing in the wagon as he crossed the plains. It seemed absurd that only recently he had felt the chill of the approaching winter.

This was Lawrence's seventh year as a traveling merchant, and his twenty-fifth since birth. He gave a huge yawn in the driver's box.

There were few grasses or trees of any notable height, so he had an expansive view. At the very edge of his field of vision, he could see a monastery that had been built some years earlier.

He didn't know what young noble was cloistered in this remote location. The masonry of the building was magnificent, and unbelievably it even had an iron gate. Lawrence seemed to remember that roughly twenty monks lived there, attended to by a similar number of manservants.

When the monastery had first been built, Lawrence had anticipated fresh clientele; the monks were somehow able to secure supplies without employing independent merchants, though, so his dreams were fleeting.

Admittedly the monks lived simply, tilling their fields, so trade with them would not be especially profitable. There was another problem in that they would probably solicit donations and leave their bills unpaid.

As far as simple trade went, they were worse partners than out-and-out thieves. Still, there were times when trade with them was convenient.

Thus Lawrence looked in the direction of the monastery with some small regret, but then his eyes narrowed.

From the direction of the monastery, someone was waving at him.

"What's this?"

The figure did not look like a manservant. They wore dark brown work clothes. The waving figure was covered in gray clothing. His deliberate approach likely meant some hassle, but ignoring him could make matters worse later. Lawrence reluctantly turned his horse toward the figure.

Perhaps having realized that Lawrence was now headed his way, the figure stopped waving but made no move to approach. He appeared to be waiting for the cart's arrival. It would hardly be the first time that a Church-associated person demonstrated arrogance. Lawrence was in no mood to take every such insult personally.

As he approached the monastery and the figure became clearer, Lawrence muttered in spite of himself:

". . . a knight?"

He at first dismissed the idea as ridiculous, but as he drew nearer he saw that it was unmistakably a knight. The gray clothing was in fact silver armor.

"You, there! What's your business here?"

The distance between them was still too far for conversation, which is why the knight yelled. He apparently felt no need to introduce himself, as if his position were obvious.

"I am Lawrence, a traveling merchant. Do you require my service?"

The monastery was now directly in front of him. He was close enough to count the number of servants working in the fields to the south.

He also noted that the knight in front of him was not alone. There was another one past the monastery, perhaps standing guard.

"A merchant? There's no town in the direction you came from, merchant," said the knight haughtily, sticking out his chest as if to display the golden cross that was engraved there.

But the mantle draped over his shoulders was gray, indicating a knight of low rank. His blond hair looked freshly cut, and his body did not look as if it had been though many battles; so his pride most likely came from being a new knight. It was important to deal with such men carefully. They tended to be excitable.

So instead of replying, Lawrence took a leather pouch out of his breast pocket and slowly undid the twine that held it closed. Inside were candies made of crystallized honey. He plucked one out and popped it in his mouth, then offered the open bag to the knight.

"Care for one?"

"Mmm," said the knight, hesitating momentarily before his desire for the sweet candy won out.

Still, perhaps because of his position as a knight, a considerable amount of time passed between his initial nod and when he actually reached out and took a honey drop.

"A half-day's travel east of here there's a small village in the mountains. I was trading salt there."

"Ah. I see you've a load in your cart. Salt as well?"

"No, but furs. Look," said Lawrence, turning around and removing the tarp that covered his load, revealing a bundle of magnificent marten pelts. A year's salary of the knight before him was paltry compared with its worth.

"Mm. And this?"

"Ah, this is wheat I received from the village."

The sheaf of wheat in the corner of the mountain of furs had been harvested in the village where Lawrence had traded his salt. It was hardy in cold weather and resisted insects. He planned to sell it in the northwest, where crops had sustained heavy frost damage.

"Hm. Very well. You may pass."

It was a strange way of speaking for someone who'd summoned him over so high-handedly earlier, but if Lawrence were to meekly say, "Yes, sir," now, a fine merchant he'd be.

"So, what occasions your post here, sir knight?"

The knight's brow knitted in consternation at the question and furrowed still deeper as he glanced at the bag of honey drops.

He was well and truly caught now. Lawrence undid the bag's string closure and plucked out another sweet, giving it to the knight.

"Mmm. Delicious. I should thank you."

The knight was being reasonable. Lawrence inclined his head gratefully, using his best trader's smile.

"The monks have caught wind of a big pagan festival that's approaching. Thus the increased guard. Do you know anything of this festival?"

If his face had betrayed any hint of his disappointment at the explanation, calling it a third-rate performance would have been generous. So Lawrence only affected a pained expression and answered, "Sadly, I know nothing." This was of course a huge lie, but the knight was just as mistaken, so there was nothing for it.

"Perhaps it truly is being held in secret, then. Pagans are a cowardly lot, after all." The knight was so mistaken it was amusing, but Lawrence merely agreed and took his leave.

The knight nodded and thanked him again for the honey drops.

Undoubtedly they had been delicious. Most of a knight's money went to equipment and lodging; even an apprentice cobbler lived a better life. It had surely been a long time since the knight had eaten anything sweet.

Not that Lawrence had any intention of giving him another piece.

"Still, a pagan festival, they say?" Lawrence repeated the knight's words to himself once the monastery was well behind him.

Lawrence had an inkling of what the knight was talking about. Actually, anyone from this area would know about it.

But it was no "pagan festival." For one thing, true pagans were farther north, or farther east.

The festival that happened here was hardly something one needed knights to guard against.

It was a simple harvest festival, of the sort to be found nearly anywhere.

True, this area's festival was somewhat grander than the typical celebration, which is probably why the monastery was keeping an eye on it and reporting to the city. The Church had long been unable to keep control over the area, which undoubtedly made it all the more nervous about goings-on.

Indeed, the Church had been eager to hold inquisitions and convert heathens, and clashes between natural philosophers and theologians in the city were far from rare. The time when the Church could command the populace's unconditional submission was vanishing.

The dignity of the institution was beginning to crumble — even if the inhabitants of the cities said nothing, all were gradually beginning to realize it. In fact, the pope had recently had to petition the monarchs of several nations for funds when tithes had come in below expectations. Such a tale would have been preposterous even ten years before.

Thus the Church was desperate to regain its authority.

"Business everywhere will suffer," said Lawrence with a rueful smile, popping another honey drop into his mouth.

The western skies were a more beautiful golden hue than the wheat in the fields by the time Lawrence arrived in the plains. Distant birds became tiny shadows as they hurried home, and here and there the frogs sang themselves to sleep.

It appeared that the wheat fields had been mostly harvested, so the festival would undoubtedly begin soon — perhaps even as soon as the day after tomorrow.

Before Lawrence lay the expanses of the village of Pasloe's fertile wheat fields. The more abundant the harvest, the more prosperous the villagers. Furthermore, the noble who managed the land, one Count Ehrendott, was a famous area eccentric who enjoyed working in the fields himself. Naturally the festival also enjoyed his support, and every year it was a riot of wine and song.

Lawrence had not once participated in it, though. Unfortunately, outsiders were not permitted.

"Ho there, good work!" Lawrence called out to a farmer driving a cart heaped high with wheat in the corner of one of the fields. It was well-ripened wheat. Those who had invested in wheat futures could breath a sigh of relief.

"What's that?"

"Might you tell me where to find Yarei?" Lawrence asked.

"Oh, Yarei'll be over yonder — see where the crowd is gathering? That field. It's all youngsters at his place this year. Whoever's slowest will wind up being the Holo!" said the farmer good-naturedly, his tan face smiling. It was the kind of guileless smile a merchant could never manage.

Lawrence thanked the farmer with his best trader's smile, and turned his horse toward Yarei's place.

Just as the farmer had said, there was a crowd gathering within its confines, and they were shouting something. They seemed to be making sport of the few who were still working the field, but it wasn't ridicule at their lateness. The jeering was part of the festival.

As Lawrence lazily approached the crowd, he was able to make out their shouting.

"There's a wolf! A wolf!"

"A wolf lies there!"

"Who will be the last and catch the wolf? Who, who, who?" the villagers shouted, their faces so cheerful one wondered if they were drunk. None of them noticed Lawrence pulling his cart up behind the crowd.

What they so enthusiastically called a wolf was in fact not a wolf at all. Had it been real, no one would have been laughing.

The wolf was the harvest god, and according to village legend, it resided within the last stalk of wheat to be reaped. Whoever cut that stalk down would be possessed by the wolf, it was said.

"It's the last bundle!"

"Mind you, don't cut too far!"

"Holo flees from the greedy hand!"

"Who, who, who will catch the wolf?"

"It's Yarei! Yarei, Yarei, Yarei!"

Lawrence got off his wagon and peered at the crowd just as Yarei caught the last bundle of wheat. His face was black with sweat and soil as he grinned and hefted the wheat high, threw his head back, and howled.

"Awooooooo!"

"It's Holo! Holo, Holo, Holo!"

"Awooooooo!"

"Holo the wolf is here! Holo the wolf is here!"

"Catch it, now! Catch it quick!"

"Don't let it escape!"

The shouting men suddenly gave chase after Yarei.

The god of the bountiful harvest, once cornered, would possess a human and try to escape. Capture it and it would remain for another year.

None knew if this god truly existed. But this was an old tradition in the area.

Lawrence had traveled far and wide, so he put no stock in the teachings of the Church, but his faith in superstition was greater even than that of the farmers here. Too many times had he crossed mountains only to arrive in towns and find the price of his goods dropping precipitously. It was enough to make anyone superstitious.

Thus he didn't bat an eye at traditions that true believers or Church officials would've found outrageous.

But it was inconvenient that Yarei was this year's Holo. Now Yarei would be locked in a granary stocked with treats until the festival was over — close to a week — and would be impossible to talk to.

"Nothing for it, I suppose . . ." said Lawrence, sighing as he returned to his wagon and made for the village head's residence.

He had wanted to enjoy some drinks with Yarei and report on the events at the monastery, but if he didn't sell the furs that were piled high in his wagon bed, he wouldn't be able to pay for goods purchased elsewhere when the bills came due. He also wanted to sell the wheat he'd brought from the other village and couldn't wait around for the festival to end.

Lawrence talked briefly of the midday happenings at the monastery to the village head, who was busy with festival preparation. He politely declined the offer to stay the night and put the village behind him.

Years before the Count began to manage the region, it had suffered under heavy taxes that drove up the prices of its exports. Lawrence had bought some of this unfavorably priced wheat and sold it for but a meager profit. He hadn't done it to win favor with the village, but rather because he simply didn't have the resources to compete with the other merchants for the cheaper, finer grain. Nevertheless, the village was still grateful for his business then, and Yarei had been the middleman for the deal.

It was unfortunate that he couldn't enjoy a drink with Yarei, but once Holo appeared Lawrence would soon be chased out of the village as the festival came to its climax. If he'd stayed the night, he wouldn't have been able to stay long. As he sat on his wagon, Lawrence felt a sense of loneliness at being excluded thus.

Nibbling on some vegetables he'd been given as a souvenir, he took the road west, passing cheerful farmers returning from their day's work.

Having returned to his lonely travel, Lawrence envied the farmers with their friends.

*   *   *

Lawrence was a traveling merchant and twenty-five years old. At twelve he'd apprenticed under a relative, and at eighteen he set out on his own. There were many places he had yet to visit, and he felt that the true test of his mettle as a trader was yet to come.

Like any number of traveling merchants, his dream was to save enough money to open a shop in a town, but the dream still seemed distant. If he could seize upon a good opportunity it might not be so, but unfortunately the larger traders seized such opportunities with their money.

Nevertheless, he hauled loads of goods across the countryside in order to pay his debts in a timely fashion. Even if he saw a good opportunity, he lacked the wherewithal to seize it. To a traveling merchant, such a thing was as unreachable as the moon in the sky.

Lawrence looked up at the moon and sighed. He realized such sighs were more frequent lately, whether as a reaction to years of frantic trading simply to make ends meet, or because recently he'd gotten slightly ahead and was thinking more about the future.

Additionally, when he should have been thinking about little else besides creditors, payment deadlines, and getting to the next town as quickly as possible, thoughts chased one another through his head.

Specifically, he thought of the people he'd met in his travels.

He thought of the merchants he had come to know when visiting a town repeatedly on business and the villagers he had become acquainted with at his destinations. The maidservant he'd fallen for during a long stay at an inn, waiting for a blizzard to pass. And on and on.

In short, he longed for company more and more frequently.

Such longing was an occupational hazard for merchants who spent the better part of a year alone in a wagon, but Lawrence had only recently begun to feel it. Until now, he'd always boasted that it would never happen to him.

Still, having spent so many days alone with a horse, he started to feel that it would be nice if the horse could speak.

Stories of carthorses becoming human were not uncommon among traveling merchants, and Lawrence had since the beginning laughed off such yarns as ridiculous, but lately he wondered if they could be true.

When a young merchant went to buy a horse from a horse trader, some would even recommend a mare with a completely straight face, "just in case she turns human on you."

This had happened to Lawrence, who'd ignored the advice and bought a sturdy stallion.

That same horse was working steadily in front of him even now, but as time passed and Lawrence grew lonely, he wondered if he mightn't have been better off with a mare after all.

On the other hand, that horse hauled heavy loads day in and day out. Even if it were to become a human, it seemed impossible that it would fall in love with its master or use its mysterious powers to bring them good fortune.

It would probably want to be paid and given rest, Lawrence mused.

As soon as this occurred to him, he felt that it was best if a horse stayed a horse, even if it did make him selfish. Lawrence smiled bitterly and sighed as if tired of himself.

Presently he came to a river and decided to make camp for the night. The full moon was bright, but that did not guarantee that he wouldn't fall into the river — and if that happened, calling it a "disaster" would be an understatement. He'd have to hang himself. *That* kind of trouble he didn't need.

Lawrence pulled back on the reins, and the horse stopped at the signal, heaving two or three sighs as it realized its long-anticipated rest was here.

Giving the rest of his vegetables to the horse, Lawrence took a bucket out of the wagon bed and drew some water from the river, setting it before the animal. As it happily slurped at the bucket, Lawrence drank some of the water he'd gotten from the village.

Wine would've been nicer, but drinking without a partner only made the loneliness worse. There was no guarantee he wouldn't get staggering drunk, either, so Lawrence decided to go to bed.

He'd halfheartedly nibbled on vegetables most of the way, so he had only a bit of beef before hopping back in the wagon bed. Normally he slept in the hempen tarp that covered the bed, but tonight he had a wagonload of marten pelts, so it would be a waste not to sleep in them. They might make him smell a bit beastly in the morning, but it was better than freezing.

But jumping right into the pelts would crush the wheat sheaf, so in order to move them aside, he whisked the tarp off the wagon bed.

The only reason he didn't shout was because the sight that greeted him was flatly unbelievable.

"..."

Apparently, he had a guest.

"Hey."

Lawrence wasn't sure his voice actually made a sound. He was shocked and wondered if the loneliness had finally broken him and he was hallucinating.

But after he shook his head and rubbed his eyes, his guest had not disappeared.

The beautiful girl was sleeping so soundly it seemed a shame to wake her.

"Hey, you there," said Lawrence nonetheless, returning to his senses. He meant to inquire what exactly would motivate someone to sleep in a wagon bed. In the worse case, it might be a village runaway. He didn't want that kind of trouble.

"... hrm?" came the girl's defenseless response to Lawrence, her eyes still closed, her voice so sweet that it would make a poor traveling merchant — accustomed only to the brothels of the cities — lightheaded.

She had a terrifying allure despite her obvious youth, nestled there in the furs and illuminated by the moonlight.

Lawrence gulped once before returning to reason.

Given that she was so beautiful, if she was a prostitute, there was no telling how much he could be taken for if he was to so much as touch her. Considering the economics of the situation was a tonic far more effective than any prayer. Lawrence regained his composure and raised his voice once again.

"Hey, you there. What are you playing at, sleeping in someone's cart?"

The girl did not awaken.

Fed up with this girl who slept so obstinately, Lawrence grabbed the pelt that supported her head and jerked it out from under her. The girl's head flopped into the gap left by the pelt, and finally he heard her irritated squawk.

He was about to raise his voice at her again, but then he froze.

The girl had dog ears on her head.

"Mm . . . hah . . ."

Now that the girl seemed to be finally awake, Lawrence summoned his courage and spoke again.

"You there, what are you doing, climbing in my wagon bed?"

Lawrence had been robbed more than once by thieves and bandits as he crossed the countryside. He considered himself bolder and more courageous than the average person. He wasn't one to quail just because the girl in front of him happened to have the ears of an animal.

Despite the fact that the girl hadn't answered his questions, Lawrence did not pose them again.

This was because the girl, slowly awakening before him and entirely naked, was unspeakably beautiful.

Her hair, illuminated by the moonlight in the wagon, looked as soft as silk and fell over her shoulders like the finest cloak. The strands that fell down her neck to her collarbone drew a line so beautiful it put the finest painting of the Virgin Mary to shame; her supple arms were so fine they seemed carved from ice.

And exposed now in the middle of her body were her two small breasts, so beautiful they gave the impression of being carved from some inorganic material. They gave off a strangely vital scent, as if housed within her arresting charm was a warmth.

But such a fascinating spectacle could just as soon go awry.

The girl slowly opened her mouth and looked skyward. Closing her eyes, she howled.

"Auwoooooooooooooo!"

Lawrence felt a sudden fear — it blew through his body like a wind.

The howl was the song a wolf would use to call its comrades, to chase and corner a human.

This was no howl like Yarei had uttered earlier. It was a true howl. Lawrence dropped the bite of beef from his mouth; his horse reared, startled.

Then he realized something.

The moonlit girl's form — with the ears on her head. The ears of a beast.

". . . Hmph. 'Tis a good moon. Have you no wine?" she said, letting the howl fade away, drawing her chin up, and smiling slightly. Lawrence came back to himself at the sound of her voice.

What was before him was neither dog nor wolf. It *was* a beautiful girl with the ears of such an animal, though.

"I have none. And what *are* you? Why do you sleep in my cart? Were you to be sold in town? Did you escape?" Lawrence meant to ask as authoritatively as he could, but the girl did not so much as move.

"What, so you have no wine? Food, then . . . ? My, such waste," said the girl unconcernedly, her nose twitching. She spied the bit of beef Lawrence had almost eaten earlier, snapping it up and popping it into her mouth.

As she chewed it, Lawrence did not fail to note the two sharp fangs behind the girl's lips.

"Are you some kind of demon?" he asked, his hand falling to the dagger at his waist.

As traveling merchants often needed to convert large amounts of currency, they often carried their money in the form of items. The silver dagger was one such item, and silver was known as a holy metal, strong against evil.

However, when Lawrence put his hand to the dagger and posed his question, the girl looked blankly at him, then laughed heartily.

"Ah-ha-ha-ha! Me, a demon now?"

Her mouth thrown open wide enough to drop the piece of meat, the girl was so adorable as to be disarming.

Her two sharp fangs only added to her charm.

However, being laughed at made Lawrence angry.

"H-how is that so amusing?"

"Oh, it's amusing, it is! That is surely the first time I've been called a demon."

Still giggling to herself, the girl picked up the meat again and chewed it. She *did* have fangs. Add in her ears, and it was clear enough that she was no mere human.

"What are you?"

"Me?"

"Who but you would I be talking to?"

"The horse, say."

". . ."

When Lawrence drew his dagger, the girl's smile disappeared. Her red-tinged amber eyes narrowed.

"What are you, I say!"

"Drawing a blade on me now? How lacking in manners."

"What?!"

"Mm. Ah, I see. My escape was successful. My apologies! I had forgotten," said the girl with a smile — a completely guileless and charming smile.

The smile didn't particularly sway him, but nevertheless Lawrence somehow felt that pointing a blade at a girl was an unseemly thing for a man to do, so he put it away.

"I am called Holo. It has been some time since I've taken this form, but, well, it is quite nice."

As the girl looked herself over approvingly, Lawrence was so caught on the first half of what she'd said that he missed the second half.

"Holo?"

"Mm, Holo. A good name, no?"

Lawrence had traveled far and wide over many lands, but there was only one place where he'd heard that name.

None other than the harvest god of the village of Pasloe.

"What a coincidence. I also know of one that goes by Holo."

It was bold of her to use the name of a god, but at least this told him that she was indeed a girl from the village. Perhaps she'd been hidden, raised in secret by her family, because of her ears and fangs. That would fit with her claim to have "escaped successfully."

Lawrence had heard talk of abnormal children like this being born. They were called demon-children, and it was thought that a

22

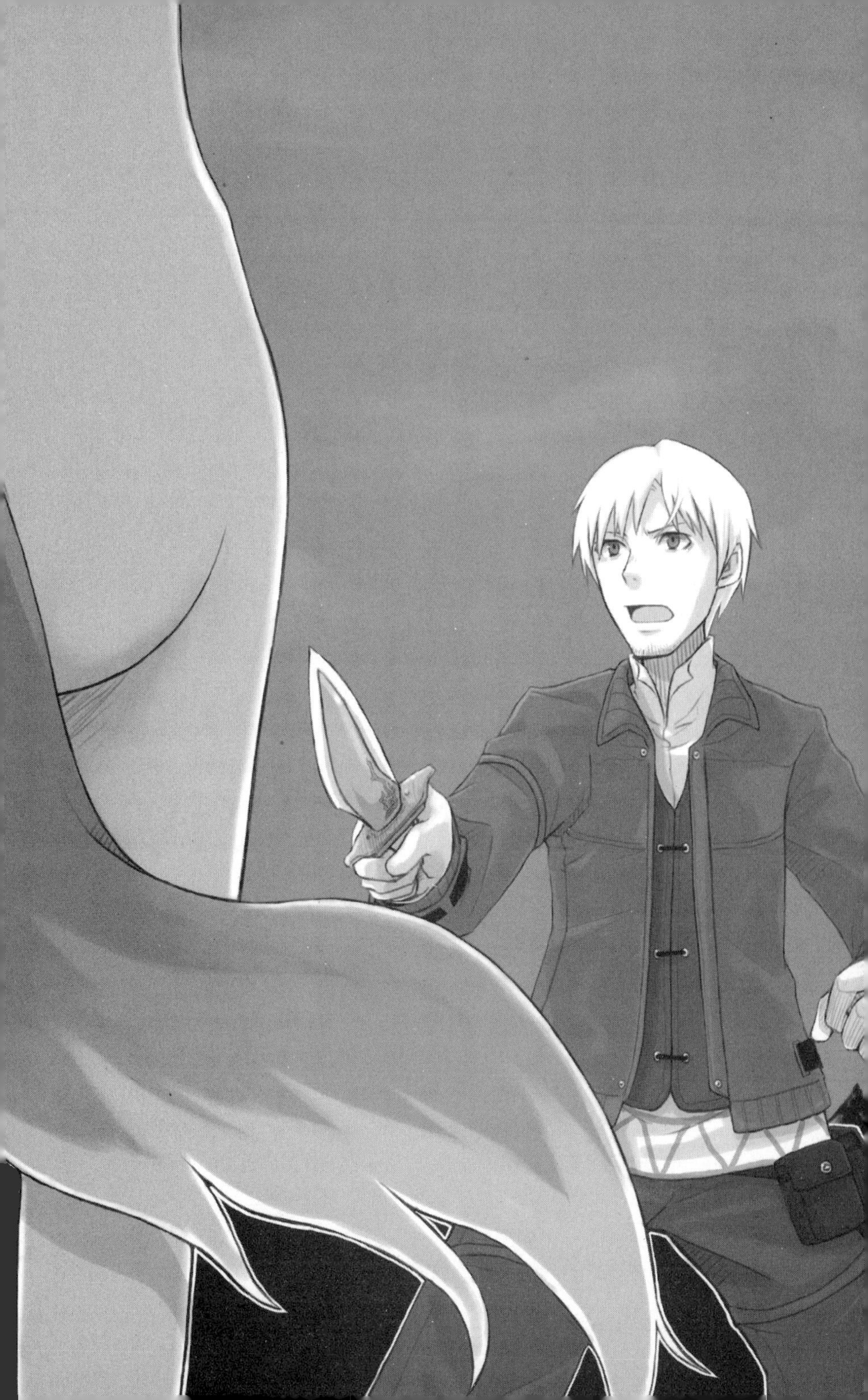

devil or spirit had possessed them at birth. If the Church discovered them they — along with their families — would be burned at the stake for demon worshipping. Such children were thus either abandoned in the mountains or raised in secret.

But this was the first time Lawrence had ever actually seen such a child. He had always assumed they would be disgustingly bestial, but judging from appearance alone, this one was a plausible goddess.

"Oh, ho, I have never met another Holo. Whence do they hail?" As the girl chewed the meat, it was hard to see her trying to deceive anyone. It seemed possible that having been raised in confinement for so long, she really did believe herself to be a god.

"It is the name of this area's harvest god. Are you a god?"

At this, the girl's moonlit face was slightly troubled for a moment before she smiled.

"I have long been bound to this place and called its god. But I am nothing so great as a deity. I am merely Holo."

Lawrence guessed that this meant she'd been locked away in her home since she was born. He felt a certain sympathy for the girl.

"By 'long,' do you mean that you were born here?"

"Oh, no."

This was an unexpected answer.

"I was born far to the north."

"The north?"

"Indeed. The summers there are short and the winters long. A world of silver."

Holo's eyes narrowed as she seemed to gaze into the distance, and it was hard to imagine that she was lying. Her behavior as she reminisced about the lands of the north was too natural to be an act.

"Have you ever been there?"

Lawrence wondered if she was counterattacking, but if Holo was lying or merely repeating things she'd heard from others, he would have been able to tell immediately.

His travels as a merchant had in fact led him to the far north before.

"I've been as far as Arohitostok. The year-round blowing snow is terrifying."

"Hm. Haven't heard of it," replied Holo, inclining her head slightly.

He'd expected her to pretend to have knowledge. This was strange.

"What places do you know?" he asked.

"A place called Yoitsu."

Lawrence forced himself to say, "Don't know it," to quell the unease that rose within him. He *did* know of a place called Yoitsu, from an old story he'd heard at an inn in the north.

"Were you born there?" he asked.

"I was. How is Yoitsu doing these days? Is everyone well?" Holo asked, slumping slightly. It was such a fleeting gesture that it couldn't be an act.

Yet Lawrence could not possibly believe her.

After all, according to the story, the town of Yoitsu had been destroyed by ursine monsters six hundred years ago.

"Do you remember any other places?"

"Mmm . . . it's been so many centuries . . . ah, Nyohhira, there was a town called Nyohhira. It was a strange town, with hot springs. I would often go to bathe in them."

There were still hot springs in the north at Nyohhira, where royalty and nobility often visited.

But how many people in this area would even know of its existence?

Ignoring Lawrence's confused reverie, Holo spoke as if she were even now relaxing in the hot water, then suddenly she sneezed.

"Mm. I do not mind taking human form, but it is unavoidably cold. Not enough fur," said Holo, laughing and hiding herself again in the pile of marten pelts.

Lawrence couldn't help laughing at her appearance. There was something that still worried him, though, so he spoke to Holo as she snuggled into the fur pile.

"You said something about changing forms earlier — what was that about?

At his question, Holo poked her head out of the pile.

"I meant just what I said. I haven't taken human form in some time. Charming, no?" she said with a smile. Lawrence couldn't help agreeing, but he kept a straight face as he replied. The girl could make him lose his composure, that was certain.

"Aside from a few extra details, you're a human. Or what else? Are you a dog turned human, like the stories of horses turning human?"

Holo stood at the slight provocation. Turning her back to him, she looked over her shoulder at him and responded steadily.

"You can doubtless tell from my ears and tail that I am a proud wolf! My fellow wolves, the animals of the forest, and the people of the village all acknowledge me. It is of the white tip of my tail that I am proudest. My ears anticipate every misfortune and hear every lie, and I have saved many friends from many dangers. When one speaks of the Wisewolf of Yoitsu, they speak of none other than me!"

Holo sniffed proudly but soon remembered the cold and dove back under the furs. The tail at the base of her back was indeed moving.

Not just ears, then — she had a tail as well.

Lawrence thought back on her howl. It was a true wolf's howl, unmistakably. Was this then truly Holo, wolf-god of the harvest?

"No, it can't be," muttered Lawrence to himself as he reconsidered Holo. She seemed unconcerned about him as she narrowed her eyes in the warm furs. Seen thus, she was rather catlike, although that was not the issue at hand. Was Holo human or wasn't she? That was the question.

People who were actually possessed by demons didn't fear the Church because their appearance was different — rather they feared it because the demon within them could cause outward calamities for which the Church made it widely known the penalty was death at the stake.

But if Holo was instead a transformed animal like in the old tales, she might bring good fortune or perform miracles.

Indeed, if she was *the* Holo, god of the harvest, a wheat trader could ask for no finer companion.

Lawrence turned his attention back to Holo.

"Holo, was it?"

"Yes?"

"You said you were a wolf."

"I did."

"But all you have are a wolf's ears and tail. If you are truly a transformed wolf, you should be able to take a wolf's form."

Holo stared absently for a while at Lawrence's words before something seemed to occur to her.

"Oh, you're telling me to show you my wolf form."

Lawrence nodded at the truth of the statement but was in fact mildly surprised.

He had expected her to either be flustered or to flatly lie.

But she had done neither, instead looking simply irritated. This expression of irritation was far more persuasive than the clumsy lie — the assurance that she *could* transform — that he expected.

"I don't want to," she said plainly.

"Why not?"

"Why do *you* want me to?" she shot back, pouting.

Lawrence winced at her retort, but the question of whether Holo was human or not was an important one to him. Recovering from his stumble, Lawrence put as much confidence as he could muster into his voice, trying to regain the conversational initiative.

"If you were a person I would consider turning you in to the Church. Demons cause calamity, after all. But if you are really Holo, god of the harvest, in human form, then I needn't turn you in."

Were she genuine, well — tales of transformed animals acting as envoys of good fortune still remained. Far from turning her in as a demon, he would happily offer her wine and bread. If not, the situation would be different.

As Lawrence spoke, Holo wrinkled her nose, and her expression grew darker and darker.

"From what I have heard, transformed animals can change to their original forms. If you are telling the truth, you should be able to do so as well, yes?"

Holo listened with the same irritated expression. At length she sighed softly and slowly extracted herself from the pile of furs.

"I have suffered many times at the hand of the Church. I'll not be given over to them. Yet —"

She sighed again, stroking her tail as she continued. "No animal can change its form without a token. Even you humans need makeup before you can change your appearance. Likewise, I require food."

"What kind of food?"

28

"Only a bit of wheat."

That seemed more or less reasonable for a god of the harvest, Lawrence had to admit, but her next statement brought him up short.

"That, or fresh blood."

"Fresh . . . blood?"

"Only a bit, though."

Her casual tone made Lawrence feel that she couldn't be lying; his breath caught, and he glanced at her mouth. Just a moment ago, he'd seen the fangs behind those lips bite into the meat he'd dropped.

"What, are you afraid?" said Holo at Lawrence's trepidation as she smiled ruefully. Lawrence would've said "Of course not," but Holo was clearly anticipating his reaction.

But soon the smile disappeared from her face, and she looked away from him. "If you are, then I'm even more disinclined to."

"Why, then?" Lawrence asked, putting more strength into his voice, feeling that he was being made sport of.

"Because you will surely quake with fear. All, be they human or animal, look on my form and give way with awe, and treat me as special. I have tired of this treatment."

"Are you saying I would be afraid of your true form?"

"If you would pretend to be strong, you might first hide your trembling hand!" Holo said, exasperated.

Lawrence looked down at his hands, but by the time he realized his mistake it was too late.

"Heh. You're an honest sort," said an amused Holo, but before Lawrence could offer an excuse, her expression darkened again and she continued, quick as an arrow. "However, just because you are honest does not mean I should show you my form. Was what you said before the truth?"

"Before?"

"That if I am truly a wolf, you would not give me over to the Church."

"Mm . . ."

Lawrence had heard that there were some demons capable of illusions, so this was not a decision he could make lightly. Holo seemed to anticipate this and spoke again.

"Well, I have a good eye for both men and beasts. You are a man who keeps his word, I can tell."

Lawrence was still unable to find his tongue at the mischievous Holo's words. He certainly could go back on his word. He was understanding more and more that she was toying with him, but there was nothing he could do about it.

"I'll show you a bit, then. A full transformation is difficult. You'll forgive me if I only do my arm," said Holo, reaching down into the corner of the wagon bed.

For a moment Lawrence thought that it was some sort of special pose she had to assume, but he soon realized what she was doing. She was picking a grain of wheat from the sheaf in the corner of the wagon.

"What are you doing with that?" asked Lawrence without thinking.

Before he could even finish the question, Holo popped the grain of wheat in her mouth and, closing her eyes, swallowed it like a pill.

The shell of the unhusked kernel was not edible. Lawrence frowned at the thought of the bitter taste in his mouth, but that thought soon vanished at the sight that came next.

"Uh, uughh . . ." Holo groaned, clutching her left arm and falling onto the pile of furs.

Lawrence was about to say something — this could not be an act — when a strange sound reached his ears.

Sh-sh-sh-sh. It was like the sound of mice running through the forest. It continued for a few moments, then ended with a muffled *thud*, like something treading on soft ground.

Lawrence was so surprised he could do nothing.

The next moment, Holo's formerly slim arm had transformed into the forepaw of some huge beast and was totally unsuited to the rest of her body.

"Mm . . . whew. It really doesn't look very good."

The limb appeared to be so large that she would have trouble supporting it. She rested the giant leg on the pile of furs and shifted herself to accommodate it.

"Well? Do you believe me now?" She looked up at Lawrence.

"Uh . . . er . . ." Lawrence was unable to reply, rubbing his eyes and shaking his head as he looked and looked again at the sight before him.

The leg was magnificent and coated in dark brown fur. Given the size of the leg, the full animal would be huge, roughly as big as a horse. The paw ended in huge, scythe-like claws.

And all that grew from the girl's slender shoulder. It would be strange to think it *wasn't* an illusion.

Unable to believe it, Lawrence finally took a skin of water and doused his face with it.

"Aren't you the doubtful one. If you still think it's an illusion, go ahead and touch it," teased Holo, smiling, curling the giant paw in a come-hither motion.

Lawrence found himself irritated, yet still he hesitated. Besides the sheer size of the limb, it also gave off a certain ineffable sense of danger.

It was the leg of a wolf. I've dealt with goods called Dragon Legs, Lawrence told himself, irritated at his cowardice. And just before his hand could touch it . . .

"Oh —" said Holo, seeming to remember something. Lawrence snapped his hand back.

"Wha —! What is it?"

"Mm, oh, nothing. Don't be so surprised!" said Holo, now sounding annoyed. Adding embarrassment to his fear, Lawrence became angrier and angrier at what he felt was his failure as a man. Getting hold of himself, he reached out once again.

"So, what happened?"

"Mm," said Holo meekly, looking up at Lawrence. "Be gentle, will you?"

Lawrence couldn't help stopping his hand short at her suddenly endearing manner.

He looked at her, and she looked back, grinning.

"You're rather charming, aren't you?" she said.

Lawrence said nothing as he made sure of what his hand was feeling.

He was irritated at her half-teasing manner, but there was another reason he failed to reply.

It was of course because of what he was touching.

The beast-leg that thrust from Holo's shoulder had bone as thick and solid as a tree's limb, wrapped in sinew that would be the envy of any soldier, and covering that, a magnificent coat of brown fur, from the base of the shoulder all the way down to the paw. Each pad of the paw was the size of an uncut loaf of bread. Past the soft pink toes was something denser — the scythes of her claws.

The leg was solid enough, but those claws were anything but illusory. In addition to the not warm, yet not cold sensation peculiar to animal claws, Lawrence felt a thrill at the sensation that these were not something that he should be touching.

He swallowed. "Are you really a god . . . ?" he murmured.

"I'm no god. As you can tell from my forepaw, I am merely

bigger than my comrades — bigger and cleverer. I am Holo the Wisewolf!"

The girl who so confidently called herself "wise" looked at Lawrence proudly.

She was every bit a mischievous young girl — but the aura that the beast-limb exuded was not something a mere animal could ever manage.

It had nothing to do with the size of the thing.

"So, what think you?"

Lawrence nodded vaguely at her question. "But . . . the real Holo should be in Yarei now. The wolf resides in the one who cuts the last wheat stalk, they say . . ."

"Heh-heh-heh. I am Holo the Wisewolf! I know well my own limitations. It is true that I live within the wheat. Without it, I cannot live. And it is also true that during this harvest I was within the last wheat to be harvested, and usually I cannot escape from there. Not while any were watching. However, there is an exception."

Lawrence listened to her explanation, impressed with her rapid delivery.

"If there is nearby a larger sheaf of wheat than the last one to be harvested, I can move unseen to that wheat. That's why they say it, you know, the villagers. 'If you cut too greedily, you won't catch the harvest god, and it will escape.'"

Lawrence glanced at his wagon bed with a sudden realization.

There was the sheaf of wheat — the wheat he'd received from the mountain village.

"So that is how it was done. I suppose one could call you my savior. If you hadn't been there, I would never have escaped."

Although Lawrence could not quite bring himself to believe those words, they were lent persuasion when Holo swallowed a few more wheat grains and returned her arm to normal.

However, Holo had said "savior" with a certain distaste, so Lawrence decided to get even with her.

"Perhaps I should take that wheat back to the village, then. They'll be in a bad way without their harvest god. I've been friends with Yarei and others in Pasloe for a long time. I'd hate to see them suffer."

He concocted the pretense on the spot, but the more he thought about it, the truer it seemed. If this Holo was the *real* Holo, then wouldn't the village begin suffering poor harvests?

After a few moments his ruminations ended.

Holo was looking at him as if stricken.

"You . . . you're jesting, surely," she said.

Her suddenly frail mien rocked the defenseless merchant.

"Hard to say," Lawrence said vaguely, trying to conceal his internal conflict and buy some time.

Even as his head filled with other concerns, his heart grew only more uneasy.

Lawrence agonized. If Holo was what she claimed to be, the god of the harvest, his best course of action would be to return her to the village. He had long associated with Pasloe. He did not wish them ill.

However, when he looked back at Holo, her earlier bravado was entirely gone — now she looked down, as apprehensive as any princess in an old knight tale.

Lawrence grimaced and put the question to himself: Should I return this girl to the village, even though she clearly does not want to go?

What if she *is* the real Holo?

He mulled the matter over in a cold sweat, the two questions battling in his mind.

Presently he became aware of someone looking at him. He

followed the look to its source and saw Holo gazing at him beseechingly.

"Please, help me . . . won't you?"

Unable to stand the sight of Holo so meekly bowing her head, Lawrence turned away. All he saw, day in and day out, was the backside of a horse. The life left him completely unable to resist a girl like Holo looking at him with such a face.

Agonizingly, he came to a decision.

He turned slowly back toward Holo and asked her a single question.

"I must ask you one thing."

". . . all right."

"If you leave the village, will they still be able to raise wheat?"

He didn't expect Holo to answer in a way that would weaken her own position, but he was a merchant. He had dealt with any number of dishonest negotiators in his time. He had confidence that if Holo attempted to lie, he would know.

Lawrence readied himself to catch the prevarication he was sure would come, but come it didn't.

When he looked at her, she wore an expression completely different from what he had seen so far; she looked angry and near tears as she stared into the corner of the wagon bed.

"Er . . . what's wrong?" Lawrence had to ask.

"The village's abundant harvests will continue without me," she spat, her voice surprisingly irate.

"Is that so?" asked Lawrence, overwhelmed by the piercing anger that emanated from Holo.

Holo nodded, squaring her shoulders. She gripped the furs tightly, her hands white from the effort.

"Long did I stay in that village; as many years as I have hairs on my tail. Eventually I wished to leave, but for the sake of the village's wheat I stayed. Long ago, you see, I made a promise with a youth of the village, that I would ensure the village's harvest. And so I kept my promise."

Perhaps because she couldn't stomach it, she did not so much as look at Lawrence as she spoke.

Earlier her wit and words had been quick and easy; now she stumbled uncertainly.

"I . . . I am the wolf that lives in the wheat. My knowledge of wheat, of things that grow in the ground, is second to none. That is why I made the village's fields so magnificent, as I promised. But to do that, occasionally the harvest must be poor. Forcing the land to produce requires compensation. But whenever the harvest was poor, the villagers attributed it to my caprices, and it has only gotten worse in recent years. I have been wanting to leave. I can stand it no longer. I long ago fulfilled my promise."

Lawrence understood Holo's anger. Some years ago, Pasloe had come under the care of Count Ehrendott, and since then new farming techniques had been imported from the south, increasing yield.

Holo thus felt that her presence was no longer necessary.

Indeed, the rumor was proliferating that not even the god of the Church existed. It was not impossible that a countryside hamlet's harvest god had gotten wrapped up in such talk.

"The village's good harvests will continue. There will be a poor yield every few years, but that will be their own doing. And they'll overcome it on their own. The land doesn't need me, and the people certainly don't need me either."

Getting her words out all in one breath, Holo sighed deeply and fell over on the pile of furs yet again. She curled up, pulling the furs around her and burying her face in them.

He could not see her face to make certain, but it seemed not impossible that she was crying. Lawrence scratched his head, unsure of what to say.

He looked helplessly at her slender shoulders and wolf ears.

Perhaps this was how a real god acted: now full of bluster and bravado, now wielding a sharp wit, now showing a childish temper.

Lawrence was at a loss at how to treat the girl now. Nevertheless, he couldn't very well remain silent, so he took a new approach.

"In any case, setting aside the question of whether or not that's all true . . ."

"You think me a liar?" snapped Holo at his preamble. He faltered, but Holo seemed to realize that she herself was being too emotional. She stopped, abashed, and muttered a quick "Sorry," before burying her head in the furs again.

"I understand your resentment. But where do you plan to go, having left the village?"

She did not answer immediately, but Lawrence saw her ears prick at his question, so he waited patiently. She had just delivered a significant confession, and Lawrence expected that she simply couldn't face anyone for a moment.

At length, Holo guiltily looked into the corner of the wagon bed, confirming Lawrence's suspicions.

"I wish to return north," she said flatly.

"North?"

Holo nodded, turning her gaze up and off into the distance. Lawrence didn't have to follow it to know where she was looking: true north.

"My birthplace. The forest of Yoitsu. So many years have passed that I can no longer count them. . . . I wish to return home."

The word birthplace left Lawrence momentarily shocked, and

he looked at Holo's profile. He himself had not visited his hometown once since embarking on the life of a wandering merchant.

It was a poor and cramped place of which he had few good memories, but after long days in the driver's seat, sometimes lonelineliness overcame him and he couldn't help thinking fondly of the place.

If Holo was telling the truth, not only had she left her home hundreds of years ago, but she'd endured neglect and ridicule at the place in which she'd settled. . . .

He could guess at her loneliness.

"But I'd like to travel a bit. I've come all the way to this distant place, after all. And surely much has changed over the months and years, so it would be good to broaden my perspective," said Holo, looking at Lawrence, her face a picture of calm. "So long as you'll not take me back to Pasloe or turn me in to the Church, I'd like to travel with you. You're a wandering merchant, are you not?"

She regarded Lawrence with a friendly smile that suggested she'd seen right through him and knew he would not betray her. She sounded like an old friend asking a simple favor.

Lawrence had yet to determine whether or not he believed Holo's story, but as far as he *could* tell, she was not a bad sort. And he'd begun to enjoy conversing with this strange girl.

But he wasn't so won over by her charm as to forget his merchant's instincts. A good merchant had the audacity to face a god and the caution to doubt a close relative.

Lawrence thought it over, then spoke quietly.

"I cannot make this decision quickly."

He expected complaint but had underestimated Holo. She nodded in comprehension. "It is good to be cautious. But I never misread a person. I don't believe you're so cold as to turn someone away."

Holo spoke with a mischievous smile playing across her lips. She then turned and hopped back into the pile of furs, albeit without the sulkiness she'd shown before. It seemed as though she was saying, "Enough talk for today."

As she'd derailed of the conversation yet again, Lawrence could only grin in spite of himself as he watched Holo.

He thought he could see her ears moving, then her head popped out and she looked at him.

"Surely you'll not tell me to sleep outside," she said, obviously aware that he could do no such thing. Lawrence shrugged; Holo giggled and returned to the fur pile.

Seeing her like this, Lawrence wondered if her actions earlier were something of an act, as if she were trying to play the part of the imprisoned princess.

Nevertheless, he doubted that her dissatisfaction with the village or her desire to return home were lies.

And if those weren't lies, then he must believe that she was the real Holo, because a mere demon-possessed girl would not be able to make it all up. Lawrence sighed as he realized that more thought would not yield any new answers; he decided to go to sleep and leave further ruminations for the morrow.

The furs that Holo slept in belonged to Lawrence. It was ludicrous to think that their owner would forgo their comfort and sleep on the wagon's driving bench. Telling her to move over to one side, he, too, snuggled into the fur pile.

From behind him, he heard the quiet sounds of Holo's breathing. Although he'd told her he couldn't make a quick decision, Lawrence had already decided that as long as Holo had not made off with his goods in the morning, he would travel with her.

He doubted that she was that sort of troublemaker — but if she was, he thought, she would surely make off with his entire load.

He looked forward to the next day.

After all, it had been a long time since he'd slept beside another. It was impossible to be unhappy with her slightly sweet scent piercing the strong-smelling furs.

The horse heaved a sigh, as if reading Lawrence's simple thought.

Perhaps horses really could understand humans and simply preferred not to speak.

Lawrence grinned ruefully and closed his eyes.

Lawrence rose early the next morning. He was like most merchants who awoke early in order to extract the most profit from the day. However, when he opened his eyes to the morning mist, Holo was already up, sitting next to him, and rummaging through something. For an instant Lawrence wondered if his estimation of her had been wrong, but if so, she was truly audacious. He raised his head and looked over his shoulder, and it appeared she had gone looking for clothes among his things and was just now tying her shoes.

"Hey, now! Those are mine!"

Even if it wasn't actual theft, even a god shouldn't be rummaging around through other people's things.

Holo turned around at Lawrence's rebuke, but there was not so much as a trace of guilt on her face. "Hm? Oh, you are awake. What think you of this? Does it look good?" she asked, completely unconcerned as she spread her arms. Far from chastened, she seemed actually proud. Seeing her like this made the uncertain, overwrought Holo of yesterday seem like something out of a dream. Indeed it seemed that the real Holo, the one he'd have to contend with from here on out, was this impudent, prancing thing.

Incidentally, the clothes she now wore were Lawrence's best, the one outfit he reserved for negotiations with rich traders and

40

the like. The top was an indigo blue shirt underneath a three-quarters-length vest. The trousers were a rare combination of linen and leather, with a skirt that wrapped fully around her lower body, tied with a fine sheepskin sash. The boots were a rare prize, made of tanned leather and triple-layered, good even in the snowy mountains. Over all this she wore a bearskin greatcoat.

Merchants take pride in their practical, dignified clothing. To buy these Lawrence had saved gradually beginning in his apprenticeship — it had taken him ten years. If he showed up to a negotiation wearing these with a nicely groomed beard, he would have most people at a disadvantage.

And Holo now wore those garments.

He couldn't find it in himself to be angry with her, though.

All the clothes were clearly too big for her, which made it all the more charming.

"The greatcoat is black — my brown hair looks lovely against it, eh? These trousers, though — they get in the way of my tail. Might I put a hole in them?"

The trousers she spoke of so lightly had been made by a master craftsman only after significant effort on Lawrence's part. A hole would likely prove impossible to repair. He shook his head resolutely.

"Hrm. Well, fortunately they're still large. I'll find a way to make them work."

Holo seemed not to harbor the faintest concern that she would be asked to take the clothes off. Lawrence didn't think she was likely to run away while wearing them, but nevertheless he rose and regarded her. If she were to go a city and sell them, they would fetch a tidy amount of gold.

"You're a merchant through and through, that's sure enough. I know just what you anticipate with that expression on your face," said Holo, smiling. She jumped lightly down from the wagon.

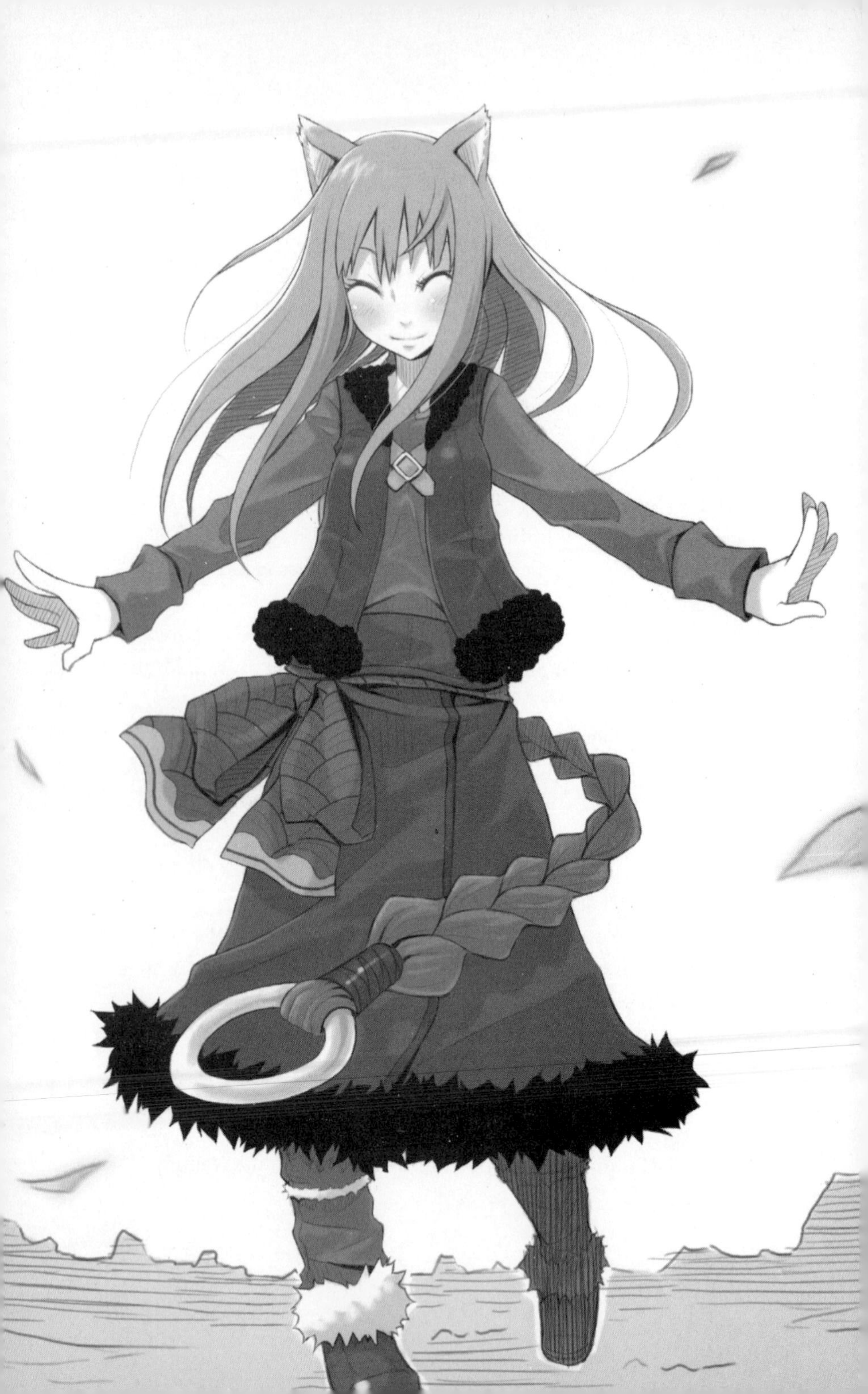

Her movement was so unassuming and natural that he had no reaction. If she'd run just then, he would have been unable to pursue.

Or perhaps he didn't react because he didn't believe she would run.

"I'll not run. If that had been my aim, I'd have gone long since."

Lawrence glanced at the wheat sheaf in the wagon bed, then looked back at the smiling Holo. She took the bearskin cloak off and tossed it back in the wagon; evidently the cloak, which had been made for Lawrence's height, was too big for her. She was even smaller than he'd realized yesterday, having seen her only in the dim moonlight. Lawrence was on the tall side, but even so she was fully two heads shorter than him.

Then, as she verified the fit of the rest of the clothes, she spoke offhandedly. "So, I wish to travel with you. May I?"

She smiled but did not seem to flatter. If she'd tried to flatter him, Lawrence felt there might have been reason to refuse her, but she simply smiled happily.

Lawrence sighed.

She didn't seem to be a thief, at least. He couldn't let his guard down, but it wouldn't hurt to let her come along. And sending her away would only make the constant loneliness harder to bear.

"This must be some kind of fate. Very well," Lawrence said.

Holo did not appear especially overjoyed — she merely smiled.

"You'll have to earn your keep, though. The life of a merchant isn't easy. I expect the god of abundant harvests to bring an abundant harvest to my coin purse."

"I'm not so shameless as to thoughtlessly freeload. I'm Holo the Wisewolf, and I have my pride," said Holo sullenly. Lawrence was not so blind as to think she wasn't making a show of childish indignation, though.

Sure enough, Holo chuckled. "Though this proud wolf made a

bit of a spectacle of herself yesterday," she said self-deprecatingly, as if her flustered demeanor reflected her true feelings. "In any case, it is good to meet you . . . er . . ."

"Lawrence. Kraft Lawrence. When I'm working I go by Lawrence."

"Mm. Lawrence. I shall sing your praises for all eternity," said Holo with chest thrust forward, her wolf ears pricking up proudly. She seemed oddly serious. It was difficult to tell if she was being childish or cunning. She was like the ever-changing mountain weather.

Apparently that ever-changing mood was part of her craftiness. Lawrence hastily revised his opinion and offered his hand from the wagon bed. It was the proof that he'd truly acknowledged her presence as a companion.

Holo smiled and took his hand.

Her hand was small and warm.

"At any rate, it will soon rain. We should make haste."

"Wha . . . ? You should have said so sooner!" exclaimed Lawrence — loudly enough to startle the horse. The previous night hadn't brought so much as a hint of rain, but looking up at the sky he could indeed see clouds beginning to gather. Holo chuckled at him as he hurriedly made preparations to depart. She scampered on board the wagon, and it was obvious enough from the ease with which she rearranged the slept-in furs that she would be more handy than some fresh-faced apprentice child.

"The river is in a foul temper. 'Twould be best to cross a short distance from here."

After Lawrence roused the horse, collected the bucket, and took the reins in hand, Holo joined him in the driver's seat.

It was too big for one person, but slightly too small for two.

But to ward off the chill, too small was just right.

With the neigh of a horse, the pair's strange travels had begun.

CHAPTER TWO

The rain was a true downpour. The threatening storm finally caught up with Lawrence and Holo, but fortunately they caught sight of a church through their rain-blurred vision and hurried into it. Unlike the monastery, the church survived on tithes from travelers and pilgrims who would stay the night and pray for a safe journey, so Lawrence and Holo were greeted warmly, without so much as a single fell glance.

Nonetheless, a girl with wolf ears and a tail would hardly be allowed to walk into a church. Holo thus covered her head and face in a hood, and they spun the lie that she was Lawrence's wife, whose face was badly burned.

He knew Holo was snickering to herself beneath the veil, but she understood her relationship with the Church, so her performance was good enough. That she had suffered many times at the hands of the Church was surely no lie.

Even if she weren't a demon, but an animal incarnation, that was little distinction as far as the Church was concerned. To the Church, all spirits besides the god it worshipped were anathema, tools of evil.

But it was through the gates of that church that the two passed easily and rented a room, and when Lawrence returned to the room after attending to his soaked wagonload, he found Holo, naked to the waist and wringing out her hair. Water fell in great, undignified drops from her beautiful brown locks. The floor was already full of holes, so a little bit of water wouldn't hurt — Lawrence was more concered with the problem of averting his eyes.

"Ha-ha, the cool water soothes my burns, it does," said Holo, indifferent to Lawrence.

Pleased by their lie or otherwise, Holo smiled. Brushing aside the hair that stuck to her face, she swept it up and back in a grand motion.

The boldness of the gesture was undeniably wolflike, and it was not hard to see that the wet hair, disarrayed as it was, resembled the stiff fur of a wolf.

"The furs will be all right, surely. They were good marten skins, and martens live in the mountains, mountains where my kind live as well."

"Will they sell high?"

"I hardly know. I'm no fur merchant, am I?"

Lawrence nodded at the entirely reasonable answer, then began to disrobe and dry his own clothes.

"Oh, that's right," he said, remembering. "What shall we do with that wheat sheaf?"

He finished wringing out his shirt and was about to do the same with his trousers when he remembered Holo's presence; he looked to her and discovered that she was now quite naked and wringing her own clothes free of water. Feeling somehow vexed, he ventured to strip nude and do the same.

"Mm, what do you mean, 'what?'"

"I mean, shall we thresh it, or shall we leave it as it is? Assuming the talk of you residing in the wheat is true, that is."

Lawrence was teasing Holo, but she only cracked a slight smile.

"As long as I live, the wheat will neither rot nor wither. But should it be burned, eaten, or ground into the soil, I will likely disappear. If it's in the way, you could thresh it and keep it safe somewhere; that might be better."

"I see. I'll thresh it and put the grains in a pouch, then. You should hold it, right?"

"'Twould be a boon. Still better to hang it 'round my neck," Holo said.

Forgetting himself for a moment, Lawrence glanced at Holo's neckline, but hastily looked away.

"I'd hoped to sell some of it elsewhere, though. Could we set aside a bit for sale?" Lawrence asked after he'd calmed himself.

He heard a rustling, and turned to see that it was Holo's tail waving wildly. The tail's fur was very fine, and shed water readily. Lawrence frowned as his face was dampened by the flying drops, but Holo seemed not the least bit contrite.

"Most of the crops grew well because of the region. They'll soon wither — that's the point. No use taking them elsewhere."

Holo looked thoughtfully at the clothes she'd finished wringing out, but as she had nothing else to change into, she put the wrinkled items back on. Since they weren't cheap like what Lawrence wore, they shed water well. Lawrence thought the situation rather unreasonable but said nothing and changed back into his own damp, wrinkled clothes, then nodded to Holo.

"Let's go dry ourselves in the great room. With this rain, there should be plenty of other people gathering around the furnace."

"Mm, a good idea, that," said Holo, covering her head with the thin cloak. Once covered, she giggled.

"What's so funny?"

"Heh, I would never have thought to cover up my face because of burns."

"Oh? What would you have done?"

"The burns would become part of me, just like my ears or tail. Proof of my uniqueness."

Lawrence was somewhat impressed with her statement. Nonetheless he wondered uncharitably if she'd feel the same way if she were actually injured.

Holo interrupted his reverie.

"I know what you are thinking," she said.

Underneath the cloak, she smiled mischievously. The right corner of her mouth curled up in a smirk, showing a sharp fang.

"Want to injure me and see for yourself?"

Lawrence was not entirely disinclined to respond to her provocation, but he decided that if he actually reacted and drew his dagger, things could really get out of hand.

It was possible that she meant it. More likely, though, it was just her mischief-loving nature.

"I'm a man. I could never injure such a beautiful face."

Hearing him say so, Holo smiled as if having received a long-anticipated gift and drew playfully near to him. A sweet scent swirled vaguely around him, rousing Lawrence's body. Completely indifferent to his reaction, she sniffed him, then drew slightly back.

"You may have been caught in the rain, but you still smell foul. A wolf can tell these things."

"Why, you —"

Lawrence threw a half-serious punch, but Holo moved adroitly aside and he hit only hair. She laughed, cocking her head and continuing.

"Even a wolf knows to keep its coat clean. You're a good man, aye, but you need to keep neat."

He didn't know whether she was joking or not, but hearing it from a girl like Holo made it impossible to deny. For as long as he could remember, Lawrence maintained his appearance only insofar as it would help his professional negotiation, with no thought given to whether it would appeal to a woman.

Had his negotiation partner been a woman, he might have taken the trouble, but unfortunately, he had not once met a female merchant.

He didn't know how to answer, so he simply turned around and fell silent.

"The beard, though, is quite nice."

The medium-length beard that grew from Lawrence's chin had always been well-received. Lawrence accepted the compliment gracefully, turning back to face her, somewhat proudly.

"I daresay I'd prefer it a big longer, though."

Long beards were not popular among merchants. The thought automatically occurred to Lawrence, but Holo drew a line from her nose across her cheeks with her index finger, continuing her jape.

". . . Like so, like a wolf."

Lawrence was now finally aware that he had been made sport of. He ignored her and walked toward the room's door, even as he felt childish for doing so. Holo giggled and followed. Truthfully, he was not actually angry with her.

"There will be many people around the furnace. Best not to let anything slip."

"I am Holo the Wisewolf! Long ago I traveled clear to Pasloe in human form. Worry not!"

The churches and inns far from the cities were important sources of information to a merchant. Churches in particular attracted all kinds of people. An inn might house poor travelers and grizzled merchants, but churches were different. One might find anyone from master brewers to wealthy nobles in a church.

The church Lawrence and Holo had stopped in housed twelve guests. A few looked to be merchants; the others were of various professions.

"Aha, so you're here from Yorenz, then?"

"Yes. I delivered salt from there to my customer and got marten furs in trade."

Most of the guests sat on the floor in the main hall, taking their meals or picking fleas from their clothing. One couple monopolized the bench in front of the furnace. Despite being a "great hall," it was not particularly spacious, so no matter where one was in the crowded room, the generously stoked fireplace would dry one's clothes. The couple's clothes did not appear wet, so Lawrence imagined they were probably wealthy, and having made generous donations to the church could be here as they pleased.

Lawrence was not wrong; he pricked up his ears to listen for a point in the couple's conversation where he could enter and waited for his chance.

The wife had gone silent, possibly because of the exhausting journey, and her middle-aged husband welcomed conversation.

"Still, going all the way back to Yorenz, isn't that rather arduous?"

"That depends on how canny the merchant."

"Oh ho, interesting!"

"When I bought the salt in Yorenz, I paid no money. Rather, I'd already sold a measure of wheat to a different branch of the same company in another city — but when I sold the wheat, I took no payment; neither did I pay for the salt. So I completed two separate deals with no money exchanged."

This system of barter had been invented by a mercantile nation in the south about a century earlier. When Lawrence's master had explained it to him, he'd agonized over the concept for two weeks before finally understanding. The man in front of him had apparently never heard of it himself and appeared similarly unable to grasp it, hearing the explanation but once.

"I see . . . what a strange contrivance," he said, nodding. "I live in the city of Perenzzo, and my vineyard has never employed such a method when selling our grapes. Will we be all right?"

"This barter system was invented by merchants who needed a convenient way to deal with people from many different lands. As the owner of a vineyard, you'd need to be careful not to let vintners claim your grapes to be poor and buy them cheaply."

"Yes. We have such arguments every year," said the man with a smile — but to the accountants he employed, the red-faced arguments they had with sly vintners were no laughing matter. Most vineyard owners were noble, but almost none of them took a personal hand in the farming or sale of their product. Count Ehrendott, who managed the region surrounding Pasloe, was highly eccentric in this regard.

"Lawrence, was it? Next time you're in Perenzzo, do come by for a visit."

"I shall, thank you."

As was common among the nobility, the man did not give his own name, assuming his name would already be known. It was seen as plebeian to give one's own name.

Undoubtedly if Lawrence were to visit Perenzzo and ask after the master of the vineyard, it would be this man. Had this been Perenzzo, though, a man of Lawrence's stature would find it practically impossible to simply arrange an audience with him. Churches were therefore the best place to establish such connections.

"Well then, as my wife appears tired, I'll take my leave of you."

"May God allow us to meet again," said Lawrence.

It was a standard phrase within the Church. The man rose from his chair and, along with his wife, gave a polite nod before leaving the hall. Lawrence, too, vacated the chair the man had requested that he bring over from the corner of the room. He then returned the chairs the couple had occupied to the corner.

The only people who sat on chairs in the great hall were nobility, knights, and the wealthy. Most people disliked all three.

"Heh-heh, you're not a man to be trifled with, master!"

Once Lawrence had cleared the chairs and returned to Holo's side in the middle of the hall, a man approached them. Given his dress and affect, he, too, was a merchant. His bearded face looked young. He had probably not been working on his own very long.

"I'm merely a traveling merchant like any other," said Lawrence shortly. Beside him, Holo straightened. The hood over her head shifted slightly; only Lawrence would know that it was her ears pricking.

"Far from it, master. I'd been wanting to speak with him for some time but couldn't find the opportunity. Yet you slipped right in. Thinking that it's traders like you that I'll be going up against in the future, why, it's hard not to despair."

The man grinned as he spoke, revealing a smile that lacked one front tooth, giving it a certain charm. Perhaps he'd pulled the tooth on purpose to lend his foolish smile persuasion. As a merchant, he'd know how to use his appearance to best effect.

Lawrence realized he'd better not be careless.

Nonetheless, he himself had struck up conversations just like this one when he was starting out, so he held a spark of empathy for the man.

"That's nothing — when I was starting out, all the established merchants seemed like monsters to me. Half of them still do. But I'm still eating. You just have to keep at it."

"Heh-heh, it's a relief to hear you say so, sir. Oh, by the way, I'm Zheren — and you've probably figured it out, but I'm just starting out as a merchant. Begging your indulgence, sir!"

"I'm Lawrence."

Lawrence remembered that when he himself had just started out, he'd also tried to strike up conversations like this one and gotten frustrated by the cold responses. Now on the receiving end of a solicitous young merchant's conversation, he understood those cold responses.

A young merchant just starting out had nothing to share and could only receive.

"So, then . . . is this your companion?"

It was unclear whether Zheren broached the subject because he truly had nothing to share or if he'd committed the common beginner's mistake of trying to gain without offering anything in return. If this had been a conversation between veterans, they would already have traded information on two or three locations by this point.

"My wife, Holo." For a moment Lawrence hesitated, wondering if he should use a false name, but ultimately decided there was no need.

Holo bowed slightly in greeting as her name was mentioned.

"My, a wife and a merchant both?"

"She is an eccentric and prefers the wagon to the village home."

"Still, covering your wife in a cloak this way, she must be very precious to you."

Lawrence had some grudging respect for the man's charisma; perhaps he'd been the town rogue. For his part, Lawrence had been taught by his relatives that it was best not to say such things.

"Heh-heh, but it is a man's instinct to want to see hidden things.

God has led us together here. Surely you can let me have a look at her."

What shamelessness! thought Lawrence in spite of the knowledge that Holo was not actually his wife.

But before Lawrence could take the man to task, Holo spoke.

"The traveler is happiest before the journey; the dog's bark fiercer than the dog itself, and a woman most beautiful from behind. To show my face in public would dash many dreams, and thus 'tis something I cannot do," she said, smiling softly underneath the veil.

Zheren could only grin, chastened. Even Lawrence was impressed with her lilting eloquence.

"Heh-heh . . . your wife is something else, master."

"It's all I can do to avoid being quite henpecked."

Lawrence was more than half-serious.

"Yes, well . . . it's certainly providential that I've met the both of you. Can you spare a moment to hear my tale?" said Zheren. Silence descended as he flashed his grin that was one tooth short and moved closer to the pair.

Unlike typical inns, churches only provided lodging — not food. However, the hearth could be used for cooking, provided one gave the proper donation. Lawrence did so and placed five potatoes into a pot to boil. Naturally the firewood for cooking had to be purchased as well.

It would take time for the water to boil, so Lawrence threshed the wheat that housed Holo and found an unused leather pouch to keep it in. Remembering that she'd said she wanted to keep it around her neck, Lawrence took a leather strap and attended to the hearth. Altogether the potatoes, firewood, pouch, and strap came to a significant cost, so he mused over how much to charge her as he brought the potatoes back to the room.

Because his hands were full, Lawrence couldn't knock on the door — but Holo's sensitive wolf ears could identify his footfalls. When he entered the room, however, her back was turned to him as she sat on the bed, combing her tail fur.

"Hm? Something smells good," she said, raising her head. Evidently her nose was as sensitive as her ears.

The potatoes were topped with goat cheese. Lawrence would never have indulged in such luxury had be been alone, but now that he was in a party of two, he decided to be generous. Holo's happy reaction made it entirely worthwhile.

Lawrence set the potatoes on the table beside the bed, and Holo immediately reached out to help herself. Just before she could grab a potato, Lawrence tossed the pouch full of wheat to her.

"Wha . . . oh. The wheat."

"And here's a strap, so you can work out a way to hang it around your neck."

"Mm. My thanks. But this takes precedence," she said, tossing the wheat aside with surprising nonchalance, then licking her lips and reaching for a potato. Apparently eating was a priority for Holo.

Once she had a potato in hand, she immediately broke it in half. Her face fairly glowed with delight at the steam that rose from the food. With her tail wagging back and forth she looked undeniably canine, but Lawrence was sure that if he pointed it out she'd be irritated, so he said nothing.

"So wolves find potatoes delicious, do they?"

"Aye. It is not as though we wolves eat meat year-round. We eat tender buds from trees. We eat fish. And the crops that humans raise are better still than tree buds. Also, I rather like the human habit of putting meat and vegetables to a fire."

It is said that a cat's tongue cannot stand hot food, but wolves did not appear to have this problem. Holo held half of the potato in her hand and popped the entire piece into her mouth at once after blowing on it two or three times. Lawrence felt that she'd bitten off more than she could chew, and indeed she soon appeared to choke. Lawrence tossed her a water-skin, and with it Holo managed to get the potato down.

"Whew. Rather surprising, that. Human throats are so narrow. It's rather inconvenient."

"Wolves swallow things whole, right?"

"Mm. Well, we lack *this*, so we cannot chew at our leisure."

Holo pulled at the edge of her lips; presumably she was talking about her cheeks.

"But I've choked on potatoes in the past, it's true."

"Oh ho."

"I suppose potatoes and I are ill-fated."

Lawrence resisted telling her that it was her gluttony that boded ill, not potatoes.

"Earlier," he began instead, "you said something about being able to tell when someone is lying?"

Upon hearing the question, Holo turned to face him mid-bite, but suddenly looked aside and moved her hand.

Before Lawrence could ask what was wrong, her hand stopped, frozen in midair as if she'd grabbed something.

"There are still fleas."

"It's that nice fur of yours. I bet it's a lovely bed for them."

Transporting fur or woven goods often involved smoking the fleas out of them, depending on the season. Lawrence spoke from experience, but Holo seemed quite shocked, and thrust out her chest as she spoke proudly.

"Well, it's a credit to your eye for quality that you can tell as much, then!" she said haughtily. Lawrence decided to keep his thoughts to himself.

"So is it true that you can tell truth from lies?"

"Hm? Oh, more or less." Wiping off the hand that had grabbed the flea, Holo turned her attention back to the potato.

"So, how good at it are you?"

"Well, I know that what you said about my tail just now was not meant as praise."

Lawrence, stunned, said nothing. Holo giggled happily.

"It's not perfect, though. You may believe me or not . . . as you wish," said Holo impishly, licking cheese from her fingers.

She'd gotten the better of him again, but if he were to react, that would only give her another opportunity. Lawrence composed himself and tried again.

"So let me ask you this — was the lad's story true?"

"The lad?"

"The one who spoke to us by the furnace."

"Oh. Heh, 'lad,' you say."

"Is something funny?"

"From where I stand you're both but lads."

If he tried a comeback she'd only toy with him more, so Lawrence stifled the reply that rose within him.

"Heh. I daresay you're a bit more grown than he, though. As for your lad, it seems to me he is lying."

Lawrence calmed himself; this confirmed his suspicions.

During their conversation in the hall, the young merchant Zheren had spoken to Lawrence about an opportunity for profit.

There was a certain silver coin in circulation that was due to be replaced by a coin with a higher concentration of silver. If the story was true, the old silver coins were of poorer quality than their replacements, but their face value would be the same. However, when being exchanged for other currencies, the new silver coins would be worth more than the old. If one knew in advance which coin was due to be replaced, one could buy them up in bulk, then exchange them for the new coins, thus realizing what amounted to pure profit. Zheren claimed that he knew which coin among all those circulating in the world would be replaced, and would share the information in exchange for a piece of the profit. Since Zheren would certainly have made the same offer to other merchants, Lawrence could not simply swallow the story whole.

Holo stared into space as if thinking back on the conversation, then popped the piece of potato into her mouth and swallowed it.

"I don't know which part is a lie, though, nor do I understand the finer points of the conversation."

Lawrence nodded and considered. He had not actually expected that much from Holo.

Assuming that the transaction itself wasn't a lie, Zheren must be lying about the coins, somehow.

"Well, currency speculation isn't rare in and of itself. Still . . ."

"You don't understand why he's lying . . . no?"

Holo plucked a bud from the surface of her potato and ate the rest. Lawrence sighed.

He had to admit that she'd long since gotten control of him.

"When someone's lying, what's important is not the content of the lie, but the reasoning behind it," she said.

"How many years do you think it took me to understand that?"

"Oh? You may have called that Zheren person a lad, but you're both the same to me," said Holo proudly.

In times like these, Lawrence wished Holo did not look so frustratingly human. To think that the youthful Holo had long understood the principles that he had suffered so much to grasp was too much for him to take.

"If I were not here, what would you do?" asked Holo.

"First I'd work out whether it was true or not, then I'd pretend to believe his story."

"And why is that?"

"If it's true, I can turn a profit just by going along with it. If it's a lie, then someone somewhere is up to something — but I can still come out ahead if I keep my eyes and ears open."

"Mm. And given that I *am* here, and I've told you he's lying, then . . ."

"Hm?"

Lawrence finally realized what had been eluding him. "Ah."

"Heh. See, there was nothing over which to agonize so. Either way you'll be pretending to accept his proposal," said Holo, grinning. Lawrence had no retort.

"I'll be taking that last potato," said Holo, snatching the potato from the table.

For his part, Lawrence was too abashed to even split the potato he held in his hand.

"I am Holo the Wisewolf! How many times longer do you think I have lived than you?"

Lawrence's mood only worsened with her concern for his feelings. He took a vindictive bite out of his potato.

He felt like an apprentice traveling with his teacher all over again.

The next day was beautiful with clear autumn skies. The church awoke still earlier than the merchants, so by the time Lawrence rose, the morning routine was already finished. Lawrence anticipated this and was unsurprised, but when he went out to the well to wash his face, he was shocked to see Holo walking out of the worship hall with the members of the Church. She had her head bowed and was wearing her cloak, but even so she stopped frequently to chat pleasantly with the churchgoers.

The sight of the devout chatting with the god of the harvest whose existence they refused to acknowledge was amusing, though Lawrence lacked the nerve to find it so.

Holo took her leave from the congregation and quietly approached a dumbfounded Lawrence. She clasped her small hands together in front of her chest and spoke.

"Lord, grant my husband courage."

The well water was chilly due to the approaching winter; Lawrence poured it over his head anyway and pretended not to hear Holo's laughter.

"It's gotten a bit more important, the Church has," said Holo.

Lawrence shook his head to clear it of water, just as Holo had done with her tail the previous day. "The Church has always been important."

"Hardly. It was not so when I came through here from the north. They'd always be going on about how the one god and his twelve angels created the world and how humanity was but borrowing it. Nature is not something created, though. Even then, I thought to myself, 'When did these people learn to tell such jokes?'"

This centuries-old harvest god was talking like a natural philosopher criticizing the Church, which made it all the more amusing. Lawrence dried off and dressed. He wouldn't forget to leave a coin in the tithe-box that was prepared there. One was expected to leave money in the box if one used the well, and the people of the church would be checking. Anyone who failed to leave a donation would have unlucky things said about him. The constantly traveling Lawrence needed all the luck he could get.

Nonetheless, what he tossed in the box was a worn, blackened copper coin that could barely be counted as money.

"I suppose this is a sign of the times, then . . . much has changed."

Presumably she referred to her homeland, given the desolate expression on her face.

"Have you yourself changed?" asked Lawrence.

". . ." Holo shook her head wordlessly. It was somehow a very childish gesture.

"Then I'm sure your homeland hasn't changed, either."

Despite his youth, Lawrence had endured much. He'd been to many nations, met many people, and gained a wide variety of experiences, so he felt qualified to say as much.

All traveling merchants — even those who had run away from their homes — couldn't help holding their homeland dear, since when in a foreign land, one could only trust one's countrymen.

Holo nodded, her face emerging slightly from underneath the cloak.

"'Twould be a disgrace to the name Wisewolf to be comforted by you, though," she said with a smile, turning and heading back toward their room. She gave him a sidelong glance that could've been interpreted as gratitude.

As long as her attitude was that of a very sly, very old person, Lawrence could cope.

It was her childish side that he found difficult.

Lawrence was twenty-five. If he lived in a town he'd be married and taking his wife and children to church. His life was half over, and Holo's childish demeanor penetrated his lonely heart.

"Hey, what keeps you? Hurry!" shouted Holo, looking over her shoulder at him.

It had been a mere two days since Lawrence met Holo, but it felt like much longer.

Lawrence decided to accept Zheren's offer.

However, Zheren could not simply rely on Lawrence's word and hand over the information; neither could Lawrence afford to pay up front. He would have to sell his furs first. Thus the two men decided to meet in the riverside city of Pazzio and sign a formal contract before a public witness.

"Well then, I'll be on my way. When you arrive in Pazzio, find a tavern called Yorend; you'll be able to contact me there."

"Yorend, is it? Very well."

Zheren smiled his charming smile again as he took his leave, hefting his burlap sack of dried fruit over his shoulder as he walked on.

Besides actual trading, the most important task that faced a young merchant was exploring the many regions, becoming familiar with the locals and their goods, and making sure his face was remembered. To accomplish this, it was best to carry something well-preserved that could be sold at churches or inns and used as an excuse for conversation, like dried fruit or meat.

Lawrence watched Zheren, feeling a certain nostalgia for the time before he'd acquired his wagon.

"Are we not going with him?" Holo asked as Zheren's form disappeared into the distance. Having checked to see that there was no one around to see her, she was grooming her tail fur.

Possibly because she had to cover her ears with the cloak, she did not bother combing her fall of chestnut hair, merely tying it back with a length of hempen rope. Lawrence felt that she could at least comb it, but he had no comb to offer. He resolved to acquire a comb and hat when the arrived in Pazzio.

"It rained all day yesterday, so he'll make better time on foot than we can on the wagon. There's no need for him to slow down on our account."

"True, merchants are always on about time."

"Time is money."

"Ho-ho! An interesting saying. Time is money, is it?"

"As long as we have time, we can make money."

"'Tis true. Though it's not how I think," said Holo, casting a glance to her tail.

Her magnificent tail was long enough to hang past the back of her knees. The abundant fur would probably fetch a good price if shorn and sold.

"I imagine the farmers you watched over for so many centuries were mindful of time."

As soon as Lawrence said it, he realized he probably shouldn't have. Holo glanced at him as if to say "I'll let you have that one," smiling impishly.

"Hmph. At what have you been looking? The farmers care nary a whit for time. It's the *air* they're mindful of."

"I don't follow you."

"They wake in the dawn air, work the farm in the morning air, pull the weeds in the afternoon air, twist rope in the rainy air. They worry over their crops in the windy air, watch them grow in the summer air, celebrate the harvest in the autumn air, and in the winter air they wait for spring. They think not of time — like me, they note only the air."

Lawrence couldn't say that he understood all of what Holo said, but there were parts he followed. He nodded, impressed, which seemed to satisfy Holo; she puffed up her chest and sniffed proudly.

The self-proclaimed Wisewolf evidently didn't feel the slightest need for humility.

Just then, a person who seemed to be another traveling merchant came across the road.

Although Holo's ears were hidden by the cloak, her tail was in plain view.

The passerby stared at Holo's tail, although he didn't speak.

In all likelihood he didn't realize it was a tail. Lawrence imagined that if it were him, he'd wonder what kind of fur it was and how much it was worth.

Still, when it came to keeping a straight face, that was a separate matter entirely.

"You're quick enough, but you lack experience."

Apparently having finished her grooming, Holo tucked her tail back underneath her skirt and spoke. The face underneath the cloak was that of a girl barely in her mid-teens, which showed occasional glimpses of someone much younger.

Yet her words had the air of someone much older.

"Still, one will grow wiser with age."

"How many hundreds of years do you think it will take?" Lawrence headed off her attempt to tease him.

Surprised, she laughed loudly. "Ah-ha-ha-ha! You *are* rather quick, aren't you?"

"Perhaps you're just old and slow."

"Heh-heh. Do you know why we wolves attack people in the mountains?"

Lawrence was unable to keep up with Holo's sudden segue, so he could only answer with a confused, "Er, no."

"It is because we wish to eat human brains and gain their knowledge." Holo grinned, baring her fangs.

Even if she was joking, Lawrence shivered unconsciously, his breath catching.

A few seconds passed; he realized he'd lost.

"You're still a pup. Hardly a match for me."

Holo sighed. Lawrence gripped the reins tightly and stifled a frustrated expression.

"Still, have you ever been attacked by wolves in the mountains?"

It was a strange feeling being asked such a question by a girl with ears, fangs, and a tail. He was having a conversation with a wolf — the same wolf whose presence in the mountains he feared.

"I have. Perhaps . . . eight times."

"They're quite difficult to handle, are they not?"

"They are. Wild dogs I can handle, but wolves are a problem."

"That's because they want to eat lots of humans, to get their —"

"I'm sorry, all right? So stop."

The third time Lawrence had been set upon by wolves, he was part of a caravan.

Two of the men in the caravan had been unable to clear the mountains. Their cries echoed in Lawrence's ears even now.

His face was expressionless.

"Oh . . ."

Apparently the perceptive wisewolf had figured it out.

"I am sorry," said a contrite Holo, slumping, almost shrinking.

Lawrence had been attacked by wolves many times. With the memories of the encounters swirling in his head, he was in no mood to answer.

Splish, splosh, went the horse's hooves in the muddy road.

". . . Are you angry?"

Such a crafty wolf — she must have known that if she asked like that, he'd be unable to truthfully answer that he *was* angry.

So he answered. "Yes, I'm angry."

Holo looked up at Lawrence in silence. When he looked back at her out of the corner of his eye, he saw her pouting — it was charming enough that he almost forgave her.

"I *am* angry. No more jokes like that," he finally turned to her and said.

Holo nodded resolutely and looked ahead. She now seemed quite meek.

After a period of silence she spoke again. "Wolves live only in the mountains, but dogs have lived with humans. That's why wolves make tougher opponents."

He probably should have ignored her, but doing so would make later conversation difficult. He turned slightly in her direction and gave a sign that he was listening.

"Hm?"

"Wolves only know that they are hunted by humans, and that they are terrifying creatures. So we are always thinking about what to do when they enter our forest."

Holo stared straight ahead as she spoke, as serious as Lawrence had ever seen her.

He didn't think she'd made that story up; he nodded, slowly.

But there was something in her vagueness that worried him.

"Did *you* ever —"

But Holo stopped him before he could continue. "There are some things I simply cannot answer."

"Oh." Lawrence chided himself for speaking without thinking ahead. "Sorry."

Holo then smiled. "Now we're even."

A twenty-five-year-old was not, it seemed, a match for a Wisewolf.

There was no further conversation, but neither was there any bad air between the two. The horse plodded along, and soon the day had passed and night fell.

A merchant never continued his travels after dark when it had rained. If the wagon became stuck in the mud, seven times out of ten it meant that the goods would have to be abandoned.

To turn a steady profit as a traveling merchant one had to minimize losses, and the road was full of dangers.

Holo suddenly spoke, nestled in the fur pile beneath a sky she'd promised would be clear the next day.

"The worlds we live in, you and I, are very different," she said.

CHAPTER THREE

The river Slaude meanders slowly across the plains. It it said to trace the path left behind by a giant snake that slithered from the mountains to the west through the plains to the eastern sea, and its wide, slow path is an essential transportation route for the region.

Pazzio is a large port town situated near the midpoint of the river. Not far upstream lie large fields of wheat; still farther are thickly forested mountains. Logs are floated downstream year-round; barges carrying wheat or corn, depending on the season, navigate up and down the river. That alone would be enough to ensure the town's prosperity, but because there are no bridges across the Slaude, its ferries make it a natural gathering place.

It was past afternoon but not yet dusk; Lawrence and Holo arrived during the busiest time of the day.

Pazzio's trade had grown since the town recovered its autonomy from the monarchy — now merchants and aristocrats ruled it. Consequently, there were heavy tariffs levied on goods entering the town, but there were no immigration checks or demands for identification. Had it been a castle town, the opposite would be true, and Holo's nonhuman status would be a problem.

"Have they no king here?" was Holo's first utterance upon arriving in the city.

"Is this your first time coming to a city of this size?"

"Times surely change. In my day, a city this large would have been ruled by a king."

Lawrence felt a slight sense of superiority — he'd been to cities many times the size of Pazzio. He tried not to let it show lest Holo point it out. And in any case, he'd been just as naive when he first started out.

"Heh. I'll just say that your intentions are admirable," quipped Holo.

Apparently Lawrence had been a bit careless about hiding his thoughts.

Although Holo's attention was focused on the many shops that lined the road, she'd still noticed his expression. Had it just been a lucky guess? The idea that she could discern his thoughts so easily was unsettling and far from funny.

"This isn't . . . a festival, is it?"

"If it were a Church celebration day, the streets would be so crowded we couldn't pass through them. Today, though, there's still space."

"Ho. Difficult to imagine that," said Holo with a smile, leaning out of the cart and scanning the merchant stalls they passed.

She looked every bit the country bumpkin on her first visit to the town, but Lawrence suddenly thought of something else.

"Hey."

"Mm?" was her only reply as she continued to stare at the many vendors.

"Will it be all right, not covering your head?"

"Huh? Head?"

"I know it's festival time in Pasloe right now, so most of the villagers will be drinking and celebrating — but not all of them, and some of the ones who don't may be visiting Pazzio right now."

"Oh, that," said Holo, sitting back down in the wagon, suddenly irritated. She looked back at Lawrence, her cloak just barely covering her ears. "Even if they could see my ears, nobody would notice. They've all long forgotten about me."

There was such vehemence in her voice it was a miracle she didn't shout. Lawrence reflexively raised his hands as if calming a startled horse. Holo was no horse, but it seemed to have some effect.

She snorted derisively and pulled the cloak down, facing ahead and pouting.

"You lived there for hundreds of years — surely there are some legends passed down about you. Or did you never take human form?"

"There *are* legends. And sometimes I'd appear as a human."

"So there are stories about you appearing as a human?"

Holo gave Lawrence a belabored sidelong glance, sighed, then spoke. "As far as I remember, it went something like this. She looks like a beautiful girl of about fifteen. She has long, flowing brown hair and wolf ears, along with a white-tipped tail. Sometimes she would appear in this form, and in exchange for keeping her appearance a secret, she promises a good harvest."

Holo regarded Lawrence flatly with a look that said, "Happy?"

"Well, it sounds like you pretty much told them everything about yourself. Is that really okay?"

"Even if they were to see my ears or tail, they would doubt — just as you did. They'll never realize the truth."

Holo slipped her hand underneath the cloak and fussed with her ears, perhaps because they pushed against the inside of the fabric uncomfortably.

Lawrence looked sideways at her. He wanted her to be more careful, but if he said as much she would surely get genuinely angry.

It seemed that discussion of Pasloe was taboo. He felt better when he considered that the legends of Holo made no mention of her actual facial features, only identifying her by her ears and tail. As long as she kept those concealed, she would go unnoticed. Legends were just legends — it was not as if she were on a Church wanted poster.

A few moments after Lawrence resolved not to press the matter, Holo appeared to be considering something. At length, she spoke.

"Hey . . ."

"Mm?"

"Even . . . even should they see me, they won't know who I am . . . will they?"

Her mood had changed completely from before; it was almost as if she wanted to be discovered.

But Lawrence was no fool. He stared expressionlessly forward at the horse. "It is certainly my hope that they won't," he answered.

Holo smiled slightly, almost ruefully. "You needn't worry."

Once Holo started looking happily at the stalls again, Lawrence realized she'd been speaking to herself as well as him.

There was no need to press the matter, however — Holo was quite stubborn.

Lawrence couldn't help smiling at Holo now. She'd cheered up completely and was excitedly looking at the delicious fruits they passed.

"There's quite a collection of fruit! Are they all picked nearby?"

"It's because Pazzio is the gateway to the south. When the season's right, you can even see fruit from regions nearly impossible to visit."

"There is much fruit in the south, and good."

"Surely you have fruit in the north as well."

"Aye, but it's tough and bitter. To make it sweet it must be dried and cured. We wolves can't do such work, so we have to take it from the villages."

Lawrence would've expected birds, horses, or sheep to be more likely targets for wolves. It was hard to imagine them driven by a desire for something sweet. Perhaps a bear — bears often took the leather bags filled with grapes that hung from the eaves of houses.

"I would think wolves would prefer spicy things. It's bears that crave sweets."

"We don't like spicy food. Once we found red fang-shaped fruit among the cargo of a shipwreck. We ate it and regretted it loud and long!"

"Ah, hot peppers. Expensive, those."

"We dunked our heads in the river and decided humans were terrifying indeed," said Holo with a chuckle, enjoying the memory for a moment as she gazed at the stalls. After a time, her smile faded, then finally reappeared as she sighed. The pleasure of nostalgia is never without its companion, loneliness.

Lawrence was trying to decide what he should say when Holo seemed to perk up.

"If it's red fruit we're talking about, I'd rather have those," she said, tugging on his clothing and pointing out a stall.

Beyond the stream of passing people and wagons, there was a stall with a generous pile of apples.

"Oh, those are fine apples."

"Are they not?" Holo's eyes glittered beneath the cloak. He

wondered if she noticed that her tail was swishing back and forth underneath her skirts. Perhaps she really did like apples. "They look rather toothsome, no?"

"Indeed."

What Holo was hinting at was clear enough, but Lawrence pretended not to notice.

"Now that I think of it, I had a friend who invested more than half his worth in apples. I'm not sure where they were from, but if they turned out like these, he's surely doubled his money." Lawrence sighed regretfully. "I should've done the same."

Holo's expression shifted as if to say "that's not the point I was trying to make," but again Lawrence pretended not to notice.

"Hmph. Well . . . that's most unfortunate," Holo replied.

"But the risk was very high. If it were me, I would've transported them by ship."

"A . . . ship, you say?" As they talked, they continued to move along the road with the clop-clopping of the horse's hooves as accompaniment. Holo was becoming anxious. She clearly wanted the apples, but was just as clearly loath to say so, hence her agitated responses to Lawrence's comments.

"You see, a group of merchants will sometimes pool their money to hire a ship. The amount of money they raise determines the amount and type of cargo, but unlike land transport, if there is an accident you may lose lives as well as money. Even a strong wind can put you in danger. However, there is profit to be had. I've twice traveled by sea this way, so . . ."

"Mm . . . ah . . ."

"What's wrong?

They passed the apple booth, and it began to recede behind them.

There is nothing more fun than knowing the heart of another. Lawrence smiled his best merchant smile.

"Right, so about shipping..."

"Mm . . . apples . . ."

"Hm?"

"I . . . I want . . . I want apples. . . ."

Lawrence thought she'd be stubborn until the end, but since she'd finally admitted her desire, he decided to go ahead and treat her.

"Earn your own food, why don't you." Holo glared at Lawrence as she munched away on an apple; he made a show of shrugging helplessly.

She'd been so charming when she finally gave in and admitted her desire that Lawrence had generously given her a silver *trenni* coin of considerable value. She'd returned with more apples than she could carry. She appeared not to know the meaning of the word *restraint*.

By the time her face and hands were sticky with juice, well into her fourth apple, she got around to complaining again.

"You . . . *munch* . . . earlier, you . . . *mmph* . . . pretended like you didn't . . . *chomp* . . . notice!"

"It's amusing knowing what someone else is thinking," said Lawrence to Holo as she ate the apple down to its core.

Thinking he'd have one for himself, Lawrence reached back to the pile of apples in the wagon bed, but Holo slapped his hand away even as she started on her fifth apple.

"Mine!"

"Hey, I paid for them."

Holo's cheeks were stuffed; she waited until she had finished swallowing to reply.

"I'm Holo the Wisewolf! I can make this much money any time I want."

"Don't let me stop you. I'd planned to use that money for lodging tonight."

"*Mmph . . . grm . . . But, I . . . munch . . .*"

"Answer once you're done eating, please."

Holo nodded and didn't speak again until her stomach contained no less than eight apples.

Did she still intend to have dinner after all that?

". . . Whew."

"You certainly ate a lot."

"Apples are the devil's fruit, full of tempting sweetness as they are."

Lawrence couldn't help laughing at her overstatement.

"Shouldn't a wisewolf be able to conquer temptation?"

"While one may lose much because of avarice, nothing was ever accomplished by abstinence." The sight of Holo licking her fingers clean of the sweet juice strengthened her argument. If it meant missing such pleasure as this, asceticism was the height of folly.

All this was merely academic, of course.

"So, what was that you were going to say earlier?"

"Hm? Oh, yes. I've no money and no immediate means to earn money, so as you do business I'll just put a few words in to help you bring in more profit. Agreed?"

No merchant worth his salt simply answers "agreed" when so asked. It's common sense to refrain from answering until making sure of the other party's intentions. A verbal contract is still a contract and must be honored, come what may.

Thus Lawrence didn't answer right away. He didn't understand what Holo was getting at.

"You'll soon be selling the marten furs, yes?" As if guessing at the reason for his hesitation, Holo turned to the wagon bed behind them.

"Today, hopefully. No later than tomorrow."

"Well, I'll try to say something to bring your profit up, if I can.

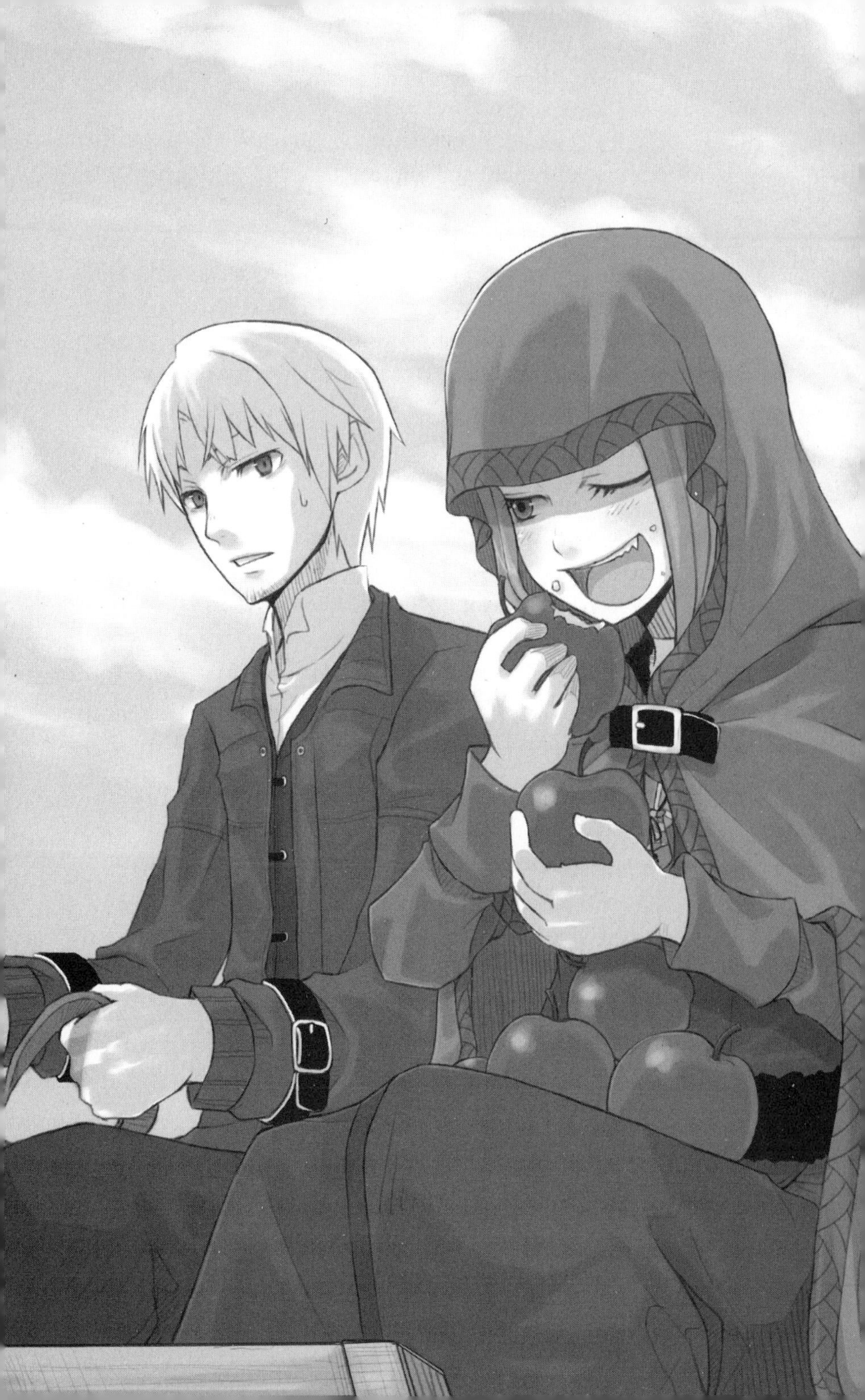

Whatever the difference I make, I keep," she said, licking her little finger clean as if it were nothing.

Lawrence mulled it over. Holo seemed confident that she could sell the marten pelts higher than he could. Wisewolf or no, he had seven years of experience as a traveling merchant. He wasn't such a weak dealer that a few words tossed in from the side would bring up his prices, and there was no guarantee the buyer would accept such prices.

Yet his curiosity at exactly how she would attempt this farce overpowered his doubt that it would actually happen, so in the end he said, "Agreed."

"It's done, then!" replied Holo, burping.

"But this isn't just limited to our pelts. You're a merchant, too — there may be no chance for me to talk up our price."

"How modest of you."

"Wisdom is knowing thyself first."

The statement would've sounded better had she not said it while casting her gaze longingly back toward the remaining pile of apples.

The pelts' destination was the Milone Company, a brokerage house that acted as an intermediary for a variety of goods. The Milone Company was the third-largest house in the city; the two above it were local businesses that had their headquarters in Pazzio. The Milone Company was headquartered in a mercantile nation far to the south and run by a powerful trader of noble lineage; the Pazzio location was a branch.

Lawrence had chosen the Milone Company over the local brokerages because it would pay higher commodity prices in order to best its competitors and also because, having so many branches in different places, it could provide valuable information.

His aim was to dig up information akin to the story he'd heard from the young merchant Zheren. Who better to ask about currency exchange than traders who routinely crossed borders to do business?

After securing lodgings for the two of them, Lawrence trimmed his beard and set out.

The Milone Company was the fifth building from the docks and the second-largest shop in the area. It had a huge gate that faced the docks to accommodate wagon traffic, which made the shop seem even bigger at a glance. Commodities of all kinds were piled around the gates, as if to show off the company's prosperity. It might have been their peculiar way of competing with the local businesses, which could trade on their long-standing local connections and didn't need flashy displays to prove they were turning a profit.

Lawrence stopped his wagon at the loading area, and presently an employee came out to meet them.

"Welcome to the Milone Trading Company!"

The smart-looking man tasked with unloading had a neatly trimmed beard and hair. Normally a trading company's unloading dock was a chaotic swirl of banditlike men shouting this way and that — Milone was an exception.

"I've sold wheat here before, but today I have furs to sell. Will you take a look?"

"Yes, yes, but of course! The man inside and to the left will be happy to see you."

Lawrence nodded and with a flick of the reins drove the wagon inside. Around the area were stacked all sorts of goods — wheat, straw, stones, timber, fruit, and more. The staff was quick and efficient, which is how the Milone Company was successful even in foreign countries, a fact that would impress any traveling merchant.

Even Holo seemed impressed.

"Ho there, sir, where are you headed?"

The two were watching the busy loading and unloading in the shop but stopped at the sound of the voice. They looked in its direction and saw a large man with steam rising from his suntanned body. He didn't seem like the man Lawrence had been directed to find, but he was certainly huge.

"Is he a knight?" Holo said under her breath.

"We're here to sell furs. I was told to come to the left side of the shop." Lawrence met the man's eyes and smiled.

"Right, then, I'll just take your horse. This way, if you please."

Lawrence did as he was told and angled his horse toward the man. The horse snorted. Apparently he sensed the man's vitality.

"Ho-ho, a good horse, sir! He looks stout of heart."

"He works without complaint; I'll say that much," said Lawrence.

"A horse that complains — now that would be something to see!"

"You're not kidding."

The two men laughed, and the worker led Lawrence's horse inside the unloading area, and after hitching him to a sturdy wooden fence, called out.

The person that answered was a man who looked more fit to be carrying a quill and ink than hay bales. He seemed to be the buyer.

"Kraft Lawrence, I presume? We thank you for your patronage."

Lawrence was used to being greeted politely, but he was impressed that the man knew his name before Lawrence had given it. He'd last visited the company during a winter three years ago, selling wheat. Perhaps the man that now greeted Lawrence in the entryway still remembered him.

"I'm told you've come to sell furs today." The buyer skipped over the usual pleasantries about the weather and jumped straight to the heart of the matter. Lawrence coughed slightly and shifted into his trader persona.

"Indeed I have. These are the very ones, here in the back of the wagon, seventy total." He hopped down from the wagon and invited the buyer to view the furs. He was followed by Holo, who jumped down from the wagon a moment later.

"Ho, these are good marten furs indeed. The year has been a good one for crops, so marten fur is scarce."

About half the marten fur that reached the marketplace came from farmers who hunted in their free time. When the harvest was plentiful, they were too busy to hunt, and marten fur was scarcer. Lawrence decided to push his position.

"You only see furs this fine once every several years. They were drenched with rain on the way here, but look — they've lost none of their luster."

"'Tis a fine luster, to be sure, and with good lie. What of their size?"

Lawrence pulled a largish pelt from the bed and offered it to the buyer, since it was generally prohibited for people other than the owner of the goods to touch them.

"Oh, ho. They're not lacking in size. You said you had seventy?" He didn't ask to see all the pelts; he was not so unrefined. Here was the challenge of trade — there was no buyer that would not want to see each pelt, but likewise was there no seller that would want to show each.

This was the intersection of vanity, propriety, and desire.

"Well, then . . . Sir Lorentz . . . ah, my apologies, Sir Lawrence, you've come to trade with us because you sold wheat here in the past?"

The same name was pronounced differently in different nations. It was a mistake Lawrence himself made often enough, so he forgave it with a smile and produced a wooden abacus from his pocket, which the man looked at. Different regions and nations had different ways of writing numbers, and because nothing was harder than trying to puzzle through these differences, merchants hardly ever wrote figures down while negotiating. Moving the wooden beads of the abacus would make the numbers completely clear, although one still had to be mindful of exactly what currency was being counted.

"I can offer . . . say, one hundred thirty-two silver *trenni*."

Lawrence pretended to think on the matter for a moment. "You don't see furs like these often. I brought them to you because I've done business with you in the past, but . . ."

"We certainly appreciate your business."

"For my part I'd like to continue our association."

"As would we, I assure you. In light of friendly relations, then, what say you to one hundred forty?"

It was a somewhat transparent exchange, but within the mutual deception was truth — which made the dealings more interesting.

One hundred forty *trenni* was a good price. It wouldn't be wise to push past that.

But just when Lawrence was about to say "It's done, then," Holo — who'd been silent up until that point — tugged slightly on his sleeve.

"Excuse me a moment," said Lawrence to the buyer, then leaned down, putting his ear level with Holo's hood.

"I don't quite know — is that a good price?"

"Quite good, yes," said Lawrence simply, smiling to the company representative.

"Well then, do we have an agreement?" It seemed the buyer was ready to conclude the deal. Lawrence smiled and was about to reply.

"Wait just a moment."

"Wha — " said Lawrence, without thinking.

Before he could say anything further, she kept speaking — just like a canny merchant would.

"One hundred forty *trenni*, you said, yes?"

"Uh, er, yes. One hundred forty in silver *trenni* pieces," answered the representative, a bit taken aback by the sudden question from the up-to-now silent Holo. Women were rare in places of trade — not unheard of, but rare.

For her part, Holo either didn't know or didn't care; she spoke as freely as she pleased. "Ah, perhaps you didn't notice?"

The buyer, quite taken aback, looked at Holo. He seemed not to understand what she was getting at; Lawrence didn't know, either.

"My apologies, but have I overlooked something?" The buyer, a merchant from a neighboring country, looked to be roughly the same age as Lawrence. He was a veteran of countless negotiations, who'd dealt with innumerable parties in his career.

It was to his credit that despite his experience, he appeared to be sincerely apologizing to Holo.

Of course it was far from surprising that he was taken aback. Holo had effectively asked him if he knew what he was looking at.

"Mm. I can see you're a fine merchant, so surely you pretended not to notice? I can see I won't need to hold back with you." Holo grinned underneath her cloak. Lawrence nervously hoped she wasn't showing her fangs, but more than anything he wanted to know what she was doing.

The buyer had been accurate and honest. If Holo was telling the truth, then Lawrence himself had also missed an important detail.

Which was impossible.

"My intention is anything but, I assure you. If you'll kindly point out what you're speaking of, we will be happy to adjust the price appropriately . . ."

Lawrence had never seen a buyer act so meekly. To be sure, he'd seen them pretend meekness, but this was no act.

Holo's words had a strange weight, and her delivery was perfect.

"Master," she said to Lawrence. "It's not polite to make sport of people."

It was hard to tell whether she called him "master" to mock him or because it was appropriate to the situation, but in either case, if he bungled his response here, he knew he'd hear about it later. He frantically groped for a response.

"Th-that was certainly not my aim. But perhaps you should be the one to tell him."

Holo grinned a lopsided grin at Lawrence, flashing a fang. "Master, pass me a fur, if you please."

"Here."

It struck Lawrence as silly that he had to exert himself to maintain his dignity in the face of being called "master." Holo was the only master here.

"Thank you, master. Now, if you please, sir . . ." said Holo, turning to the buyer and showing him the fur. At a glance its lay, size, and luster did not seem to merit an increased price. Even if she were to talk up the lay as being especially fine, the buyer would unavoidably ask to examine the fur more closely, and would inevitably find flaws. The price was unlikely to drop, but the relationship between buyer and seller would suffer.

"These are fine furs, as you can see," Holo said.

"I quite agree," replied the buyer.

"You won't see their like in many years. Or perhaps I should put it this way — you won't *smell* their like in many years."

Holo's words froze the air in an instant. Lawrence had no idea what she was talking about.

"'Tis a scent, but to miss it you'd need to be blind!" Holo laughed. She was the only one. Lawrence and the buyer were too stunned to be amused.

"Well, a smell is worth a thousand words. Would you care to sample the scent?" Holo handed the pelt to the buyer, who took it and looked uncertainly toward Lawrence.

Lawrence nodded slowly, hiding his confusion.

What was the point in smelling the pelts? He had never heard of such a thing in all his dealings.

Neither had the buyer, surely, but he had no choice but to placate his vendors. He slowly brought the fur up to his nose and sniffed.

At first, his face showed a mixture of confusion and surprise. He sniffed again, and only the surprise remained.

"Oh? Smell something, do you?" Holo said.

"Ah, er, yes. It smells like fruit, I'd say."

Lawrence looked at the fur in surprise. Fruit?

"Fruit indeed. Just as fur is scarce this year because of the harvest, so did the forest overflow with fruit. This marten was scampering about in that same forest until just a few days ago, and it ate so much of that plentiful fruit that the scent suffused its body."

The buyer sniffed the fur again. He nodded, as if to say "true enough."

"The truth is that while the fur's luster might be better or worse, it generally changes little. Does the problem not come, then, when the fur is made into clothing, when it is actually used? Good fur is durable; bad fur soon wears thin."

"True, as you say," said the buyer.

Lawrence was astonished. How much did this wolf know?

"As you can tell, this particular fur has the sweet scent of a marten that has eaten very well indeed. It took two strong men to pull the hide clear of the body, it was so tough."

The buyer tugged on the fur experimentally.

He couldn't pull too hard on goods he hadn't yet purchased, though — something Holo knew full well.

She was a perfect merchant.

"The fur is as strong as the beast itself was, and will keep the wearer as warm as a spring day, shedding rain from dawn 'til dusk. And don't forget the scent! Imagine coming across a perfumed piece of clothing like this among coats made from nose-wrinkling marten fur. Why, 'twould sell so dear your eyes would pop out."

The buyer was indeed imagining the scenario, gazing off into the distance. When Lawrence thought about it, he could see that the goods would sell high — or perhaps, he could *smell* as much.

"So, what do you think would be a fair price, then?"

The buyer snapped out of his reverie and straightened himself, then played with some figures on his abacus. The beads flew back and forth with a pleasant *tak-tak-tak* sound, finally displaying a figure.

"What say you to two hundred *trenni*?"

Lawrence's breath caught in his throat. One hundred forty pieces was already a respectably high price. Two hundred was unimaginable.

"Mmm," Holo murmured to herself. He wanted to beg her to stop — this was going too far, but she was implacable.

"How about three pieces for each fur — two hundred ten in total?"

"Er, well . . ."

"Master," she said to Lawrence. "Perhaps we should try elsewhere —"

"Uh, no! Two hundred ten pieces, then!" said the buyer.

Hearing this, Holo nodded, satisfied, and turned to her "master." "You heard the man, master."

She was definitely teasing him.

The tavern called Yorend was on a slightly removed alleyway, but it looked well-kept enough. Local craftsmen appeared to make up the bulk of its clientele.

Lawrence found himself suddenly tired when they arrived at the Yorend tavern.

Holo, on the other hand, was quite energetic, probably because she'd managed to outwit two merchants at once. The hour was yet early, so the tavern was mostly empty, and their wine was out very quickly — Holo drained hers in one huge draught, while Lawrence was content to nurse his.

"Ah, wine!" said Holo, belching a fine belch. She lifted her wood cup and ordered another round, which the tavern girl acknowledged with a smile.

"What troubles you? Aren't you going to drink?" said Holo, munching away on some fried beans.

She didn't seem to be particularly dizzy with success, though, so Lawrence decided to broach the subject directly.

"Have you ever worked as a merchant?"

Holo, still munching the snack and holding her refilled glass, smiled ruefully. "Oh, I'm sorry, have I injured your pride?"

Naturally, she had.

"I don't know how many deals you've done in your life, but I watched countless transactions when I was in the village. Long ago, I once saw a man use that technique — I didn't invent it myself. When was that, anyway . . . ?"

Lawrence didn't speak, but his eyes held the question: Is that true? Holo looked slightly troubled as she nodded, and Lawrence sighed even as he felt somewhat relieved.

"I really hadn't noticed, though. Last night when I slept in the furs, I didn't smell any fruit."

"Oh, that. That was from the apples we bought."

Lawrence was speechless. When had she pulled that trick?

And suddenly, he felt a chill of worry.

It was fraud!

"It's his own fault for being tricked," said Holo. "He'll be impressed once he figures it out."

". . . You may have a point."

"There's no point in being angry when you've been tricked. A real merchant knows to be impressed."

"That's quite a sermon. You sound like a wizened old trader."

"Heh. And you're just a babe in arms, yourself."

Lawrence had to laugh. He shrugged as he drank his wine. It had a keen taste to it.

"All this aside, did you do as you were supposed to?" Holo was talking about the Zheren matter.

"I asked around the Milone Company to see if anybody knew about nations that would be issuing new silver currency, but they didn't seem to be hiding anything. As long the information isn't something that needs to be monopolized, they'll normally share it. Makes for good business relations."

"Hm."

"But chances for this kind of deal aren't common. That's why we're involved."

It wasn't vanity. It was reality. In currency speculation, prices either rose, fell, or held steady. Even if the details became complex, all one had to do was turn it over in one's head until one hit upon the solution.

Once the proposed deal was reduced to the party that would gain and the one that would lose, there were few decisions to make.

However . . .

"Still, whatever the trick, as long as we can avoid getting fleeced and come out ahead, we'll be fine. "

Lawrence drank some wine and popped some beans into his mouth — Holo was paying, so he decided he might as well take advantage of it.

"I don't see the owner anywhere. I wonder if he's out," he said.

"Zheren did say we could contact him through the bar. He must be on good terms with the establishment."

"Well, traveling merchants usually base their operations out of either a tavern or a trading house. In fact, I've got to get to a trading house later on. And the owner really isn't around, is he?" said Lawrence, scanning the tavern yet again. It was a fairly spacious establishment, with fifteen round tables; only two other people — craftsmen from the look of them — were in the tavern.

He couldn't very well just go talk to them, so he asked the girl when she brought them another round of wine along with some roasted herring and smoked mutton.

"The owner?" said the girl as she set the wine and food on the table. Her arms were very slender; Lawrence wondered where she got the strength to handle the heavy food. "He's gone to buy ingredients at the marketplace," she continued. "Do you have some business with him?"

"Could you possibly tell him we're trying to get in touch with a man named Zheren?"

If they didn't know Zheren here, that was fine, too. Many merchants used taverns as convenient points of contact, so a misunderstanding was entirely possible.

But it turned out to be unnecessary concern on Lawrence's part. The girl's eyes brightened immediately at the mention of Zheren.

"Oh, Mr. Zheren? I know of him."

"Do you?"

"He normally comes soon after sundown. Feel free to stay here until then."

She was a shrewd girl indeed, but she had a point. It was an hour or two until dusk, which would be just enough time to enjoy a nice leisurely drink.

"We'll take you up on that, then," said Lawrence.

"Do enjoy yourselves!" said the girl with a bow, then turned to attend to the tavern's other two patrons.

Lawrence drank from his cup of wine. Its tart scent wafted across his nose, fading to sweetness on his tongue. Some liquors, like rum, traded on their intensity, but Lawrence preferred the sweetness of wine or mead. Sometimes he'd have cider just for a change.

Beer was good, too, but its flavor depended on the skill of the craftsman and the tastes of the person drinking it. Unlike wine, whose quality depended entirely on price, a beer's deliciousness was unrelated to its cost, so merchants tended to avoid it. There was no way to know if the particular brew would suit your taste unless you were from the region or town — so when he wanted to appear local, Lawrence would order beer.

Lawrence thought on this when he noticed that Holo, sitting opposite him, had stopped eating. She appeared to be deep in thought. Lawrence spoke up to get her attention, but she was slow in answering.

". . . That girl, she's lying," she finally said, once the girl had disappeared into the kitchen.

"Lying how?"

"Zheren doesn't necessarily come in here every day."

"Hm." Lawrence nodded, looking into his wine cup.

"Well, I hope we'll see Zheren soon, as she says."

The girl's lie meant that she was already in touch with Zheren. If not, things would be complicated now for both Lawrence and the mysterious young merchant.

"As do I," said Holo.

The reason for the lie was unclear, though. It could be that she was able to call Zheren anytime she wanted and simply wanted to keep Lawrence and Holo at the table and ordering wine for a little while longer. Merchants and traders told lies large and small all the time. Worrying over every single one would soon drive one to distraction.

So Lawrence wasn't particularly worried, and he imagined Holo was the same.

And other than Holo's delight at the honeycomb-shaped honeyed stew, the sun set without incident, and soon customers began filtering into the tavern.

Among them was Zheren.

"I rejoice at our reunion!" said Zheren, raising his wine cup. It knocked against Lawrence's with a pleasant *klok*. "How fared your furs?"

"They fetched a good price — as you can tell from the wine."

"I envy you! I daresay you had an angle?"

Lawrence didn't reply immediately, instead taking a drink of wine. "That's a secret."

Holo was busily devouring the beans, possibly to hide her smirk.

"Well, in any case, I'm glad you were able to sell them for a good price. For my part, more capital means more profit."

"Just because I have more capital doesn't mean I'll be increasing my investment."

"Say it's not so! I've prayed for your good fortune in anticipation of just that!"

"Then you've been praying at the wrong place. You should've just prayed for me to up my investment."

Zheren gazed upward, his face a mask of exaggerated tragedy.

"So, to business, then," said Lawrence.

"Ah, right." Zheren composed himself and looked at Lawrence, but looked briefly to Holo as well, as though he knew she, too, was a figure not to be underestimated.

"In exchange for selling me the information of which silver currency is due to become purer, you want a portion of the profit I'll make. Does that sum it up?"

"Indeed."

"Is this story of a purer coin true?"

Zheren faltered slightly at the directness of the question. "Well, I'm predicting it based on information I got from a small mining town. I think it's trustworthy, but . . . there are no guarantees in business."

"True enough."

Lawrence nodded, satisfied at seeing Zheren cringe. He brought some stew to his lips and continued.

"If you'd told me it was a sure thing, I'd have had to walk away. Nothing is more suspicious than a guarantee."

Zheren sighed in relief.

"So, what would you want for a percentage?"

"Ten *trenni* for the information, plus ten percent of your profit."

"That's a very conservative demand given the potential gain."

"It is. If you should take a loss, I won't be able to compensate you. If I had to, all my assets would be forfeit. So I'll take ten percent of whatever you make, but if you take a loss, I'll refund you the information fee, and no more."

Lawrence mulled the issue over, his mind long since fuzzy from liquor.

Zheren's proposal boiled down to roughly two possibilities.

The first was that he, Lawrence, would sustain a loss, and Zheren would use that for his own gain.

The second was that Zheren's proposal was basically sound.

However, thanks to Holo, he knew that Zheren's claim that the currency in question would rise in value owing to an increased silver content was a lie. If so, Zheren planned to profit from Lawrence's loss, but Lawrence didn't yet know how.

Given this, Lawrence began to wonder if Holo's estimation of Zheren was mistaken after all. It didn't make sense that Zheren's goal was the paltry information fee.

But it wouldn't matter how much time he spent thinking about it. Only when he got the information from Zheren would he be able to get a fresh perspective.

If it became obvious that he would sustain a loss, he could just get his information fee back. With a little bit of speculation he could dodge any problems, and now his interest in whatever Zheren was planning was greater than ever.

"That sounds good enough to me."

"Oh, er, thank you very much!"

"Just to confirm, you want ten *trenni* to provide me with the information, and ten percent of my earnings. However, if I lose money, you'll return the fee to me, and you won't be liable for further losses."

"Yes."

"And we'll sign a contract to this effect before a public witness."

"Yes. As for the settlement day, can we make it three days before the spring market? I expect the currency to change within the year."

The spring market was still half a year out. It was enough time for the currency to settle into its new value, be it up or down. If it actually rose, there would be an accompanying increase of confidence in the currency, and people would be happy to do business using it. Its market value would rise rapidly. Those who sold it impatiently would lose out.

"That will do. It should be sufficient time."

"In that case, I look forward to seeing you at the public witness's office early tomorrow morning."

There was no reason to refuse. Lawrence nodded, and raised his cup. "To profit for both of us!"

At the sight of both men raising their cups, the listless Holo scrambled to get her cup in her hand.

"To profit!"

There was a pleasant *klok* as the cups knocked against each other.

The public witness, just as the name implies, is a public service for providing witnesses for contracts. However, just because a contract was signed before a public witness, the town guard would not necessarily catch someone who breached it. Even the monarchy, in charge of the public good as it was, would not do that.

Instead, the offending party's identity would be spread around by the public witness. This was fatal to a merchant. For larger deals, this was even truer — a merchant with a bad reputation wouldn't even be able to deal with traders from foreign countries, at least not in that particular city.

The consequences weren't particularly effective for people who were going to retire from trading, but as long as they planned to continue as a merchant, the incentive was enough.

It was before such a public witness that Lawrence signed the contract, paid Zheren the ten *trenni*, and received the information without incident. Lawrence and Holo then parted ways with Zheren and headed into the town marketplace. The empty wagon would only cause problems in the crowded town center, so they left it at the inn and went in on foot.

"This is the silver the boy mentioned, yes?" Holo held a silver *trenni*. It was the most widely used currency in the region because among the hundreds of different kinds of currency in the world, it was one of the most trusted, and also simply because this town and the region around it were within the nation of Trenni.

Nations that did not have their own currency were doomed to either collapse or become client nations of larger powers.

"It's a well-trusted coin in this region," said Lawrence.

"Trusted?" Holo looked up at Lawrence as she played with the coin on which the profile of the eleventh ruler of Trenni was engraved.

"There are hundreds of currencies in the world, and the amount of gold or silver in each varies constantly. Trust is an important part of currency."

"Huh. I only knew of a few different kinds of money. It used to be that business was done in animal skins."

Lawrence wondered exactly how many hundreds of years ago she was talking about.

"So, how about it? Have you worked something out now that you know which coin he was talking about?"

"Well, there are several possibilities."

"For example?" asked Holo as they walked past the stalls in the marketplace. She stopped suddenly, and a big man who had the look of a worker about him bumped into her. He was just about to shout at her when Holo looked up from underneath her cloak and apologized. The man reddened and managed to say, "W-well, be more careful."

Lawrence silently resolved not to be swayed by this particular tactic of Holo's. "What's wrong?" he asked.

"Mm. I want to eat one of those."

Holo was pointing at a bread stall. It was just before midday, so fresh-baked bread was lined up in neat rows. In front of a stall, a maid was buying more bread than she could possibly eat, probably for the midday meal of some craftsman and his apprentice.

"You want some bread?"

"Mm. That one, there, with the honey on it."

Holo indicated some long, thin loaves that were being showily displayed from the eaves of the stall. The honey-drizzled bread was popular in most places. Lawrence seemed to remember that the tradition was started in a certain city where a baker had hung the loaves from the eaves of his shop as he drizzled them with honey as a way to attract customers. The tactic had been so successful that fights broke out among the people who wanted to buy the bread, and the baker's union had made it official policy that all honey bread would be henceforth hung from the eaves.

The bread did look delicious, but Lawrence couldn't help grinning at Holo's sweet tooth showing itself yet again.

"You have money," he told her. "Go ahead and buy some if you want."

"I don't imagine bread and apples are far apart in price. Will you carry the mountain of bread I'll bring back with me? Or shall I ruin the baker's day by asking him for so much change?"

Lawrence finally understood. All Holo had were silver *trenni* coins — each of which was worth far more than it took to buy a loaf of bread. She'd bought more apples than she was able to carry with a similar coin.

"All right, all right. I'll give you a smaller coin. Here, hold out your hands. One of these black coins should get you one loaf."

Lawrence took the silver coin from Holo's hands and replaced it with several brown and black copper ones, pointing at the coin he wanted her to use.

Holo scrutinized the currency carefully. "You'd best not be cheating me," she said suspiciously.

He thought about kicking her, but Holo soon turned on her heel and headed for the baker's stall.

"Always with the quick tongue," retorted Lawrence, but in truth he couldn't claim he wasn't enjoying himself.

When he saw Holo walking back, her face the very picture of contentment as she sank her teeth into the bread, he couldn't help laughing.

"Don't bump into anybody else," Lawrence said. "I don't want to have to deal with a fight."

"Don't treat me like a pup, then."

"It's hard to see you as anything else when your mouth is covered in sticky honey."

"..."

For a moment Lawrence thought she was sulking in anger, but the aged wolf was not so easily provoked.

"Am I charming, then?" She looked up at Lawrence with her head cocked slightly, whereupon he slapped her on the head. "You certainly can't take a joke," she grumbled.

"I'm a very serious person," said Lawrence.

Her faintly flustered demeanor went unnoticed.

"So, what was it you were thinking about?"

"Oh, right, right." It was better to bring up the previous topic of conversation than stay in this uncomfortable territory. "So, back to the *trenni* coin. Zheren may well be telling the truth."

"Oh?"

"There are reasons to raise the silver content. So . . . here, take this coin, a silver *firin*. It's from a nation three rivers south of here. It's got a respectable silver content and is quite popular in the marketplace. You could say it's the *trenni*'s rival."

"Huh. Seems one thing never changes: a nation's power is in its money." The always-quick Holo munched away on her bread.

"Exactly. Nations do not always fight through strength of arms. If your country's currency is overwhelmed by a foreign coin, you've been just as thoroughly conquered. All the foreign king needs to do is cut off your supply of money, and your marketplace will die. Without money, you can neither buy nor sell. They control your economy."

"So they're increasing the silver content in order to gain advantage over their rival," said Holo, licking her fingers after finishing the bread.

Having come that far, Lawrence imagined that Holo might realize she had something to say.

"I suppose my ears aren't completely omniscient." Evidently she did.

"It's entirely possible that Zheren wasn't actually lying," agreed Lawrence.

"Mm. I quite agree."

She was being so reasonable that Lawrence found himself taken aback. Even though she'd admitted she wasn't perfectly accurate, he fully expected her to angrily chide him for doubting her senses.

"What, did you think I was going to be angry?"

"I surely did."

"Well, I might be angry at *that*!" she said with a mischievous smile.

"In any case, Zheren might not have been lying."

"Hmm. So where are we going now?"

"Now that we know which coin to look into, we're going to look into it."

"So, to the mint?"

Lawrence couldn't help laughing at her naive question, which earned him a sharp, angry look. "If a merchant like me showed up at the mint, the only greeting I'd get would be the business end of a spear. No, we're going to see the cambist."

"Huh. I guess there are things even I don't know."

Lawrence was understanding Holo's personality better and better. "Once we're there, we'll see how the coin has been performing recently."

"What do you mean?"

"When a currency's value changes drastically, there are always signs."

"Like the weather before a storm?"

Lawrence smiled at the amusing analogy. "Something like that. When the purity is going to increase a lot, it increases a little at a time, and when it's going to drop, it will drop gradually."

"Mmm . . ."

It didn't seem like Holo fully understood, so Lawrence launched into a lecture, sounding for all the world like a determined school-teacher.

"Currency is based on trust. Relative to the absolute value of the gold or silver in them, coins are obviously more highly valued. Of course, the value is set very carefully, but since what you're actually doing is arbitrarily assigning a value to something with no inherent worth, you can think of it as a ball of trust. In fact, as long as the changes to a coin's purity aren't large, they're impossible to detect. Even a cambist has difficulty with it. You have to melt the coin down to be sure. But because a currency is based on trust, when it gains popularity its actual value can exceed its face value — or do the opposite. There are many possible reasons for changes in its popularity, and one of the biggest is a change in the gold or silver purity of the coin. That's why people are so sensitive to changes in a currency — so sensitive that even changes too small to detect with eyeglasses or a scale can still be considered major."

He finished his lengthy digression. Holo stared off into the distance, appearing to be deep in thought. Lawrence suspected even the canny Holo wouldn't understand everything from the first explanation. He prepared himself to answer her questions, but none were forthcoming.

When he looked more carefully at her face, she seemed not to be trying to piece things together in her head, but rather as if she was confirming something.

He didn't want to believe it, but she may well have understood perfectly the first time.

"Hmph. So when whoever makes the coins wants to change the purity, first they'll make a minute change to see what the reaction is, then they'll adjust it up or down, yes?"

Having an apprentice like this was certainly a mixed blessing. A superior apprentice was the pride of any merchant, but humiliation lurked.

Lawrence hid the frustration he felt — it had taken him a full month to understand the concept of currency valuation. "Y-yeah, that's about right," he answered.

"The human world certainly is complicated." Despite the admission, her comprehension was terrifyingly quick.

As the two conversed, they approached a narrow river. It wasn't the Slaude that flowed by Pazzio, but rather an artificial canal that diverted water from the Slaude, so that goods coming down the river could be efficiently transported into the city center without having to bring them ashore first.

To that end, rafts were constantly floating along the river, tended by boatmen whose voices as they shouted at one another were now audible.

Lawrence was headed for the bridge that spanned the canal. Cambists and goldsmiths had long situated their businesses on bridges. There they would set up their tables and their scales and do business. Naturally, they were closed on rainy days.

"Oh ho, it's quite crowded," remarked Holo as they reached the largest bridge in Pazzio. With the sluice gates closed, flooding was impossible, so a bridge far larger than could ever be constructed over an ordinary river connected both sides of the canal, with cambists and goldsmiths packed elbow-to-elbow along its sides. All were highly successful, and the cambists in particular were kept busy changing money from lands near and far. Next to them, the goldsmiths busied themselves with their jewelry and alchemy. There were no crucibles for melting metal, but small jobs and orders for larger ones were common. As one would expect from a place where the bulk of the city's taxes were levied, the place fairly smelled of money.

"There are so many; how does one choose?"

"Any merchant worth his salt has a favorite cambist in each town. Follow me."

They walked up the congested bridge, Holo scurrying to keep up with Lawrence.

The bridges were crowded with passersby even in the best of times, and even though it was now illegal everywhere, the apprentices of the cambists and goldsmiths would jump from the bridge on errands for their masters, turning the milieu carnivalesque. The liveliness inevitably resulted in fraud — and it was always the customers who risked being cheated.

"Ah, there he is." Lawrence himself had been swindled many times in the past, and only once he'd made friends with certain money changers had it stopped.

His favored cambist in Pazzio looked a bit younger than him.

"Ho, Weiz. It's been a while," said Lawrence to the fair-haired cambist, who was just finishing business with another customer.

Weiz looked up at the mention of his name and smiled broadly upon recognizing Lawrence. "Well, if it isn't Lawrence! It has indeed been a while! When did you get into town?"

The association between the two professionals had been long. It was like a friendship, formed not out of kindness but necessity.

"Just yesterday," replied Lawrence. "Took a detour from Yorenz to do some business."

"You never change, old friend. You look well!"

"I'm all right. How about yourself?"

"Hemorrhoids, my friend. Finally caught the curse of our trade! It's not pleasant."

Weiz spoke with a smile, but it was the unpleasant proof of the true cambist. Sitting all day in one place so as not to miss a customer, nearly all of them suffered from hemorrhoids eventually.

"So, what brings you here today? Coming by at this hour means you must have need of my services, eh?"

"Yeah, actually, I have a favor to ask . . . uh, are you all right?" asked Lawrence. As if coming out of a dream, Weiz looked back to Lawrence from somewhere else. His eyes soon drifted away to elsewhere, though.

He was looking at the figure next to Lawrence.

"Who's the girl?"

"Picked her up in Pasloe on my way here."

"Huh. Picked her up, you say?"

"Well, more or less. Wouldn't you say?"

"Mm? Mm . . . might not be quite the word for it, but more or less, I'll allow," said Holo with some reluctance, pausing her curious glancing here and there to answer Lawrence.

"So, what's your name, miss?"

"Mine? 'Tis Holo."

"Holo, eh? Good name."

Weiz grinned shamelessly; Holo returned it with a not-altogether-displeased smile that Lawrence did not particularly appreciate.

"Well, if you have nowhere in particular to go, why not work here? I just happen to find myself in want of a maid. Someday you might follow in my footsteps, or perhaps even become my bride —"

"Weiz, I've come for a favor," said Lawrence, cutting him off. Weiz looked suitably offended.

"What? Have you already had your way with her?" Weiz had always had an indelicate manner of speaking.

Far from having "had his way with her," Lawrence found himself being toyed with by Holo, so he answered with an emphatic negative.

"Well, then, you should let me have a go," snapped Weiz, looking to Holo and smiling sweetly. Holo fidgeted nervously, occasionally pausing to say things like "Oh, my," an affectation Lawrence failed to find amusing.

Naturally, he concealed his irritation. "We'll discuss that later. Business first."

"Hmph. Fine, then. What do you want?"

Holo snickered.

"Have you any recently minted *trenni* coins? If you can, I'd like the three most recently issued coins."

"What, do you know something about the purity changing?"

Weiz knew his business — he'd immediately realized what Lawrence was up to.

"Something like that," said Lawrence.

"Well, watch yourself, friend. 'Tisn't so easy to get ahead of the crowd," said Weiz — which meant that even the cambists hadn't heard of any imminent changes.

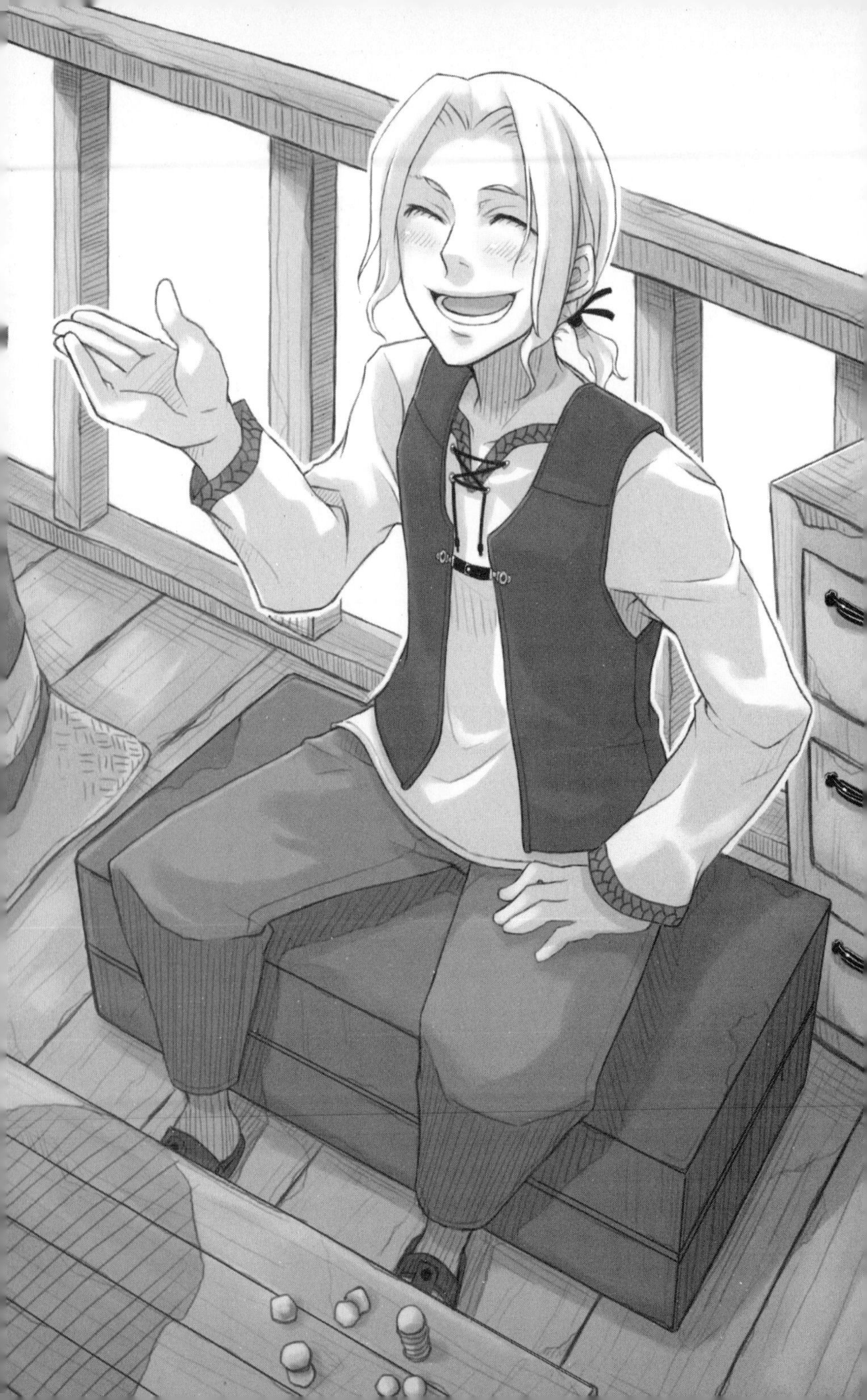

"So, do you have any or don't you?"

"I do indeed. There's a new coin came out just last month, at Advent. Then the one before that . . . here it is."

Weiz produced four coins from slots in the wooden box behind him and gave them to Lawrence. The year of issue was carved in the wood.

There was no visible difference between any of the coins.

"We handle money all day and haven't noticed anything. They're cast in the same mold, using the same ingredients. The lineup of artisans at the mint hasn't changed in years. There've been no coups, and there's no reason to change the coin," said Weiz.

The weight and color of the coins had already been scrutinized, but Lawrence still held them up to the sun and looked at them carefully. It seemed there really hadn't been any change.

"It's no use, friend. If you could tell just by looking, we'd have noticed long ago," said Weiz, his chin in his cupped hands. "Give it up," he seemed to be saying.

"Hm. What now, I wonder," said Lawrence with a sigh, returning the coins to Weiz's outstretched palm. They made a pleasant clinking sound as they fell.

"Don't want to melt them down, eh?" said Weiz.

"Don't be ridiculous. I can't do that," Lawrence retorted.

Melting down currency was a crime in any country. Weiz laughed at the preposterous notion.

However, Lawrence was now at a loss. He'd been sure that if there had been any change in the coin, Weiz would've had some idea of it.

What to do?

It was then that Holo spoke up.

"Let me see them," she said, at which point Weiz looked up and gave her his best smile.

"Oh, certainly, certainly," he said, handing the coins over —

though when she reached out to take them, he took her hands, not letting go for some time.

"Oh, sir, you're such a cad!" said Holo with a smile, to shattering effect. Weiz reddened and scratched his head.

"Can you tell something?" Lawrence asked, ignoring Weiz. He doubted even Holo would be able to discern the purity of a coin.

"Well now, let's see," she said.

Just when he wondered what she would do, Holo brought the hand that contained the money to her ear and shook it, jingling the coins.

"Ha-ha, now *that's* impossible," said Weiz with a grin.

It was said that master money changers with decades of experience could tell a coin's purity just by listening to its sound, but that was mostly legend. It was like saying a merchant's goods would always appreciate.

But Lawrence wondered. Holo had a wolf's ears, after all.

"Hmm," said Holo once she was finished. She chose two coins and returned the rest to the money changing table.

She jingled those two coins together, then repeated the process with different combinations of coins, a total of six times to check all possible combinations. Then she spoke.

"I cannot tell," she said.

Perhaps possessed by the memory of how bashful Holo had been when he'd grabbed her hands, Weiz put on an expression of sympathy so exaggerated it was hard not to wonder if he'd ever return to normal. "Oh, too bad! Too bad, indeed!" he said.

"Well, we've wasted enough of your time," said Lawrence. "We'll have a drink sometime."

"Indeed! That's a promise — a promise, you hear me!"

Overpowered by Weiz's vehemence, Lawrence promised, then the pair put the cambist's stall behind them.

Nonetheless, Weiz waived enthusiastically at them as they left. Holo looked back several times and waved shyly in return.

Once the crowds closed around them and Weiz could no longer be seen, Holo looked ahead again. She burst into laughter.

"He's an interesting sort!"

"For a matchless philanderer, I suppose so." It wasn't a lie, but Lawrence felt he had to take Weiz down a notch anyway. "So, what about the silver purity? Has it risen or fallen?" he asked, smiling down at Holo. Her grin disappeared and she seemed surprised.

"You've gotten quite good at ferreting the truth out, haven't you?"

"I'm the only one who knows about those ears of yours, after all. I know I saw them twitch."

Holo chuckled. "Can't let my guard down."

"But what surprised me is that you didn't say anything about it there. Your lie was unexpected."

"Whether or not he would've believed me, aside, we don't know what the other people nearby would've done. The fewer people as know a secret, the better, no? I suppose you can consider it compensation."

"Compensation?" Lawrence parroted back. He wondered what he'd done that merited compensating.

"You were a bit jealous back then, no? This is in exchange for that."

Lawrence's expression stiffened at Holo's teasing glance.

How had she known? Or was she just a little too good at luring him into tipping his hand?

"Oh, don't worry about it. All men burn with foolish jealousy."

It was painfully true.

"But women are fools to take delight in it. This world is full of fools no matter where you look," said Holo, drawing slightly nearer to Lawrence.

It seemed that Holo had experience with romance as well as matters mercantile.

She chuckled. "Though to me, you're both just lowly humans."

"Yet here you are, in human form. Best not bare your fangs now, in front of your beloved wolves."

"Ha, a flick of my lovely tail charms human and wolf alike!" Holo put a hand on her hip and swayed insouciantly. Somehow Lawrence got the feeling that she wasn't lying.

"Joking aside," she said, to Lawrence's relief, "it was just a bit, but the new coins have a slightly duller sound."

"Duller?"

Holo nodded. A duller sound meant that the silver purity had dropped. A small change was hard to discern, but if the purity dropped enough for the silver coins to become visibly darker, any plebian could tell the difference in sound. If what Holo said was true, it could be a sign that the *trenni* was going to become less pure.

"Hmm . . . but if that's true, it's reasonable to assume that Zheren was lying all along," said Lawrence.

"I wonder. The boy will have to return your ten *trenni*, depending on how this plays out."

"I'd gotten that far. If he'd just wanted to swindle some money by selling bad information, he'd have done it at the church without going to all the trouble of meeting at a bar."

"'Tis a puzzlement."

Holo laughed, but in his mind Lawrence was frantically trying to figure out the situation.

But the more he thought about it, the stranger it got. What was Zheren planning? He was unquestionably planning something. If Lawrence could figure out the motive, he knew he might be able to profit as well. That's why he'd taken this risk in the first place, but the fact that he still hadn't the faintest idea of Zheren's true motivation bothered him.

How did anyone make money from a drop in silver price and coin purity in the first place? All he could think of was long-term investment. If gold or silver fell from a high price to a low, you could sell at the high price, then buy up exactly what you sold after it fell. You'd end up with exactly as much gold as you started with, plus the difference in price. Speculation on gold and silver was always fluctuating. If you waited for it to return to its original price, you could realize a profit in the end.

However, he didn't have time for that kind of long-term planning. For one thing, half a year simply wasn't enough time.

"Well, Zheren brought me the deal, so he must have something to gain. He *must*."

"Assuming he's not some kind of fool," added Holo.

"He did mention not being responsible for losses. Which means . . ."

"Heh-heh," Holo began to laugh.

"What?"

"Heh. Ha-ha. Ha-ha-ha! You've been taken, my friend!"

Lawrence turned to Holo, startled. "Taken?"

"Oh, yes."

"For . . . what? The ten *trenni*?"

"Hee-hee-hee. Forcing money out of someone isn't the only kind of swindle."

Lawrence had heard of and seen many scams in his seven years of experience, but he had trouble understanding what Holo was talking about.

"What a scam! A plan where his opponent may or may not gain, but he is guaranteed to never lose!"

Lawrence's head swirled, white-hot. He nearly forgot to breathe. Soon the blood rose to his face.

"That boy will never lose. In his worst case, his profit is zero. If silver drops, all he does is return your money to you. If it rises, he gets part of whatever you make. It's a business that requires no capital. Even if no profit appears, he'll be fine."

Lawrence was overwhelmed by exhaustion. To have been had by such a frivolous scheme!

But it was true. He had been the one who'd sworn there was some larger ulterior motive. A traveling merchant so used to using every trick he could would naturally assume so. And so he had.

Zheren had predicted a profit was almost sure to appear.

"Heh. Humans are pretty smart," said Holo, as though they were talking about somebody else's problem. Lawrence could only sigh. Fortunately, he hadn't yet gone out of his way to invest in *trenni*. All he had risked was what he had on hand. There was nothing in the contract he had with Zheren about how many he was obligated to purchase. All he could do now was pray there were no fluctuations in the marketplace. He could then point out Zheren's lie, and there'd be nothing stopping him from getting his ten silver pieces back. Naturally if the price dropped, he'd be able to regain them legitimately, so losing only a single piece to him felt downright inexpensive.

When a merchant let his guard down, normally he lost everything.

But here, all Zheren had really done was hurt Lawrence's pride. He slumped a bit before Holo, who snickered at him out of the corner of her mouth.

"Although . . ." Holo began.

Lawrence looked at her beseechingly, as if to say, there's more? Holo looked back predatorily.

"Isn't it quite common for the silver purity to drop slightly?"

Suspecting that his redemption might start with this, Lawrence forced himself to straighten his leaden back. "No, normally the purity is controlled with extreme care."

"Hm. And yet out of nowhere, there's a deal that hinges on the purity of silver coins. Can that just be chance, I wonder?"

"Uh . . ."

The grinning Holo seemed to be enjoying this state of affairs. No — she was *definitely* enjoying it.

"Now, you being in that village, at that time, with that sheaf of wheat — that was chance. There is nothing so hard as discerning chance from fate. It's harder than romance for a shut-in."

"That's a strange analogy," was all Lawrence could answer.

"You're lost in the maze of your own thoughts. When that happens, you need a new perspective. When I'm hunting prey, sometimes I'll climb a tree. The forest looks different from on high. For example" — said Holo the Wisewolf with a crooked grin that bared her left fang — "what if the person who's planning something isn't that kid?"

"Oh . . ."

Lawrence felt like he'd been struck over the head.

"There's no reason Zheren's profit had to come from you. For example, perhaps he was hired by somebody else, and those wages motivated him to pull you into the strange deal."

Though she was fully two heads shorter than him, Holo seemed a giant.

"If you're looking at a single withered tree, it can seem like a grievous wound to the forest. But from the forest's perspective, that tree's remains will nourish other plants, acting for the good of the whole forest. If you change your perspective, a situation right in front of you can reverse itself. So — have you seen anything new?"

113

For a moment, Lawrence suspected that Holo already knew something, but from her tone it seemed that she was not testing him but rather was genuinely trying to help. Nothing was more important to a merchant than knowledge. But such knowledge was no mere commodity to be priced.

The situation before him. His knowledge of that technique.

Lawrence thought — thought about it from a different perspective.

Zheren, the only man he'd talked to directly — what if Zheren's gains were coming not from Lawrence, but from some other party?

Lawrence's breath caught in his chest the instant the thought came to his mind.

If that were indeed the case, he could think of only one possible explanation.

He'd heard the setup from another traveling merchant when they drank together in another town. The sheer scope of the tale was so huge he'd assumed it was yet another tavern-story.

Still, the story could conceivably explain why someone would do something so apparently meaningless as buying up a depreciating silver currency.

He could also see why Zheren would be lying even as he signed a contract before a public servant, and would use his influence in a tavern, acting in a way that didn't make sense for a swindler.

Zheren had been trying to lend the transaction as much credibility as he could in order to tempt Lawrence into buying up silver coins.

If Lawrence was right, Zheren had been hired by another party to buy up silver coins. Whoever it was wanted to collect silver as discreetly as possible.

The best way to collect a particular currency without attracting any attention would be to hire merchants to do it for you, appealing to their self-interest. Merchants who stood to turn a profit by buying up silver currency would not want to share information with others and would naturally be extremely careful. Then, you could just wait for an opportune moment and smoothly take over the collected currency, accomplishing your goal without influencing the marketplace or tipping anybody off.

It was a common technique for buying up a commodity in advance of a higher price.

The really clever part of this plan was that if the silver currency fell, the merchants would want to unload their silver in order to minimize their losses. This would make taking over their silver holdings far from difficult, and pride would keep the merchants who'd sustained losses from admitting that they'd invested in silver currency.

It was a perfect plan for colleting coinage without anyone knowing.

The massive scale of the plan could yield obscene profits. At least, the profits mentioned in the stories about such plans were stupendous.

Lawrence chuckled in spite of himself.

"Heh. You've figured something out, have you?" said Holo.

"Let's go."

"Hm? Uh, where?"

Lawrence had already started jogging away. He turned to Holo, impatient. "The Milone Company. That's how the plan works. The more depreciating silver currency that can be bought up, the more profit there will be!"

Once he'd discovered the motivation behind someone's plan, he could profit from it.

And the bigger their plan, the better.

CHAPTER FOUR

The whole of the Milone Company went from shocked to vigilant upon Lawrence's visit. Unsurprisingly—as Lawrence proposed that together they deal with the plot behind Zheren's swindle. If Lawrence had found Zheren's initial proposal difficult to believe, the Milone Company found Lawrence's scheme that much harder to swallow.

And of course there was the matter of the furs. They weren't so angry as to have it color future transactions, but the supervisor did smile ironically upon seeing Lawrence.

Even so, what spurred the Milone Company into tentative action was seeing the contract that Lawrence had signed with Zheren before the public witness, proving that they could investigate the deal as much as they wished before proceeding.

Lawrence also asked them to check into Zheren's background, impressing upon them that this was no simple fraud.

If they did so, the Milone Company would naturally have to wonder why the plan was so intricate for a mere swindle. They'd want to investigate it simply for their own future reference, Lawrence anticipated — and he was right.

After all, if everything Lawrence said was true, the Milone Company stood to reap enormous profit.

The Milone Company, like any company, was ever-watchful for a chance to get ahead of its competitors. Lawrence's expectation that they would overlook a proposal's shadiness if it promised sufficient gain was correct.

Having sparked an initial interest in the plan on their part, Lawrence's next task was to prove Zheren's existence. He and Holo hurried to the Yorend tavern that evening and informed the barmaid that they wished to meet with Zheren. As expected, Zheren did not frequent the place every night, and the barmaid told Lawrence that he'd not yet come by that particular day. But at length as the sun sank low Zheren arrived.

Lawrence made idle merchant chatter about this subject and that, and all the while a Milone employee sat at a nearby table, eavesdropping. In the days to come, the Milone Company would investigate Zheren and determine whether Lawrence's proposal was true or not.

Lawrence believed that Zheren had to have the support of a powerful merchant. If that was true, it would be easy for the Milone Company to trace.

There was, however, a problem.

"Will we be in time?" Holo asked upon returning to their inn that evening.

Just as Holo suggested, the problem was time. Even if Lawrence's expectations were correct, depending on circumstances they could miss the chance to realize any gain. No — there would be profit either way, but perhaps not enough to induce the Milone Company to act. Without them, it would be difficult for Lawrence to turn a profit on his own. On the other hand, if the Milone Company moved quickly, the potential gain would be stunning.

Both his own plan and the plan he suspected Zheren of being a part of depended on time.

"We *should* have enough time. That's why I came to the Milone Company in the first place."

By candlelight, Lawrence poured some wine he'd bought at the tavern into a cup. He looked down into the cup briefly before draining half of it in one go. Holo was sitting cross-legged on the bed; she drank her cup dry and looked at Lawrence.

"Is this company really so capable?" she asked.

"Doing business in foreign countries requires very keen ears — hearing merchants talking in a bar or customers in the market-place. If they weren't much better at collecting information than their competition, they'd never be able to open up branches in foreign countries, much less have those branches flourish. The Milone Company is very good at this sort of thing. Investigating someone like Zheren is child's play for them."

Lawrence poured more wine for Holo — at her urging — as he spoke. By the time he finished, Holo had already drained her cup again. It was astonishing.

"Huh."

"What is it?" Holo asked, staring listlessly off into the distance. At first Lawrence thought she must have been pondering some-thing, but soon it was clear that she was merely drunk.

"You've had quite a bit," he said.

"The charms of wine are many."

"I suppose this *is* a good vintage. Normally I never drink any-thing so fine."

"Is that so?"

"When there's no money, I'll drink wine thick with grape drip-pings, wine so bitter it can't be drunk without adding sugar, honey, or ginger to it. Wine transparent enough to see the bottom of the cup is a true luxury."

Hearing this, Holo looked vaguely into her cup. "Hm. And I thought this was normal."

"Ha! Well, you're higher and mightier than I."

Holo's expression stiffened. She set her cup down on the floor, then immediately curled up into a tight ball on the bed.

Her reaction was so sudden that Lawrence could only look on in shock. He assumed that it wasn't simply because she was now sleepy.

"What's wrong?" he asked, not having the faintest idea what her problem was, but Holo's ears didn't so much as twitch.

He said nothing more as he racked his brain trying to figure out her problem, and finally hit upon it — the conversation he'd had with her when they'd first met.

"Are you angry because I said you have more status than I do?"

When Lawrence had demanded to see Holo's wolf form, she'd said she hated being feared.

She also despised being celebrated as some kind of deity.

Lawrence remembered a song he'd heard from a traveling minstrel. It claimed that the reason a god needed a festival every year was because it was lonely.

"I'm sorry. I didn't mean anything by it."

Holo didn't move.

"You're a . . . how shall I say it? You're nothing special — wait, no, that's wrong. You're not a commoner. Ordinary? No, that's not it . . ."

Lawrence became more and more agitated as he failed to find the right words.

All he wanted to say was that Holo wasn't special, but he simply couldn't articulate that.

As he continued to cast about for something to say, Holo's ears finally pricked, and he heard her snicker slightly.

Holo rolled over and smiled indulgently at Lawrence. "How inarticulate. You'll never attract a female that way."

"Urgh."

Lawrence immediately remembered a time when he had stayed over at a certain inn, waiting for a blizzard to pass, and become taken with a girl there. She flatly rejected him, for no reason other than the one Holo gave: he was desperately inarticulate.

The sharp-eyed wolf soon discerned this. "I was right, eh?" she chuckled. "Still, that was . . . immature of me."

Lawrence softened at Holo's apology, and he offered his own again. "Sorry."

"I do truly dislike it, though. Younger wolves were friendly enough, but there was always a line. Weary of it, I left the forest. I suppose" — Holo looked off into the distance then down at her hands again — "I was looking for a friend."

Holo gave a self-deprecating smile.

"A friend, eh?"

"Mm."

Lawrence would have thought this topic unpleasant for her, but Holo's answers had been strangely upbeat, so he asked the question that was on his mind.

"And did you find one?"

Holo smiled bashfully and did not immediately answer.

Given her expression, her answer was obvious. She smiled as she was thinking of the friend she'd made.

"Yes."

But Lawrence didn't find her happy nodding at all funny.

"He's a fellow from the village of Pasloe," she continued.

"Oh, the one whose wheat you borrowed?"

"Mm. He's a bit foolish, but very cheerful. He wasn't the least bit surprised when he saw my wolf form. I suppose he is a bit odd, but a good fellow nonetheless."

To hear her speaking as though of a loved one, Lawrence wrinkled his nose but hid it behind his wine cup — he didn't want her to see.

"He really *is* a fool though. Sometimes I'm at a loss."

Holo spoke happily, seeming slightly bashful to be discussing the past. She no longer looked at Lawrence but hugged her tail, playing absently with its fur.

Suddenly she let out a childish giggle and tumbled back on the bed, sounding for all the world like a child sharing a secret with a friend.

She was probably just tired, but to Lawrence's eyes it seemed as though she had left him behind and was letting her memories flood over her.

That was no reason to rouse her, though, so with a small sigh, he drained his wine cup.

"Friends, eh?" he murmured, then placed the cup on the table and stood. He walked over to the bed and drew the blanket up over Holo.

Her cheeks were slightly flushed as she slept innocently, but the longer he looked at her the more clouded his thoughts became, so he turned his back to her and headed for his own bed.

But as he blew the tallow candle out and lay down, he felt a certain regret.

He wished he'd claimed a lack of money and gotten a room with a single bed.

Lawrence sighed more deeply this time as he faced away from her.

If his horse had been there, it probably would've sighed at him, too, he thought.

"We accept your proposal," said the head of the Milone Company's Pazzio branch, Richten Marheit, in an even tone. It had been only two days since Lawrence had come to the Milone Company with his proposal. The company was indeed very efficient.

"I am very grateful. May I assume that you've discovered who is backing Zheren?"

"He has the support of the Medio Company. I hardly need mention that they're the second-largest company in the city."

"The Medio Company, eh?"

Based in Pazzio, Medio had many branches. They were the largest agricultural broker in Pazzio, particularly for wheat, and were all the more impressive for having their own ships with which to move their product.

Yet something stuck in Lawrence's mind. The Medio Company was large, but he'd expected Zheren's backer to be even larger — perhaps a nobleman.

"We believe there is a still-larger figure behind the Medio Company. With their resources alone, it would probably be impossible to enact the plan you've described. There is probably a nobleman operating behind the Medio Company, but there are many such figures who deal with them, and we've been unable to narrow it down to a single person. But as you yourself said, it won't matter as long as we're first to act."

Marheit smiled slyly, showing a confidence borne of having the immense resources of the Milone Company to call on, the likes of which Lawrence could barely imagine. Their main branch was patronized by none but royalty and high priests. They had nothing to fear from a deal like this.

It was important for Lawrence not to betray any temerity. In negotiation, showing weakness or servility was tantamount to losing. He had to be bold.

He replied in an even tone.

"Well, then, shall we discuss how to split the profits?"

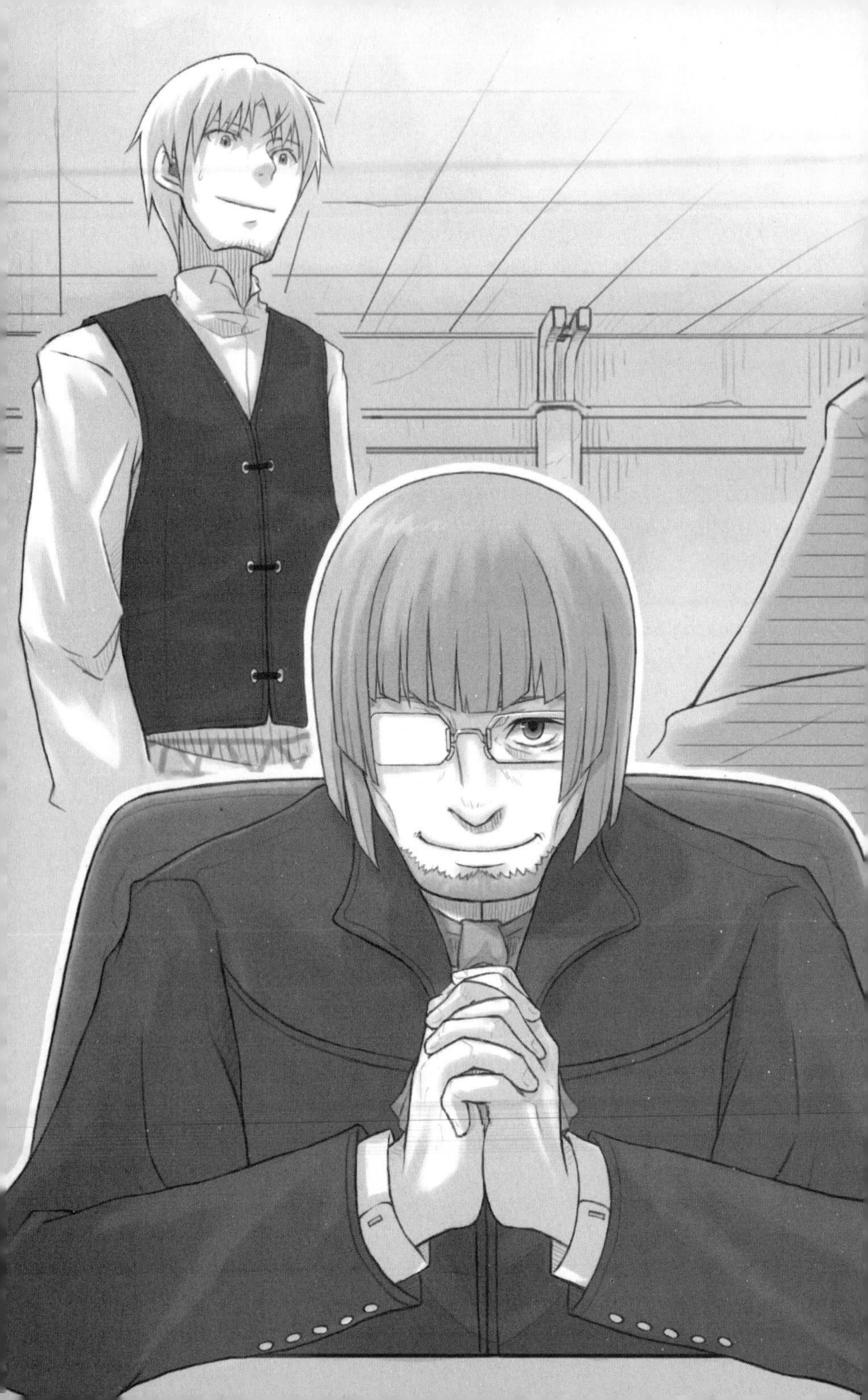

It went without saying that these negotiations would give rise to his dreams.

Seen off by all the employees of the Milone Company branch except the boss, Lawrence left humming a tune, unable to suppress his happiness.

He'd proposed that the company give him five percent of its profits from the currency exchange. This was a mere one-twentieth of its take, but Lawrence couldn't stop smiling.

After all, if the Milone Company moved as he suggested, the amount of *trenni* silver that could be bought up was not one or two thousand, but rather two or three *hundred* thousand. If — as the rough estimates suggested — they exacted a ten-percent return from the deal, Lawrence's share could exceed a thousand coins of pure profit. If he topped two thousand coins, and wasn't too extravagant, he would be able to set up a shop in a town somewhere.

However, when compared to the gain the Milone Company was anticipating, the profit made from unloading the silver coin was a mere bonus. They moved as a company, so such profits were insignificant.

Lawrence could never actually hold that kind of gain. It was simply too huge and would never fit in his purse — but if the Milone Company could realize the profit, Lawrence would be owed a significant debt and, once he opened his shop, could make a large profit on that loan.

So it was no surprise that he was humming so cheerfully.

"You seem pleased," said Holo, finally at the end of her patience as she walked beside him.

"I'd like to see the man who wouldn't be pleased at a time like this. This is the greatest day of my life." Lawrence gestured expansively. The gesture matched his mood — as if he were ready to catch anything in those outstretched arms.

The shop he'd long dreamed of opening was right before him.

"Well, I'm glad it's going so well," said Holo listlessly, her mood in stark contrast to Lawrence's. She covered her mouth with her hand.

It was nothing — she was merely hungover.

"I told you to go sleep in the hotel if you're feeling unwell."

"I was worried you'd get sucked into something unsavory unless I came with you."

"What do you mean?"

"Why, precisely what I said . . . *urp*."

"Honestly — just bear up a little longer. There's a shop ahead. We'll rest there."

". . . All right." Holo nodded with a vulnerability that seemed deliberate and grabbed hold of his outstretched arm. Wisewolf or not, one could hardly accuse her of having any self-restraint.

Lawrence, at a loss, muttered "honestly," again. Holo had no response.

The shop they entered was a tavern attached to a small inn. Though it was ostensibly a drinking establishment, it specialized in light meals and morning to night had a constant stream of merchants and travelers that used it as a rest stop. It was about a third full when they entered.

"Juice for one — any kind's fine — and bread for two," said Lawrence.

"Coming right up!" said the shopkeeper behind the counter cheerfully, then repeated the order to the kitchen.

Lawrence listened to the shopkeeper as he led Holo to an empty table inside the tavern.

Holo's manner was more kitten than wolf as she sprawled over the table. The walk from the Milone Company exacerbated the fatigue of the alcohol working its way through her system.

"Your tolerance is far from weak — you drank a lot yesterday." said Lawrence.

Holo's ears pricked under her hood at Lawrence's statement, but she seemed to lack the energy to look at him.

"Uugh," she groaned.

"Here y'are, apple juice and two servings of bread."

"The bill?"

"You'll pay now, then? It comes to thirty-two *lute*."

"One moment, please," said Lawrence, opening the coin purse that was attached to his waist and rummaging inside it. As he collected the black coins that could easily be mistaken for bronze, the shopkeeper noticed Holo's condition and smiled ruefully.

"A hangover, eh?"

"Too much wine," said Lawrence.

"Such are the mistakes of youth! It's the same with drinking as it is with anything else — there's a price. Plenty of young merchants stagger out of here with pale faces."

Any traveling merchant had indeed experienced this a few times. Lawrence himself was guilty of it on any number of occasions.

"Here you are, thirty-two *lutes*."

"So it is. You should rest here awhile. I take it you couldn't make it all the way back to your own inn?"

Lawrence nodded, at which point the shopkeeper laughed heartily and retreated behind the counter.

"Have some juice," said Lawrence. "It was pressed at just the right time." Holo raised her head lethargically. Her features were so fine that even her pained expression had a certain charm. No doubt Weiz would've been happy to take the day off to nurse her back to health. Even the slightest smile from her would've been thanks enough. Lawrence chuckled at the thought as Holo sipped the juice and regarded him strangely.

"Whew . . . I've not been hungover in centuries," sighed Holo after drinking half the juice and regaining a bit of vigor.

"A hungover wolf is a sad sight indeed. I suppose I can imagine a bear drinking too much, but a wolf . . ."

Bears often took bags filled with fermenting grapes hanging from the eaves of buildings. They had to be fermented to make wine, and as they did, they exuded a sweet scent.

There were even stories of bears making off with such bags only to later collapse drunkenly in the forest.

"It was probably bears I drank with the most in the forest," said Holo. "There was a bit of tribute from humans, too."

The idea of bears and wolves drinking wine together sounded like something out of a fairy tale. What would the Church make of this if they overheard?

"No matter how many times I'm hungover, though, I never seem to learn."

"Humans are the same way," said Lawrence to the ruefully grinning Holo.

"Now that you mention it . . . what was I going to say? I had something to tell you, but now it's gone. I feel like it was something rather important, too . . ." said Holo.

"Well, if it's that important, you'll remember eventually."

"Mmm . . . I suppose. Ugh. It's no good. I can't remember," she said, slumping back down on the table and closing her eyes.

She had probably felt like this all day. The shopkeeper hadn't said it, but it was a good thing they weren't about to depart. The wagon's shaking wouldn't make her feel any better.

"Anyway, all we have to do is leave the rest to the Milone Company. 'Good things come to those who wait,' after all. Just rest until you feel better."

"Ugh . . . it's so undignified," said Holo, sounding even more pathetic than before — she would likely feel ill for some time yet.

"I suppose you'll be off all day, then."

"Mm . . . it's pathetic, but you're right," she answered, still sprawled on the table, opening a single eye to look at Lawrence. "Did you have plans of some kind?"

"Hm? Well, I was thinking of doing some shopping after checking in with the Company."

"Shopping, is it? You can go on your own. I'll rest here awhile then return to the inn on my own," said Holo, raising her head and sipping the apple juice again. "Or what — did you want me to come along?"

Her teasing was by now standard, almost a greeting; so Lawrence simply nodded.

"Oh, you're no fun," Holo pouted at Lawrence's tranquility. Sipping perfunctorily at her drink, she must have expected him to become flustered, but even Lawrence could maintain his composure at times.

Lawrence couldn't help smiling down at Holo again as he chewed on a piece of bread.

"I was thinking of buying you a comb or a hat," he said. "Perhaps some other time."

Holo's ears twitched underneath the cloak.

". . . Just what are you planning?" she asked, her eyes half-lidded, but watching Lawrence carefully nonetheless.

Lawrence could hear the *swish, swish* of her restlessly twitching tail. Apparently she was worse than he expected at hiding her thoughts.

"What a way to talk."

"As the saying goes, one has to be even more careful with meat in one's mouth than with meat that's about to be taken away."

Hearing Holo's bitter words, Lawrence drew close to her face and whispered into her ear.

"If you're going to act the prudent wisewolf, at least do something about your restless ears and tail."

Surprised, Holo felt for her ears. "Oh!" she said.

"That should make us even," said Lawrence with a hint of arrogance. Holo glared at him, thin-lipped and frustrated.

"You've got such lovely hair, it seems a shame for you not to have a comb for it," he continued briskly.

He was happy having finally gotten the best of her, but if he pushed, it was quite possible she'd put him in his place again.

However, upon hearing Lawrence's words, the bored-looking Holo sniffed and sprawled across the table once more. "Oh, you're talking about my hair," she said shortly.

"All you do is bind it back with a hempen string. You don't even comb it."

"My hair isn't important. A comb would be nice, though — for my tail." A *swish, swish* sound could be heard after she spoke.

". . . Well, if you say so."

Lawrence did think that her flowing, silken hair was beautiful, and hair of any kind that was so long was very rare. It was difficult for anyone other than nobility to be able to wash their hair in hot water daily, so having such long, beautiful hair was a mark of high birth.

So like anyone else, Lawrence had a weakness for a girl with long, beautiful hair. Holo's hair was so lovely that few among even the nobility could match it, yet she seemed not to understand its value at all.

If she were to hide her ears with a veil rather than a heavy cloak and wear fine robes instead of the rough clothes of a traveling merchant, she'd be the equal of any maiden from a minstrel's poem — but Lawrence shied away from saying so.

There was no telling how she'd react, after all.

"So, then."

"Hm?"

"When will you buy this comb?"

Holo looked up at Lawrence from her prone posture on the table, her eyes shining with a certain anticipation.

"I thought you didn't need one," said Lawrence without rancor, his head cocked slightly.

"I never said that. I would like a comb. A fine-tooth one, if possible."

Lawrence didn't see the point of buying a comb if it wouldn't be used to comb hair. In his mind, a fine brush of the sort used by weavers would be best for her tail.

"I'll buy you a brush. Shall I introduce you to a good weaver?"

It was best to leave fur to experts with specialized tools, after all. Lawrence was only half-serious, but when he finished speaking and looked at Holo, his voice caught.

She was angry — so angry she was gnashing her teeth.

"You . . . you would treat my tail as a simple piece of fur?" she said, her intonation flat — surely not because she was afraid that talk of tails would be overheard by the other patrons.

Lawrence winced at her vehemence, but Holo looked as unwell as she had all day. There was a limit to how much she could counterattack.

"I cannot take this anymore," she said.

Lawrence suspected that her threats were empty.

He imagined that she might try crying, so he nonchalantly drank some apple juice. "What, are you going throw a tantrum now?" he asked, a note of accusation in his voice.

Naturally his resolve would waver if she actually burst into tears, but he didn't say this.

Perhaps chastened by his words, or possibly for some other reason, she opened her eyes slightly to regard Lawrence then looked away.

Her childish demeanor was rather charming. With a small smile, Lawrence mused that it would be nice if she were always like this.

Holo was silent for a moment. Then, in a small voice, she said, "I can't take it. I have to vomit."

Lawrence almost tipped the cup of apple juice over as he scrambled to his feet and called out for the shopkeeper to bring a bucket.

Well after the sun had set in the west and the clamor from outside his window had subsided, Lawrence looked up from the desk. Pen in hand, he raised both arms and stretched expansively. His back popped gratifyingly, and he turned his head left and right to work out the kinks in his neck, which also popped.

He looked back down to the desk. On it was a sheet of paper with simple plans for a shop — the town it would be situated in, the goods it would sell, and plans for its expansion. Written separately were construction costs, plans for securing citizenship, and a variety of other anticipated expenditures.

It was a plan for realizing his dream — to own a shop.

Even a week ago, this remained only a fantasy, but since Lawrence had made his deal with the Milone Company, it suddenly felt much more imminent. If he could bring in two thousand *trenni*, then after selling some ornaments and jewels that amounted to his savings, he would be able to open his shop. Lawrence would be a traveling merchant no longer, but a town merchant.

"Mmph . . . what's that sound?"

While Lawrence had been absorbed in gazing at the picture of the shop he'd drawn, Holo had at some point awoken. Her eyes were still blurry with sleep, but she appeared mostly recovered. She looked at Lawrence, blinked a few times, and dragged herself out of bed. Her eyes were slightly swollen, but she looked well enough.

"How do you feel?"

"Better. A bit hungry, though."

"If your appetite's back, you must be fine," said Lawrence, smiling and indicating the bread on the table. It was dark rye bread — the worst, cheapest bread you could get, but Lawrence enjoyed its bitter flavor and bought it frequently.

Unsurprisingly, Holo made her displeasure with the bread known after a single bite but ultimately gave up, since there was nothing else to eat.

"Is there anything to drink?"

"The water jug's right there."

Holo checked to see that the jug actually contained water and, after taking a drink, moved next to Lawrence as she munched away on the bread.

". . . A drawing of a shop?"

"*My* shop."

"Oh ho, not bad," said Holo, looking intently at the paper as she ate.

When traveling in a country whose language he didn't speak, Lawrence would use drawings to make deals. Sometimes he simply couldn't remember the name of a particular commodity, and interpreters were not always available. Hence, most traveling merchants were good at drawing. Whenever Lawrence turned a healthy profit, he would draw a picture of his future shop. It made him feel even better than drinking wine.

And while he had confidence in his drawing abilities, it was nice to be praised.

"What's this writing?"

"Location and expense planning. I don't expect it to go exactly like this, of course."

"Hmm. You've drawn parts of a city, too, I see. What city is it?"

"None in particular — just an idealized city for my shop."

"Ho-ho. You've been very detailed here — I suppose you're planning to open it soon, then?"

"If the deal with the Milone Company goes well, I will probably be able to."

"Hm." Holo nodded, not looking terribly excited at the idea. She popped a piece of bread into her small mouth, then walked back over to the table. Lawrence imagined that the ensuing gulping sound was her finishing the water.

"It's every traveling merchant's dream to have a shop. I'm no different."

"Heh. I know. You've even gone so far as to sketch out your ideal city, so you must have done this many times before."

"When I draw it, I feel that it will happen someday."

"An artist I knew long ago said something like that — that he wanted to paint all the scenes he saw before him." Holo bit into a second slice of bread and sat on the corner of the bed. "I doubt the artist would have fulfilled his dream even now, but it seems that yours is getting closer."

"Indeed. When I think about it, I can hardly stay still — I want to run around the Milone Company, swatting the ass of every employee I see."

It was a bit of an exaggeration, but far from a lie. Perhaps that was why Holo refrained from making fun, simply chuckling and saying, "I hope your dream comes true, then."

She continued. "Still, is having a shop such a good thing? Can't you do well as a traveling merchant?"

"If you profit, sure."

Holo cocked her head slightly. "What else would there be?"

"A traveling merchant might make the rounds between twenty or thirty towns — if you don't keep moving, you won't make any money at all. Most of your year is spent on a wagon." Lawrence sipped a bit of wine from the cup on the table. "The life being what it is, you don't really make any friends — just business associates."

Hearing his explanation, Holo seemed to realize something and to regret asking the question.

She really is a good sort, Lawrence thought, and he continued, hoping to assuage her regret. "But if I could open a shop, I'd become a true citizen of a town. I could make friends, and it would be simple to search for a wife. It would be a great solace to me to know where I would be buried when I die. Though finding a bride who'll stay beside me even in death . . . that will take some luck."

Holo laughed slightly.

Among traveling merchants, the act of going to a new city to dig up new goods was known as "searching for a wife," as it carried the sense of going to find something rare and valuable.

In reality, though, simply opening up a shop did not guarantee that one would be close to the citizens of the town.

Nonetheless, being able to stay on the same piece of land for a long time was every merchant's dream.

"It will be bad for me if you open a shop, though," said Holo.

"Why's that?" said Lawrence, turning around. Although her smile had not disappeared, it was tinged with sadness.

"If you open a shop, you won't want to leave it. I'll have to either travel alone or find a different companion."

Lawrence then remembered that Holo had said she wished to travel the world for a while then return to her homeland in the north.

But she had her wits. She had the money she'd made from the fur sale. Surely she would be fine on her own.

"You could travel alone, though, right?" Lawrence had no particular agenda behind the words, but upon hearing them, Holo silently looked down as she ate her bread.

"I'm tired of being alone," she blurted out, looking suddenly childish as she swung her legs — which didn't quite reach the floor — over the edge of the bed. She fell back and seemed so small that even the flickering candlelight threatened to swallow her.

Lawrence recalled the time Holo had so fondly reminisced about her friend from centuries earlier.

Dwelling so nostalgically on the past proved she was lonely. He remembered how she looked then, curled up as if to protect herself from a storm of isolation.

Lawrence chose his words very carefully to avoid hurting her feelings — she didn't often show this side of herself. "I expect I'll stay with you until you're back home in the north country, though."

He had little choice but to say as much, but nonetheless Holo looked up with an expression that said "Really?" in a rather humble manner. Lawrence carefully concealed the excitement he felt and continued.

"Even when the money comes in I won't be able to open up a store right away."

"Truly?"

"Why would I lie?" said Lawrence. He couldn't help smiling bitterly; Holo, too, smiled, but in relief. The slight downward cast of her eyes made her seem somehow tinged with loneliness. Lawrence was struck with the incongruous realization that her eyelashes were really quite long.

"So come on, don't make that face," he added.

A city merchant would probably have been able to come up with something more effective to say, but unfortunately Lawrence was always traveling and forced into a life absent of women. Still, Holo looked up and smiled slightly. "Mm-hm," she assented with a nod.

Seeing such a small girl so meek made her seem almost fleeting somehow. The wolf ears she normally held so high lay flat and directionless, and her proud tail curled up uncertainly next to her body.

It was suddenly silent.

Lawrence continued to watch Holo, who seemed unable to return his gaze.

She glanced at him just once, then quickly looked away. Lawrence felt he'd seen this before. Sifting through his memories, he realized it had been the apple incident, shortly after they'd arrived in Pazzio.

She'd wanted apples then — what did she need now?

Understanding another person's desire was a singularly important skill for a merchant.

Lawrence took a deep breath and stood. Surprised by the sudden noise, Holo's ears and tail twitched, and she regarded Lawrence. Flustered by his sudden approach, she looked away.

She reached her hands out to him as he stood before her — tremulously, almost frightened.

"Was it crying in your sleep that made your eyes red?" Lawrence took her hand and sat beside her. He pulled her close and held her gently.

"When I . . ."

"Hm?"

"When . . . when I open my eyes, they're gone. Yue, Inti, Paro, and Myuri . . . they're all gone. They're nowhere."

She was talking about her dream. Lawrence stroked her head softly as she sniffled. The names she'd mentioned must have been her wolf friends, perhaps even fellow wolf-gods — but he was far from insensitive enough to ask.

"I — I can live for centuries. So I thought I would go traveling. I was sure, so very sure, that I'd see them all again. But . . . they were gone. There was no one."

Holo's hand trembled as she grasped Lawrence's shirt. Lawrence himself didn't want to be plagued by such dreams.

If he were to return to his hometown, not a soul would remember him — sometimes he had similar nightmares.

There were tales of merchants who'd left their homeland and not returned for twenty or thirty years. They would finally return home to find their village simply gone. It might have been razed to the ground in a war or stricken by plague or famine — there were any number of possible reasons.

This is why traveling merchants dreamed of owning a shop.

A shop meant a home, making a place for oneself.

"I don't want to open my eyes and find no one there . . . I'm tired of being alone. It's cold. It's . . . lonely."

Lawrence remained silent at her outpouring of emotion, only stroking her head. She was so distressed that anything he said would likely fall on deaf ears, and he couldn't think of anything appropriate to say anyway.

He himself had been assailed by the winds of loneliness when riding his wagon or entering a new town.

There was nothing one could do in such times — nothing one could hear and find consoling. The only thing to do was find something to grab hold of and wait out the storm.

Holo continued to cry.

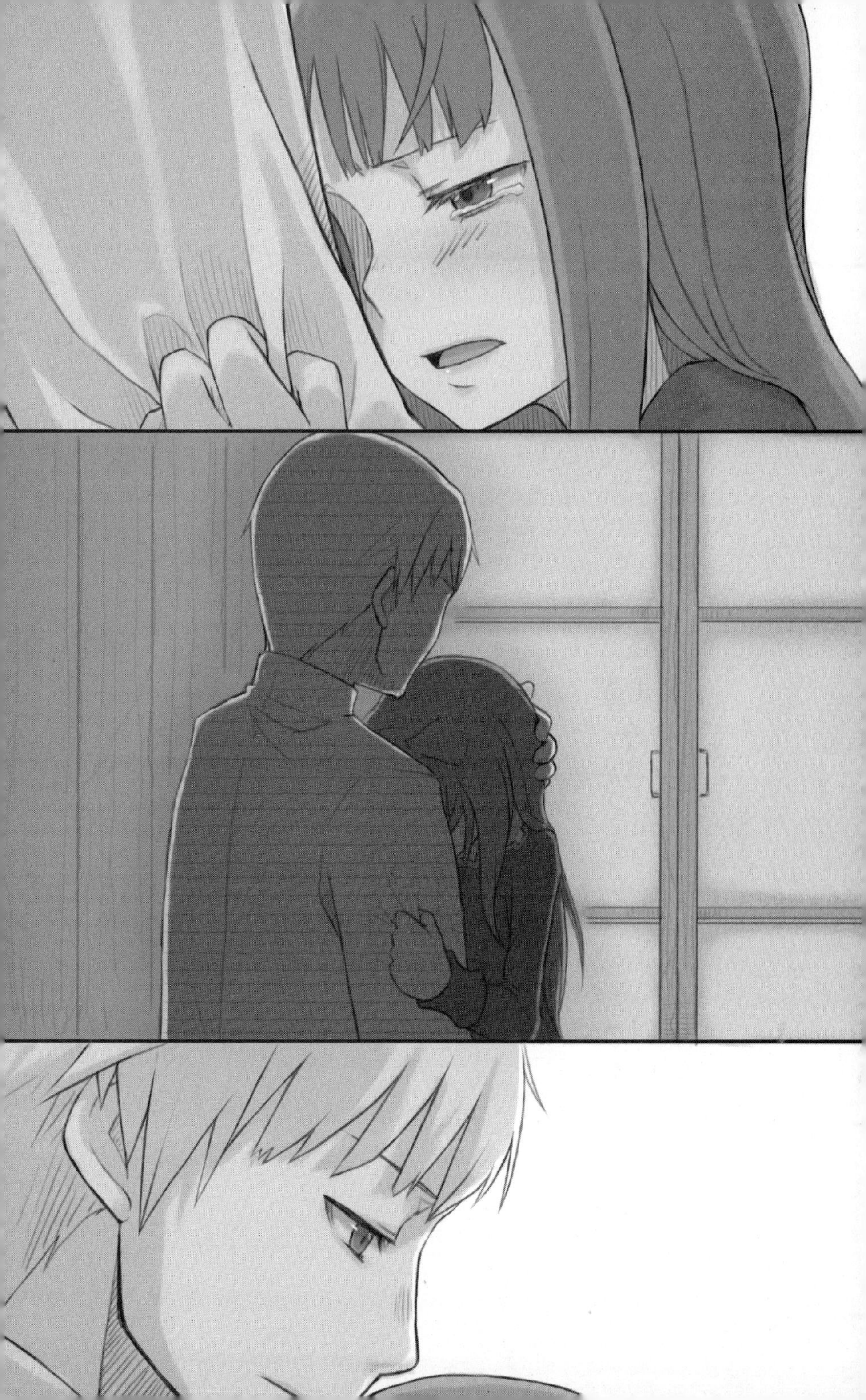

Lawrence held her, and at length the waves of emotion subsided and she let go of his clothes, looking up at him.

He let go of her, and she sat up, still sniffling.

"... How humiliating," said Holo, her nose and eyes still red but her voice calm.

"Traveling merchants have dreams like that, too," said Lawrence.

Holo giggled shyly and sniffled through her stuffed-up nose.

"Your face is a mess. Hang on."

Lawrence stood and took the paper from the desk. The drawings and figures on the sheet were dry, so he thought it would be okay for her to blow her nose on it.

"But . . . this is your . . ."

"I always throw them away when I'm done. The deal isn't even finished yet — it's too early to be optimistic," said Lawrence with a smile.

Holo returned his smile and took the paper. After blowing her nose mightily on it and wiping her eyes, she looked much better. She sighed and took a deep breath, then looked sheepish once more.

Seeing her like this, Lawrence wanted to embrace her again but refrained. Holo was herself again, and he would likely be made light of.

"I'm in your debt now," she said, picking up the now-crumbled bread and eating it. It was unclear whether or not she'd discerned his thoughts.

Relieved in any case that he hadn't been chided, he watched her as she finished eating and yawned, dusting her hands free from crumbs. She was probably tired from crying.

"I'm still sleepy. Can you sleep?" she asked.

"Soon, yes. Staying awake any longer would be a waste of candlelight."

"Heh, spoken like a true merchant," said Holo, smiling as she sat cross-legged on the bed, then lay down.

After taking one last look at her, Lawrence blew the candle out.

Darkness fell instantly. As his eyes were still used to the light, it seemed pitch-black. The weather was clear and the stars were out. He couldn't yet see the faint light that filtered through the wooden window. As he waited for his eyes to adjust, Lawrence felt his way to his own bed beneath the window in the corner of the room, careful not to trip over Holo's bed on his way.

Finally he made it and, after feeling the edge of the bed, lay down on it. In the past, Lawrence had bruised himself by carelessly flinging himself toward the bed and accidentally hitting the edge. He'd learned to be careful.

But there was no way for him to be prepared for what awaited him.

As he started to lie down in the bed, he realized someone was already in it.

"Wha — what are you —"

"Don't be such a prude," said Holo in an irritated voice that was nonetheless flirtatious.

Lawrence let himself be pulled down, and Holo pressed herself against him.

Unlike before when he'd held her gently, this embrace was tight. He felt her unmistakably soft body.

Lawrence's rising heartbeat could not be controlled. He was a healthy man, after all. He'd embraced her tightly almost before he realized it.

". . . Can't breathe . . ." came Holo's constricted voice. He returned to his senses and relaxed his arms but did not let go of her. She made no move to push him away.

Instead, she drew close to his ear and whispered.

"Have your eyes adjusted yet?"

"What do you —"

— Mean, he was about to say, but Holo cut him off with a finger pressed to his lips.

"I finally remembered what I was going to say to you."

Her whispering voice was itchy. Itchy, indeed — though her sweetly intimate tone was gone, replaced by an alarming edge to her voice.

"It's a bit late. There are three people outside the door. I doubt they are guests."

Lawrence finally realized that Holo was already wearing her cloak. She rummaged around quietly, and soon all of Lawrence's belongings appeared on his chest.

"We're on the second story. Fortunately there is no one outside. Are you ready?"

Growing excited in a completely different sense now, Holo got up. Lawrence pretended to draw the blanket over himself, and put on his clothes. Just as he was affixing his silver dagger to his waist, Holo spoke loudly, her voice purposely carrying beyond the closed door.

"Come, see my body 'neath the moonlight!"

As soon as she finished, Lawrence heard a window clatter open. Holo perched on the windowsill and jumped down without hesitation. Lawrence scrambled after her, putting his foot on the sill. He didn't hesitate, either — because behind him came the sound of the door being pried open, followed by heavy footsteps.

He felt unpleasantly weightless for a moment, but his feet soon collided with the hard ground.

Unable to bear the force of the impact, Lawrence landed in a squatting position.

He was lucky not to have broken his leg, but Holo still laughed loudly at him, although she did extend her hand.

"We'll have to run. We've no time to collect the horse."

A stunned Lawrence glanced back at the stables. The horse had been strong and cheap but more importantly was the first thing he'd ever bought.

Part of him wanted to make a break for the stables, but prudence told him not to. Holo's course of action was the right one.

Lawrence clenched his teeth and restrained himself.

"They will gain nothing by killing your horse; we'll wait for things to calm before retrieving it, yes?" said Holo by way of consolation. Lawrence could only hope that it was true. He nodded and took a deep breath, grabbing her outstretched hand and pulling himself up.

"Oh, also —"

Holo took the pouch that hung from her neck and undid the string that bound it closed. She poured roughly half of the wheat it contained into her hand.

"Just in case. You should take some, too," she said, casually thrusting the grains into the pocket on his chest without waiting for his reply. They felt warm; it was probably Holo's body heat.

After all, it was the wheat in which she lived.

"Right, now let's run."

Holo smiled as though speaking with a trusted friend. Lawrence was about to reply but simply nodded his head and dashed with her toward the town in the night.

"So, what I was going to say to you was this — if the Milone Company could check up on that boy, surely the reverse is true. His backers were bound to be alerted. If they discover we're gone to another company with a deal, they'll try to silence us, no?"

The only light on the cobbled path was the moon, but it was enough to see by. They continued to run without spotting another person, then turned down an alley.

Lawrence could barely see anything in the darkness there. Holo led him on, tugging on his hand as she ran, Lawrence stumbling after her.

They ran near an intersection and saw a group of men behind them, shouting. He caught the words "Milone Company" among their shouts.

They, too, knew that the only place Lawrence and Holo would find sanctuary was the Milone Company.

"Oops. I don't know the way," said Holo, still pulling on Lawrence's hand as they came to a fork. Lawrence looked up and checked the moon's position and phase and mentally roughed out a map of Pazzio.

"This way."

They ran down the western fork. This part of Pazzio was old. Buildings were constantly being rebuilt, and the road wound through them like a snake. But Lawrence had visited Pazzio many times. Furtively checking their position against the main road as they went, the pair came closer and closer to the Milone Company.

But their opponents were no fools.

"Stop. There's a guard."

They needed only to turn right at this intersection, follow the road to its end, then turn left. Four blocks later, they'd be at the Milone Company. There should still be men loading and unloading wagons at this hour. If they could make it there, the thugs wouldn't be able to touch them. In a city of commerce, the best security was the wealth implied by the signboard of a large business.

"*Tch*. We're so close."

"Heh-heh. I've not hunted in many years, but this is my first time *being* hunted."

"This is no time for jokes. Oh, well, we'll have to take the long way around."

Lawrence backtracked to the original road, turning right along it. He decided that they'd take an alley after the next block and circle around to the Milone Company.

But he was stopped after he made his first right turn.

Holo grabbed his shirt and pushed him against the wall.

"Did you find them? They should be close by! Find them!"

The current of fear that ran through him was worse than when he'd been chased by wolves in the forest. Two men came dashing violently out of a nearby alley. If Holo hadn't stopped, she and Lawrence might have run right into them.

"Damn. There are too many of them. And they know the area."

"Mmm . . . 'tis a bad situation," said Holo. Her hood was down, exposing her wolf ears as she scanned left and right.

"Shall we split up?"

"Not a bad idea, but I've a better one."

"Which is?"

Footsteps could be heard nearby. Undoubtedly every main road now had a guard on it. They'd be cornered as soon as they tried to use one.

"I'll head down the main road and draw them off. Then you can take the chance to — "

"Wait. You can't —"

"Now you listen. If we split up, you're the one that will be caught. On my own, I won't be caught, but you will. And when that happens, who is going to go to the company? Shall I show them my ears and tail and beg for your rescue? Well?"

Lawrence had no retort. He had already informed the Milone Company about the depreciating *trenni* silver. They might even abandon him and Holo both. Should that happen, his only recourse would be to play himself as a trump card and threaten to invest in their opponent.

And only he could conduct those negotiations.

"Either way it's no good. If the Milone Company sees your ears and tail, they may turn you over to the Church. And I needn't mention the Medio Company."

"So all I need do is avoid capture? And should I be caught, I'll just hide my ears and tail for a day while you come to rescue me."

Perhaps because of her bravado, Lawrence wanted to stop her from doing this that much more. She smiled up at him.

"I'm Holo the Wisewolf. Even if my ears and tail are discovered, I'll pretend to be a mad wolf, and none will want to come near me." She grinned, showing her fangs.

Yet all Lawrence could think of was embracing the sobbing girl who spoke of loneliness, with her impossibly slight form. He couldn't imagine turning her over to these hired thugs.

Still smiling, Holo continued. "Your dream is to own a shop, is it not? And just a moment ago I said I was in your debt. Are you trying to make a dishonorable wolf of me?"

"Don't be foolish! If you're caught, you'll be killed! What honor is there in that? I'll wind up owing you a debt I can never repay!" raged Lawrence, his voice low.

Holo smiled thinly and shook her head. She poked him lightly in the chest with her slender forefinger. "Loneliness is a deadly illness. We *are* even."

Lawrence had no words at the sight of her calm, grateful smile.

Holo took advantage of the silence and continued. "Besides, you're a quick thinker and clever — I promise. I trust you. I know you'll come for me."

She quickly embraced the silent Lawrence and then slipped free of his grasp, dashing away.

"There they are! On Loinne Road!"

As soon as Holo ran out of the alley, the shouts could be heard, and the pursuers' footsteps grew distant.

Lawrence clamped his eyes shut for a moment, the forced them open and ran. If he missed this chance, he might never see Holo again. He quickly ran down the dark alley — stumbling a few times, but always moving forward. He crossed the wide road and entered another alley, heading west. The commotion continued, but his opponent could not afford to make noise for long lest they alert the town guard.

He continued running, sprinting again across the main road, and heading down another alley. He needed only to turn right, then left on the next main road, to reach the Milone Company.

"Just one? There should be two!"

Lawrence heard the voice come from behind him. Had Holo been captured? Did she escape? If she'd escaped, that was fine. No — he hoped desperately that it was so.

He jumped onto the moonlit boulevard and turned immediately left. Soon he heard voices behind him. "There he is!"

Ignoring them, he sprinted with all his strength, hurling himself against the gates of the Milone Company's loading area.

"I'm Lawrence — I came earlier today! Help! I'm being pursued!"

Wakened into action by the commotion, the men on duty opened the iron gate.

Immediately after Lawrence disappeared behind it, a group of men carrying wooden staves rushed up to the gate.

"Wait, you! Give that man to us!" said one of them, hitting the gate with his stave. The men began trying to use force to pull the gate open.

But those who held the gate closed on the opposite side were used to long days of loading and unloading. The gate would not open so easily.

A bearded man on the far side of middle age emerged from within the company building. "Scum!" he roared. "Whose house do you think this is? It is the Milone Company's Pazzio branch, owned by the honorable Marquis Milone, recognized by His Grace, the thirty-third Archduke of Raondille! Anyone within these walls is a guest of the Marquis! Know that when you strike these gates, you strike His Grace's throne!"

Cowed by the man's grand speech, the attackers faltered. Just then, the whistle of the city guard sounded.

The men seemed to realize this was their chance to escape. They soon scattered.

Within the gates, everything was still for a while. At length, the sounds of footfalls and guard whistles faded, and the man who'd delivered the impressive speech finally spoke up again.

"That's quite a commotion so late at night. What's going on here?"

"My humblest apologies, sir. I offer my deepest gratitude for your sanctuary."

"Save your thanks for the Grand Marquis of Milone. What did they want?"

"I expect they were from the Medio Company. Undoubtedly they are displeased with the deal I've struck with your company."

"Oh ho. You're a merchant who'll take risks. I haven't seen many of your kind lately."

Lawrence wiped the sweat from his forehead and smiled. "It's my partner that's the reckless one."

"Must be rough."

"I don't want to think about it, but that same partner may have been captured. Would it be possible for me to speak with the branch manager, Sir Marheit?"

"We're a foreign company. Raids and arson are a fact of life for us. He's already been contacted," said the man with a hearty laugh.

It drove home to Lawrence how formidable the man who ran this operation must be.

Perhaps they really *would* be able to guarantee his safety.

Uncertainty swirled in his mind, but Lawrence soon composed himself. He would get them to guarantee not only his safety, but his profit, too.

His pride as a merchant and his debt to Holo, who'd taken such a risk for him, demanded no less.

Lawrence took a deep breath.

"Anyway, come inside, will you? Even wine gets better with time," said the man. Lawrence, thinking about Holo as he was, found it hard to calm himself.

Still, the old man was used to situations like this, and seeing Lawrence's agitated state, he offered some consolation. "In any case, if your partner's all right, he'll come here, eh? As long as you give us his name and description, we'll shelter him even if the Church itself comes after him!"

It was an exaggeration, but it put Lawrence at ease.

"My thanks. Surely . . . no, without question she'll come. Her name is Holo. She's a small girl, and wears a hood over her head."

"A girl, eh? Is she a beauty?"

Lawrence understood that the man was asking in order to ease his fears, so he smiled and answered. "Of ten people, all of them would turn to look at her."

"Ha-ha-ha! That's something to look forward to, then," laughed the big man heartily, and he led Lawrence into the company building.

"Eight or nine out of ten of them will be Medio men."

Although he had probably just been awakened, Marheit's manner was no different than it had been earlier in the day as he skipped the pleasantries.

"I agree. They have discovered that I came to you for assistance with my plan for the silver coin and are trying to stop us."

Lawrence didn't want his agitation to be obvious, but he couldn't help worrying about Holo as he talked. Holo being who she was, he thought there was a chance she'd escaped, but it was best to assume the worst. In any case, he needed guarantees of both his and Holo's safety as fast as he could get them.

And for that, he needed the Milone Company.

"I believe my companion may have been captured. If so, it seems obvious to me that negotiations will be impossible. Will the Milone lend its aid?" asked Lawrence, only avoiding leaning over the table with effort. Marheit seemed deep in thought and did not face Lawrence.

Finally he looked up, slowly.

"You say your companion may have been captured?"

"Yes."

"I see. After the commotion here, I sent some of my men to follow them. They reported seeing a girl taken, apparently against her will."

Despite more than half-expecting Marheit's words, Lawrence felt them grab hold of his heart and shake him desperately.

He swallowed his shock and managed to get some words out. "That is probably my companion, Holo. She acted as a decoy so I could make it here."

"I see. But what would make them want to capture your partner?"

Lawrence had to almost physically restrain himself from shouting. He couldn't afford to lose his temper in the presence of a man like Marheit. "I expect it's because we joined with your company in trying to thwart their plans."

Marheit's countenance remained impassive in spite of Lawrence's heated response. He stared down at the table and appeared deep in thought. Lawrence, distressed, couldn't help bouncing his leg impatiently. He was about to jump up from the chair and begin shouting when Marheit spoke again.

"It's a bit strange, though, don't you think?"

"What's strange?!" demanded Lawrence, finally jumping out of his chair, causing Marheit to blink rapidly for a moment before regaining his composure.

Marheit reached his hand out to his distressed visitor. "Please calm yourself. Something is strange about all this."

"What's strange about it? Just as your company was able to easily check up on Zheren, it was simple for the Medio Company to see if anybody was interfering with their plan!"

". . . True, given that their headquarters are here . . ."

"So what is strange?"

"Indeed, I understand now. This truly *is* strange," said Marheit. Lawrence had no choice but to hear him out. "I was thinking, how did they come to realize that you were conspiring with our company?"

"Surely because I came here frequently. Also, if they noticed that you'd started collecting *trenni* silver, all they'd have to do is put two and two together."

"That is the strange part. You're a traveling merchant, after all — visiting us several times to negotiate is entirely natural."

"But if they linked that to your company's interest in *trenni* silver and the fact that I'm the one Zheren contacted . . ."

"No, it's still strange."

"Why?"

Lawrence did not understand. Impatience colored his voice.

"Naturally, the point at which we started gathering *trenni* silver was after we finished negotiating with you. Consider this, Mr.

Lawrence: 'I cannot say how it will happen, but if you collect *trenni* silver your profit is guaranteed.' We certainly wouldn't do anything based on that alone, would we?"

"T-true . . ."

"The fact that we are indeed collecting *trenni* silver means we understand the entirety of this opportunity. Undoubtedly the Medio Company also knows this. There's simply no reason to take you as hostages."

"Surely you don't mean —"

Marheit nodded, his face expressing sad regret. "I do. We already have all the information we need to turn a profit. What happens to you now is not our concern."

Feeling dizzy, Lawrence listed to one side. It was true. Lawrence was a single traveling merchant; no one was looking out for him.

"I hope you will understand how difficult it is for me to say this. But we've already invested a significant amount of capital based on the information you brought us. The profit will be immense. If we must choose between bearing your grudge or giving up the return, then . . ." Marheit sighed. "I'm sorry, but I must choose the former," he said quietly. "Still . . ."

Lawrence didn't hear what Marheit said after that. In some small corner of his mind, he wondered if this was what it felt like to meet with bankruptcy. His arms, legs — indeed, his entire body — felt frozen. He wasn't even sure if he was still breathing.

He was now, as of this moment, abandoned by the Milone Company.

Which meant Holo had also been abandoned; Holo, who'd given herself up to let him escape believing that Lawrence would be able to negotiate her rescue with the Milone Company.

Lawrence recalled the expression on her face when she spoke of returning to the north country.

When hostages had outlived their usefulness, their subsequent prospects were clear. Men were sold to slave ships and women to brothels. Although Holo had her wolf ears and tail, there were rich eccentrics who collected such "demon-possessed" girls. Undoubtedly the Medio Company knew one or two such collectors.

Lawrence thought of Holo being sold — he thought of how a wealthy, demon-obsessed collector would treat such a girl.

No. He would not allow it.

Lawrence straightened himself in the chair and immediately began thinking. He had to save her.

"Please wait," he said after several moments. "If your company has come to this conclusion, surely the other side has done so as well."

The Medio Company wasn't run by fools. They had gone after Lawrence and his companion and had dispatched many men to do it, even risking confrontation with the town guard.

"Yes. That is what struck me as so strange. I hadn't finished speaking, you see — if the need arises, I will bear the grudge that you would harbor toward the company."

Lawrence now remembered that Marheit had ended his statement with a "still" and hung his head in red-faced shame.

"I can see that your companion is very precious to you. But letting your emotions dull your thinking is misplacing your priorities."

"My apologies."

"Not at all — if my wife were in danger, I, too, would likely find it impossible to calm myself," Marheit said, smiling.

Lawrence saw this and bowed his head again, though his heart thudded at the word "wife." He realized that if Holo were a mere traveling companion, he would not be so upset, and Holo herself would not have sacrificed herself to help him escape.

"Back to the problem at hand, then. Our opponent is a canny company that will not easily be thwarted. You and your partner

155

have no theoretical value to them, yet they've targeted you — there must be a reason. Do you have any idea what it might be?"

Lawrence did not have any such idea.

When he thought the situation through, though, he realized that there must be some special reason for them to be captured.

He mulled it over.

There was only one possibility.

"No, that can't be . . ."

"Have you thought of something?"

Lawrence had immediately dismissed the possibility when it first occurred to him. It simply couldn't be — yet it was the only thing he could think of.

"The profit before us is almost unimaginable. We need only realize it. If you've thought of something, no matter how trivial, please tell me."

Marheit's request was entirely reasonable, but Lawrence's realization was not something to be shared lightly.

Lawrence thought about Holo, who was undeniably not human. Most people would call her a demon. Such "demons" were either hidden away at home or given over to the Church. Neither was any way to live. Once the Church cast its eye on such a person, he or she would certainly be executed.

Holo was indistinguishable from such a possessed individual. The Medio Company could use her to blackmail the Milone Company.

If the Milone Company did not want it revealed to the Church that they'd had dealings with someone possessed by a demon, they would have to withdraw.

If it came to an Inquisition, the Medio Company could righteously accuse the Milone Company and Lawrence of having entered into an evil contract with a demonic entity. It went without saying that Holo would be burned at the stake.

Yet Lawrence still found himself skeptical.

Who had discovered Holo's wolf's ears and tail, and when?

Given Holo's normal appearance, it wasn't something easily discernible. He believed that no one except himself knew the truth of her identity.

"Mr. Lawrence," said Marheit, putting an end to Lawrence's musings. "Have you thought of something?"

Lawrence couldn't help nodding at Marheit's patient question, which meant he would now have to divulge the truth. But if the real reason for their pursuit was something else, he would have exposed Holo's secret for naught.

In the worse case, the Milone Company could turn the tables on the Medio Company by accusing them of using a demon girl to blackmail them.

If that happened, there would be no hope for Holo.

Marheit gazed seriously across the table.

Lawrence saw no avenue of escape.

But they were interrupted.

"Excuse me," said a Milone Company representative, entering the room.

"What is it?"

"We just received a letter. It regards our current situation."

The employee held out a neatly sealed envelope. Marheit took it and flipped it over. The sender's name was missing, but it did have a destination.

"'To the wolf . . . and the forest in which it resides?'"

In that instant, Lawrence realized he'd been right.

"I'm sorry, but might I look at that letter first?"

Marheit looked at Lawrence dubiously but at length nodded and handed the envelope over.

Lawrence thanked him and, taking a deep breath, broke the seal.

There was a letter inside and a bit of what might have been Holo's brown fur.

The letter was brief.

"We have the wolf. The Church's doors are always open. If you don't want the wolf in your home, shut your doors and keep your family inside."

There was no longer any room for doubt.

Lawrence returned the letter to Marheit. "My companion, Holo, is the wolf-god of the harvest," he said in a wrung-out voice.

Marheit's eyes opened as wide as they ever got.

CHAPTER FIVE

Marheit was everything one would expect from a trader who'd opened a branch in a foreign land.

Though initially shocked by Lawrence's revelation, he soon calmed himself and began to think the situation through. He uttered not so much as a single word of blame for Holo, who'd been captured, or Lawrence, who'd made his escape. He was entirely focused on protecting the interests of the Milone Company and extracting any available profit from the situation.

"There's no doubting the threat implied by this letter. They wish you, Mr. Lawrence, to know that if you don't want your partner given up to the Church you must stay inside and not interfere."

"They must want us to keep out of their way until their plan for the *trenni* silver is concluded, but that doesn't mean they won't still turn Holo in when they're through."

"Quite right. Furthermore, we've already invested quite heavily in the coin. Pulling out now means our losses would be huge because the *trenni* is guaranteed to depreciate."

In such a situation, there was essentially no choice at all.

They could sit and await ruin, or they could strike.

The former was hardly an option.

"I suppose this means we have no choice but to strike first," said Lawrence.

Marheit took a deep breath and nodded. "However, merely rescuing your companion won't be enough. Even if we hide her here, once the Church gets involved, we'll have no choice but to roll over and let them have their way. She can't hide as long as she's in this city."

"What if we flee the city entirely?"

"It's a great plain as far as the eye can see, and even if you reached another city, there's a chance you could be extradited. Then there'd be no hope for you at all."

They were cornered. Even meek compliance with the Medio Company's demands would probably still result in Holo being delivered to the Church. There was no reason for them to avoid ruining a foreign company — in fact, the fewer competitors they had, the better.

Yet striking first carried with it a host of difficulties. No — "difficult" was the wrong word. Every possibility available to them was the height of recklessness.

"Is there nothing we can do?" mused Marheit as if talking to himself. "At this rate, we won't even be able to avoid unfounded accusations, to say nothing of actually making a profit."

Lawrence felt as if he were sitting on a carpet of needles as he listened to Marheit speak, but he bowed his head and listened — he would do whatever it took to bring about a favorable result. Merchants lacked the pride of knights or nobility. They were prepared to lick a stranger's boots if it meant coming out ahead.

So Lawrence did not hear sarcasm or scorn in Marheit's words, simply analysis. He had clearly summarized the situation they now faced.

"You're saying we need some kind of card we can play against them."

"You could put it that way. But even if we invest more capital, it's meager compared with what they stand to gain from *trenni* silver. So the problem can't be solved with money. We could report their abduction of your companion to the Church, but that would cause problems for you, and you might even deliver an unfavorable testimony about our company."

"That . . . is quite possible."

There was no point in lying, so Lawrence told the truth. He simply couldn't cut Holo loose, but if he did, unquestionably that would solve the problem.

Marheit was undoubtedly aware of that fact. If it came down to it, he would certainly try to persuade Lawrence to take that option, though unsuccessfully. Lawrence knew he would choose death with Holo first.

Though naturally he hoped he wouldn't have to.

This left him no alternative but to come up with some kind of plan to alter this indefensible position.

"All I can think of," Lawrence interjected, "is to finish negotiating the *trenni* silver deal and use the resulting profit as a trump card."

Marheit's eyes went wide at Lawrence's proposal. He didn't want to lose the Milone Company's profit — that almost-magical return made possible by exploiting a depreciating currency — any more than Lawrence wanted to lose Holo.

Such opportunities came around only once in a great while.

That was what made Lawrence's proposed trump card so potent. If it came down to it, the Medio Company would happily turn Holo over rather than lose the profit.

Still — or perhaps because of that — Marheit covered his eyes in worry. Losing that opportunity would be like losing a child.

This magical trading partner could bring them staggering gains.

That partner was none other than the King of the Kingdom of Trenni.

"The greatest gain that can be extracted from *trenni* silver is securing special privileges from the king. According to our research, the finances of the royal family are in decline. In other words, if this deal succeeds, we'll have substantial favor with the royal family. Abandoning that . . ."

"Abandoning it for my companion makes no sense at all," said Lawrence.

"Are you suggesting that they purchase it from us?"

Lawrence nodded. He had heard of deals on this scale before but had never been involved with one. He had no assurances that it could actually be done, but his long experience as a merchant suggested that it could.

"If it comes down to a choice between destroying the Milone Company or obtaining special privileges from the king, perhaps we could simply have them pay the equivalent value."

Lawrence was speaking off the top of his head, but it seemed plausible.

The idea that you could make money from a depreciating currency by collecting as much of it as possible was predicated on the presupposition that the same Kingdom of Trenni that minted the coins would be willing to buy up the currency.

They would do so because after recalling the currency, they could melt it down. They would then mint more coins with a lower silver content, resulting in more physical currency. If ten coins became thirteen coins, that meant a gain of three coins.

This was the best way to increase immediately available funds, but it hurt the nation's credibility, which would result in a loss over the long term. For the royal family to be willing to do this implied that it was in dire financial straits. What was worse, if they didn't have enough of the crucial coin, diluting it wouldn't create the extra funds the nation needed for breathing room.

The Medio Company was trying to assemble a large amount of *trenni* silver to exploit this opportunity. Depending on the circumstances, they might attempt to collect all of the *trenni* silver circulating in the marketplace.

Then they would go to the king, and say something like "If you will agree to the price we set and give us certain considerations, we will sell you the currency."

With a few exceptions, a king was a king only because his fortune or lands were greater than those of other nobility — and because he had garnered the support of the population who did not question his legitimacy. But simply being the monarch did not guarantee perfect control over the lands of the kingdom. The royal family could not simply control assets administered by other nobility.

Thus, the assets of royalty were not appreciably more significant than those of the various nobles. What made them special were the assorted duties that fell under royal prerogative: authority over mines, mints, tariffs, market administration, and so on. While such authority didn't bring with it automatic gains, if one knew how to manipulate the authority, it was like shaking money out of a tree.

In all likelihood, the Medio Company wanted control over one of these domains. Precisely which one was unclear, but if whatever they were planning was successful, they stood to gain a major advantage for their business.

What Lawrence brought to the Milone Company was a proposal to snatch this opportunity away. They aimed to collect more *trenni* silver than the Medio Company and negotiate with the king first.

From the king's perspective, dealing with two companies competing for the same privileges would be troublesome. Thus, if he were to deal with anyone, it would be with a sole company.

If the Milone Company could conclude the negotiations first, it would be impossible for the Medio Company to secure any privileges.

Those privileges were entirely unique.

For the Medio Company's part, if said privileges were something that could be simply purchased, they would pay any price. The Milone Company was no different, but held by the scruff of the neck as they now were, they would have to be content with moderate compensation.

"Still . . . if they play their card, it won't just destroy this branch — we'll be burned at the stake. Will they deal with us?"

Now was the time for nerve. Lawrence leaned forward and murmured, "Surely the king would be troubled to learn that the company with which he was dealing was to be burned as heretics."

Marheit gasped at the realization. The Church's authority surpassed even national borders. Its power was significant even within mighty empires, to say nothing of small kingdoms like Trenni.

And in any case, the king of Trenni was having financial difficulties. The last thing he would want was trouble with the Church.

"If we can sign a contract with the king, the Medio Company won't be able to touch us. Even if they try to turn us over to the Church, the king will not be pleased with the company that brought such trouble down upon him."

"I see. Still, they won't just stay silent. They might just try to bring us down with them."

"True."

"So in addition to the price for the privileges we'll hand over, we'll be demanding your companion."

"Yes."

Marheit stroked his chin, his face expressing admiration. He looked down at the table. Lawrence knew what Marheit was going to say next. He took a deep breath and gathered his wits in anticipation of his answer. This unique plan could break the deadlock and bring both Lawrence and the Milone Company great profit.

But it had its difficulties.

If Lawrence couldn't overcome those difficulties, he would either have to cut Holo loose or be burned alongside her by the Church.

The former would not happen — not ever.

Marheit looked up.

"Hypothetically, it's a sound strategy. But I'm sure you realize it will be nearly impossible to execute."

"You're talking about how we'll surpass the Medio Company, yes?"

Marheit put his hand to his chin and nodded.

Lawrence was prepared for this. "As far as I can tell, the Medio Company has not yet collected a significant amount of silver."

"And your basis for saying so is . . . ?"

"My basis is that they didn't immediately turn Holo over to the Church upon capturing her. If they already had enough silver, they would've gone directly to the Church in order to destroy us. Instead, they're trying to prevent us from moving, probably because they're concerned that in the time it would take for the Church to conclude our trial and sentencing, we would reach an agreement with the king. To put it another way, they think you've already collected enough silver to begin negotiations. It shows they have no confidence in their own position."

Marheit listened with eyes closed. Lawrence took a breath and continued.

"Also, I don't think the Medio Company wants anyone to know they are collecting *trenni* silver — this helps them take advantage of the king's weak position. From the standpoint of a nobleman dealing with the king, it shows consideration for the king's position and their relationship in the future to say that he just happened to have a large amount of silver on hand, no matter how transparent the lie. But to have people like Zheren target traveling merchants and suck us into the deal, I think their aim is to begin by having merchants gather the silver for them, then buy it up at the opportune moment. Even if they suspect Zheren's motives, if someone's willing to buy the currency, they'll be happy to sell. This is all speculation on my part, but I don't think I'm wrong. If the Medio Company started buying *trenni* silver in bulk, every company in the area would notice the strange trend in the coin, and we'd be far from their only problem."

Marheit nodded slowly. "Given all that, this may be possible," he murmured reluctantly, his eyes still closed.

The speculation was plausible, but it was still mere speculation. Perhaps they hadn't turned in Holo because they didn't wish to provoke the main branch of the Milone Company.

For whatever reason, the Medio Company was hesitating.

Given that hesitation, Lawrence and his partners had no choice but to take advantage.

"All right, we'll assume the Medio Company is not prepared to move. Based on that assumption, what action do you suggest, Mr. Lawrence?"

Lawrence took those words at face value. He couldn't afford to show any weakness.

He took a deep breath and spoke. "I will find Holo, rescue her, and we'll run until the negotiations are finished."

Marheit's breath caught. "You can't be serious."

"Escape may be impossible, but we'll buy you some time. Use it to gather as much silver as you can and conclude the negotiation."

"It's not possible."

"So you're going to turn Holo in, then? I'll be forced to publicly denounce the Milone Company."

It was an unmistakable threat.

Marheit's mouth gaped at Lawrence's near-betrayal, stunned.

The fact remained, though, that even if they chose to sacrifice Holo, the Milone Company had a contract with her and Lawrence. If it came to a Church trial, the company had perhaps a four-in-ten chance to be judged blameless, and even then, heavy fines would be levied. It went without saying that Lawrence would testify against the Milone Company.

Marheit agonized.

Lawrence took the opportunity to push.

"With the Milone Company's help, we should be able to escape for a day or two. She is a wolf spirit, after all. If she sets her strength to escape, none will be able to catch her."

Lawrence had no idea if that was true, of course, but it sounded convincing.

"Mm . . . hm . . ."

"Holo was caught because she acted as a decoy. If we hadn't had a destination and sought only escape, that would've been easy. Might I ask how long your company will need to assemble sufficient coin to command the king's attention?"

". . . How much time, you say?"

Though Marheit appeared overwhelmed by Lawrence's bravado, his mind was racing at the possibilities. His gaze flicked around the room, and it was clear he was deep in thought.

Lawrence thought that if he could rescue Holo cleanly and the

Milone Company was willing to help, he'd be able to stay on the run for an even two days.

Pazzio was an old city. There were many buildings, and the roads and alleyways were complex. If one wanted to hide, there were innumerable places to do so.

Assuming he was running from only the Medio Company, Lawrence believed he could stay hidden.

Marheit opened his eyes. "If we send a rider to Trenni now, he'll make it there by sunset if all goes well. Assuming we can commence negotiation immediately, he'll return here by dawn tomorrow. Longer negotiation will lengthen his stay."

"Can you send a rider immediately? You haven't confirmed the amount of silver you have."

"There's a limit to how much coin we can house, so we can place a rough estimate on how much we'll be able to collect. As long as we have that much by the day of the actual transaction, we'll be fine."

Even if they negotiated optimistically, there would be no problem as long as the currency was assembled by the day of the settlement.

The idea was sound enough in theory, but it took a big merchant to actually accomplish such reckless dealing. Additionally, they had to be able to offer enough capital that the king would think he couldn't afford to depend solely on his own resources. Using a mere approximation of available monies to carry out such negotiations was the height of recklessness, but the very fact that Marheit was proposing the idea lent it credence, Lawrence thought.

"We wanted to negotiate only after we discovered who was backing the Medio Company, which would reveal their funding. Then we'd be able to both preempt their deal and estimate our own. But we've neither time to think nor to look for more information."

Though he knew it was impossible, Lawrence worked the problem around in his head and came up with nothing. He sighed as if to voice his powerlessness.

He had to keep looking ahead. He straightened himself and regarded Marheit.

"Can you reach a fast settlement with the king?"

Lawrence would have to run whether or not negotiations were speedy. He was powerless to change the situation but would feel better knowing.

"If the Milone Company wills it, negotiations will be brief."

Lawrence couldn't help chuckling bitterly, but Marheit certainly sounded reliable.

He reached out with his right hand. "I imagine you know where Holo is, then?" he asked, as though inquiring about the weather.

"We *are* the Milone Company."

Lawrence shook Marheit's hand, glad to have chosen the right company to deal with.

"Assassination of our employees and arson of our facilities are facts of daily life for us. That's why we make it a point to know the city better than anyone. We have contingencies for any emergency. Even if a legion of knights should storm the city walls, we'll survive. But we do have a rival."

"The Church?"

"Indeed. The Church, like us, has a far-reaching presence. Their front-line missionaries are especially like us in this regard, exceeding even our abilities. You're aware of this, no doubt."

"They are ubiquitous and elusive, yes."

"Should the Church launch a search in earnest, you must not run before thinking — stay hidden in one place. Of course we hope to have the deal concluded by then. The password will be 'Pireon, numai.'"

"Two great gold coins, then?"

"It seemed auspicious. I shall pray for your success."

"I understand. Your hopes will be well met."

Lawrence shook Marheit's hand again, then climbed into the cart. The cart was completely unremarkable, the kind you'd see anywhere, but it had a roof that made it impossible to see who was riding within. This was not, however, to help Holo escape, but rather to deliver Lawrence to Holo. In fact, it was less about delivering Lawrence than it was about hiding his whereabouts.

Agents of the Milone Company had caught wind of the commotion the previous day and had followed the thugs without knowing at the time what was going on. Just as they'd learned where Holo was being held, they assumed that the Medio Company had people watching them as well. There was no such thing as too much caution.

Merchants would try to deceive each other just as soon as look at one another — all the more so when they *weren't* looking.

Together with another Milone employee that was riding along, Lawrence dismantled the floorboards of the carriage and looked down at the slowly passing cobblestones.

"Once I've descended, I should touch the right-hand wall and go forward, right?"

"Your destination is at the end. If all goes well, a hatch will open above you. Should you hear the word 'racche,' please wait for the escort to arrive. If you hear 'peroso,' though, make your escape with Holo along the planned route immediately."

"The good outcome and the bad, eh?" said Lawrence.

"Easy to understand, isn't it?"

Lawrence gave a wry grin and nodded his comprehension.

"We'll be there soon."

Immediately after the Milone employee spoke, the horseman on the driver's seat knocked on the wall. It was the stop signal.

The carriage braked to the sound of neighing horses as the driver shouted angrily at someone. Lawrence jumped down through the hole left by the missing floorboards and pushed aside a large stone at his feet. Beneath the stone was a dark hole. Lawrence jumped into it immediately and landed on his feet with a splash. Having confirmed their passenger's safe drop-off, his companions above slid the stone back into place, returning the passage to total darkness.

A few moments later, the carriage resumed its advance as though nothing had happened.

"I'm surprised they're so prepared," said Lawrence, half-shocked as he put his hand to the wall on his right and walked slowly forward.

The tunnel had once been used to carry water, but since water pipes now connected the marketplace, it was no longer used. That's as much as Lawrence knew about it, but the Milone Company's knowledge of the system was complete, and they had dug unauthorized extensions to the tunnels to connect various buildings.

The Church also excelled at such subterfuge. It was said they would use the digging of graves as a pretense to construct secret underground passageways to be used for spying on heretics and evading taxation. The Church was powerful, which meant it had many enemies. Escape routes were always useful.

Large towns that housed main branches of the Church or companies like Milone were so riddled with passageways that they were scarcely different from fell catacombs where demons lived. It was like making your living on a spider's web, a merchant had once said to Lawrence.

Lawrence now understood the terrifying truth of that statement.

The tunnel was dark and clammy but still better than some

of the alleys he'd walked down, which meant it was well-maintained.

This reassured Lawrence. The Milone Company was powerful. "Ah, here it is."

Lawrence heard the echoes of his splashing footfalls and realized he'd reached the end. He reached out and soon felt the wall.

A traveling merchant was used to being attacked by wild dogs on moonless roads. Lawrence was confident that if the worst happened and he had to run down this tunnel, he'd be able to find the wall.

Above and to the right, there was supposedly the warehouse of a general store with connections to the Medio Company. This was where Holo was being held. Directly above Lawrence was their temporary base of operations, and apparently they'd secretly constructed a path between the two. The degree of preparation was chilling, but it might also have been built to facilitate the company's expansion into other lands, Lawrence reminded himself.

A distant bell sounded from somewhere. It was the signal to open the marketplace. It was also the signal to begin the plan, so undoubtedly all hell was breaking loose above him. If they couldn't free Holo in the time between now and the bell that signaled the beginning of work, they would be in real trouble — the general goods merchant would return to his warehouse.

He might have been a Medio protégé, but bills came due whether or not he was housing a hostage. Commerce never stopped, after all.

The problem was the number of people guarding Holo. If their opponents used too many people, it would be obvious to the Milone Company, but if they used too few, it wouldn't be an effective guard. Lawrence hoped they had allocated people with the intention of keeping Holo's location secret their top priority.

The more people there were, the worse the fight would be. The attackers wouldn't be holding ropes and blindfolds, but edged weapons and clubs.

This would further complicate an already difficult situation, and Lawrence desperately wanted to avoid that.

Lawrence wondered how much time had passed while he'd been thinking. He was calm initially, but his legs now shook enough to splash the water around him. He was deeply troubled. He tried to calm his trembling legs, to no avail.

He tried stretching, but it only exacerbated his worry and made his heart pound harder.

He looked up, hoping the trapdoor above him would open soon.

Suddenly he froze, stricken with fear.

Had he come to the wrong place?

"S-surely not," he answered himself, making sure that it was the correct dead end.

Just then, he heard a voice above him.

"Racche," it said, immediately followed by the sound of floorboards cracking free of a foundation.

"Racche," said the voice again, to which Lawrence said, "Numai!" "Pireon," came the reply, along with a blaze of light as the floorboards slid aside.

"Holo!" exclaimed Lawrence in spite of himself when he saw her face.

Unmoved, Holo said something to the person standing next to her. She looked back down at Lawrence.

"How am I to get down there if you don't make way?"

It wouldn't be wrong to say Holo was her usual self, but when he heard her speak, Lawrence realized he wanted to see her happy face and hear her lively voice.

He did as Holo suggested and stepped aside, waiting for her to descend — yet what filled his heart was not satisfaction at seeing her face, but rather disappointment at missing her joyful voice.

Of course, he knew it was nothing more than wishful thinking and said nothing, but once Holo descended and looked up to receive a bundle from above, paying him not the slightest heed, the discontent in his heart grew stronger.

"What are you daydreaming about? Here, this is for you. Take it, and let's go."

"Wha — oh."

Lawrence held the bundle that was shoved at him and headed down the tunnel as if pushed. Something jingled in the bundle — they must have stolen some valuables to give the appearance of thieves. Soon another person descended from the trapdoor, whereupon it shut. The tunnel was completely dark again. That was the signal to move. Lawrence said nothing to Holo and began walking.

They would turn right at the end of the passage, feeling along the left-hand wall until reaching its end. They would then climb out of the tunnel and into the carriage that awaited them there to be taken to another underground passage.

Walking the tunnel wordlessly, they finally reached their destination.

Lawrence climbed the ladder that had been prepared and knocked three times against the ceiling.

If the escort failed to make the rendezvous, they would have to take a different route — but just as the possibility crossed Lawrence's mind, a hole opened in the ceiling, and immediately above it sat the carriage.

After confirming each other's identities with an exchange of "Pireon," "Numai," Lawrence crawled up into the carriage.

176

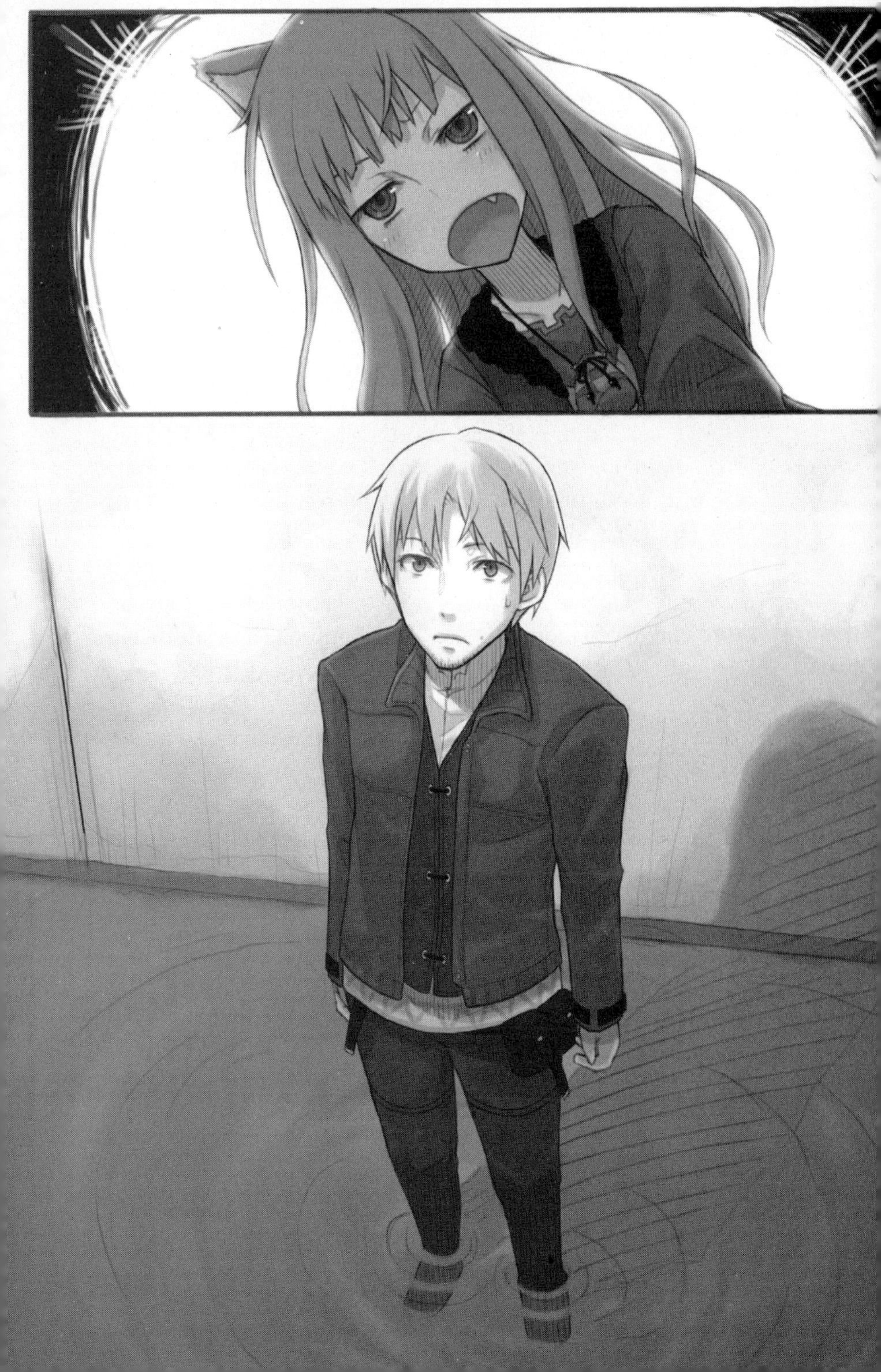

"Looks like you made it safely," said the Milone employee as he pulled Holo up. He was understandably surprised to see her wolf ears. "Business is full of surprises," he said with a smile, sliding the large cobblestone back into its original position.

"There was another with us," said Lawrence.

"He'll be collecting the ladder and emerging elsewhere," said the employee. "Once he's delivered the information about those Medio rascals to our friends, he'll leave the city."

The almost frightening efficiency was due to their daily execution and refinement of plans and counterplans. Once the employee replaced the carriage floorboards, he said a quick "good luck to you" and took Lawrence and Holo's bundles before exiting the cart. At the employee's signal, the driver started the carriage moving. So far, everything was going according to plan.

Everything except for Holo's reaction, that is.

"I'm so glad you're all right," was all Lawrence could manage. He could say no more to Holo, who sat opposite him, unfolding a strip of cloth that had been around her neck in an attempt to cover her ears.

She only replied after finishing a few adjustments to the fit of her makeshift hood. "It's good that I'm all right, is it?"

Lawrence wanted to say yes, but the words caught in his throat. Holo was glaring at him as if she were about to bite his head off.

Perhaps she *wasn't* well.

"Say my name, then!"

If she could shout like that, she wasn't in the condition Lawrence feared. Still, her vehemence made her seem twice her normal size, and he flinched at it.

"Uh . . . Holo?"

"Holo the Wisewolf!"

It sounded almost like a threatening growl, but Lawrence had no idea what she was angry about. If she wanted an apology, he was ready to apologize a hundred times over. She'd been a decoy for him, after all.

Or had something happened to her that she couldn't say?

"I can remember every single person that's ever shamed me in my life. And now I must add another name to that list. Yours!"

Something *had* happened to her. Still, her anger seemed different from the manner of girls he'd seen in villages that had been taken by thugs or brigands. And if he said something foolish, it would only be throwing oil on the fire of her rage.

Thus the silence grew longer; and perhaps the silence itself began to irk her because she rose from her seat and closed in on Lawrence.

Her white, clenched fists trembled.

There was nowhere for Lawrence to run. Holo stood directly in front of him.

Their heads were at the same height, which lent Holo's level gaze an incredibly penetrating quality. She opened her small fists and grabbed the chest of Lawrence's shirt. Her strength matched her appearance — Lawrence hadn't imagined her grip would be so weak.

Again he noticed how long her eyelashes were.

"You told me, didn't you — you told me you'd come for me."

Lawrence nodded.

"And I . . . I utterly believed that you would come . . . grrh . . . just thinking about it is infuriating!"

Just then, Lawrence came to a sharp realization, as if waking from a dream.

"You're a man, aren't you? You should've been in the front, fighting tooth and nail! But you were in that hole in the ground — you let me make a fool of myself —"

"But you're unhurt, right?" asked Lawrence, interrupting her. Holo sneered at him, displeased.

She hesitated for some time before finally nodding, as if forced to drink something very unpleasant.

Holo had probably been blindfolded. She may have mistaken whoever came to her aid for Lawrence and said something meant for him alone. That was probably why she felt — and blamed him for — such needless shame.

The realization made Lawrence happy. He knew that if he'd been the one to rescue her, she would have shown the expression he longed to see.

Slowly putting his arms around Holo, who was still gripping his shirt, he drew her closer. Holo resisted a bit, irritated, but soon relented. The once angry-looking ears that were clearly visible underneath her makeshift hood now drooped. A mildly sulky expression replaced her original anger.

Though he might travel the world and amass a great fortune, the one thing Lawrence could never have was right here.

"I'm glad you're all right," he said.

The eyes that had flashed in anger only a moment earlier threatened to close. Holo nodded, her lips slightly pouting.

"So long as you carry that wheat with you, I'll not die." Holo poked his breast pocket without moving his arms away. "For a girl, there is a kind of suffering no easier than death."

Lawrence took Holo's hand, and Holo drew near to him, resting her chin on his shoulder. He felt her weight intensely, heavier than a burlap sack full of wheat.

"Heh. I'm so lovely that even human males fall for me. Not that a one of them is fit to be my mate," said Holo mischievously.

When she finally released Lawrence, she wore her usual grin. "If they tried to touch me, I'd just remind them that they might lose a limb, or worse — they'd pale at that, oh yes! Hee-hee-hee," she chuckled, her sharp fangs visible behind her pink lips. It was true; anyone would falter at such a sight.

"But there was an exception," she added, her delight vanishing. This was a new anger, a quiet anger, Lawrence thought.

"Who do you think was there among those who captured me?"

Her expression was the height of disgust. She bared her fangs slightly in rage, and Lawrence unconsciously let go of her hand.

"Who was there?" he asked.

Who was it who could so enrage Holo? Perhaps someone from her past.

Holo wrinkled her nose as Lawrence considered. She spoke.

"It was Yarei. You remember him, no doubt."

"That —"

Can't be, he was going to say — but Lawrence never got that far because something else suddenly occurred to him.

"That's it! The figure backing the Medio Company is Count Ehrendott!"

Holo had been ready to vent her spleen at Lawrence, but now her eyes widened in surprise at his outburst.

"As someone with huge tracts of wheat, he can request payment in whatever coin he wants! And if he could arrange favorable duties for his wheat, it would be like a gift from heaven to the Medio Company, the count, or even the villagers! Of course! And that explains why there was someone there who knew you were a wolf!"

Holo looked at Lawrence blankly, but Lawrence didn't notice her as he leapt up to the window that faced the carriage drivers. He opened the small window, and one of them leaned down to listen.

"Did you hear what I just said?"

"I did indeed."

"The one backing the Medio Company is Count Ehrendott. The count and the merchants that deal with his wheat are the reason silver is being collected. Please inform Mr. Marheit."

181

"It shall be done," he said, then jumped immediately off the carriage and took off running.

Lawrence imagined that the horses carrying the negotiators bound for Trenni had already left, but if the negotiations were at all prolonged, they would be able to propose additional conditions. Knowing the source of the Medio Company's silver meant it might be possible for a company with the reputation and resources of Milone to snatch the deal right out from under them.

If he'd figured this out earlier, perhaps Holo's capture could have been avoided and this entire transaction could have gone much more smoothly.

It frustrated Lawrence to think about it, but there was nothing to do about it now. It was good they'd discovered the truth when they had.

". . . I do not follow you."

Lawrence returned to his seat, arms folded as the possibilities raced through his head, when he heard Holo's complaint. That's when he realized he'd cut her off mid-sentence.

"Explaining it all could take some time. Let's just say that your information was the key to figuring everything out."

"Huh."

Lawrence knew that it would not take much effort on Holo's part to understand what was going on, but she didn't seem inclined to bother.

Holo simply nodded her head, uninterested, and closed her eyes.

She seemed irritated at the sudden change of subject.

Lawrence chided himself for finding her sulking as charming as he did.

It might have been a trap she'd set for him, after all, to demonstrate how irritated she was at the interruption.

"I'm sorry I interrupted you," said Lawrence by way of an honest apology.

She opened a single eye briefly to glance at him, then brushed off his apology with a small "It's nothing."

Undaunted, Lawrence continued speaking. Holo was either childish or cunning — one extreme or the other.

"Yarei *should* still be locked away in the storehouse for the harvest festival. If he's in the city, that means he's involved in the deal. He's acquainted with the merchants that buy wheat from the village, and the village leader trusts him to do the dealing. Also, the bulk of the wheat sales are conducted immediately after the festival," said Lawrence.

Her eyes closed, Holo seemed to consider this, finally opening both eyes at length. Her mood appeared to have brightened.

"He must have heard my name from that boy Zheren. That Yarei was wearing clothes far too fine for any village and thought rather highly of himself."

"He must be deeply connected to the Medio Company. Did you talk to him?"

"Just a bit," said Holo. She rid herself of the last of her anger with a sigh. Perhaps it was the recollection of her conversation with Yarei that had angered her so.

Lawrence wondered what he could have possibly said to her. Holo had no love for the villagers, that was true enough, but she had decided to leave. He didn't think her grudge went any further than that.

As Lawrence pondered these things, Holo spoke.

"I don't know how many years I lived there. Maybe as many as there are hairs on my tail."

Holo's tail swished beneath her coat.

"I am Holo the Wisewolf. In order to provide the greatest

harvest, there were years I had to let the land rest, so there were seasons of meager harvest, too. Still, the fields I lent my aid should've been more productive than others over time."

This was the second time she'd explained this, but Lawrence nodded for her to continue.

"The villagers did treat me as the god of the harvest — but not out of respect. It was akin to a desire to control me. Do they not chase after the person who cuts the last sheaf of wheat, after all? Do they not bind him with rope?"

"I've heard they lock the harvester away in the storehouse for a week with treats to eat and all the tools they'll use in the following year."

"The pork and duck were tasty, 'tis true."

It was an amusing reflection. The tales were apparently true — tales of people locked up for a week only to be relased with no recollection of having eaten all the food. And the perpetrator sat right in front of him.

The vague fear that accompanied these stories now possessed a concrete form: the image of Holo in her wolf form, devouring duck and pork.

"Still," said Holo seriously as she set out to explain the reason for her anger. Lawrence composed himself.

"What do you think Yarei said to me?" Holo bit her lip, momentarily at a loss for words. She rubbed the corner of her eye with her finger and continued. "He said he heard my name from Zheren, and it made him wonder. I . . . it is pathetic, but I was so happy to hear that . . ."

Holo's head hung low, and tears overflowed from her eyes.

"Then he told me that the days when they had to worry about my mood were over. That they need no longer fear my fickle nature. That since the Church was already after me, they should just hand me over and be done with the old ways for good!"

Lawrence knew about Count Ehrendott's exchanges with natural philosophers and how he'd introduced new agricultural techniques to boost crop yield.

Even the most devout prayer must eventually show results, or the spirit or god responsible will be discarded, and people will begin to find the idea of depending on their own efforts much more appealing. If new farming methods brought prosperity where prayer failed, it was not surprising that the people would start to believe that the god or spirit to whom they prayed was capricious, unreliable.

Lawrence himself sometimes ascribed the vicissitudes of fortune to some inscrutable god.

But the girl before him was not what came to mind.

She had said her reason for staying in the village was that she got along with the villagers, that her friend from long ago had asked her to see to the harvest. She had always meant for the fields to prosper. But after she oversaw the land for centuries, people began denying her existence, and now to hear that they wished to be rid of her — how must that feel?

Tears fell freely from Holo's eyes. Her face showed a mixture of frustration and sorrow.

She'd said she hated being alone. When a god forced people to worship it, perhaps it was only out of loneliness.

If Holo's predicament elicited such wild-eyed notions in Lawrence, it was hardly surprising it also made him want to wipe her tears away.

"It doesn't really matter, in the end. I want to return to the northland, so I must leave one way or another. If they have no love for me, I'll simply kick the dust from my hind legs and leave. 'Twill be a cleaner break that way. Still . . . I can't just leave it like this."

She seemed to have stopped crying, but Lawrence could still

hear her sniffing as he stroked her head gently. He smiled as broadly as he could manage and spoke.

"I — no, *we* — are merchants. As long as we profit, we triumph. We laugh when money comes in, and cry only in bankruptcy. And we will *laugh*," he said.

Holo glanced up momentarily, then down again, tears falling from her eyes once more. She nodded, then looked back up. Lawrence wiped her tears away a second time, and Holo took a deep breath. She wiped the lingering tears from the corners of her eyes almost violently.

For several moments afterward, her long, damp eyelashes sparkled.

Holo sighed. ". . . I feel better."

She smudged away the final remnants of tears with one hand and, looking sheepish over her outburst, lightly punched Lawrence in the chest with a small fist.

"It's been centuries since I've had a proper conversation. My emotions are far too fragile. I've cried before you twice now, but I would have done it even if you had not been here. Do you understand what I'm saying?"

Lawrence raised his hands and shrugged. "You're telling me not to misunderstand."

"Mm-hm."

Holo happily rubbed her balled-up fist around on Lawrence's chest.

She was being almost unbearably dear just then, and Lawrence couldn't help but tease her a bit.

"I only brought you along to help me make money anyway. Until the Milone Company concludes its negotiations, our job is to escape. Having someone crying and carrying on in the middle of that is just a burden. So regardless of who was crying in front of me, I'd —"

Lawrence could proceed no further with his jape.

Holo looked at him as if stricken.

". . . That's not fair," he grumbled.

"Mm-hm. Female privilege."

Lawrence poked her head lightly for being so shameless.

The window by the driver's seat opened, as if the driver had been waiting for the opportune moment. He smiled reluctantly.

"We have arrived. Are you quite finished with your conversation?"

"We surely are," said Lawrence with affected enthusiasm as he removed the carriage floorboards. Beside him, Holo snickered madly.

"It's true, then, that people who bring talk of profit are rather odd," said the driver.

"What, you mean my ears?" said Holo mischievously.

The driver laughed — she'd gotten the better of him. "It makes me want to return to my traveling merchant days, looking at you two."

"I wouldn't if I were you," said Lawrence, shoving the stone and confirming the tunnel was the right one. He then climbed back into the carriage to let Holo go first. "You might end up running into someone like her."

"Ah, but a wagon bench is too wide for just one. I'd wish to be so lucky!"

Lawrence chuckled; nearly any merchant would feel the same way.

Without another word, he descended into the tunnel. Had he continued, he was sure he'd embarrass himself. And in any case, Holo awaited him.

"Surely *I* am the unfortunate one, to be picked up by the likes of you!" said Holo there in the darkness once the driver replaced the stone and drove away with a quiet rumble.

Lawrence thought about how to turn the tables while the sound of a horse's neigh echoed faintly above them, but ultimately decided that no matter what he said, Holo would win in the end. He gave in.

"You're too clever by half."

"'Tis what makes me so charming," said Holo, as if it were the most obvious thing in the world. What could he say to that?

No, it's because I'm always searching for a retort that I fall into her trap, he thought to himself.

He decided to take the most unexpected route.

Lawrence coughed quietly.

Then he looked away. "Well . . . yes, you're quite charming," he said in the shiest, most bashful tone he could manage.

There was no way she would anticipate such an answer, he was certain.

He forced himself not to laugh in the darkness. As he expected, she was silent.

Now, for the finishing blow, he thought.

As he turned to face her, the softest sensation filled his hand.

His mind went blank at the realization that it was Holo's small, impossibly soft hand.

". . . I'm so happy."

Lawrence's heart couldn't help stirring at those sweet, reticent, girlish words. As if to punctuate it, her hand squeezed his ever so slightly, as if she were embarrassed with her admission of happiness.

So it was Holo who dealt the finishing blow.

"You really are an adorable boy," she said, amused at her own joke — which was even more irritating. Lawrence wasn't angry with her for saying so, but rather himself for giving her the chance.

And yet he didn't think of letting her hand go, which felt some-how pathetic — and Holo's holding his hand made him feel un-reasonably pleased.

"Too clever by half," he murmured to himself.

It was quiet in the tunnel.

Then it filled with the echoes of Holo's giggling.

CHAPTER SIX

Holo stopped short, surely not because of the rat that scampered away with a squeak at her feet.

There in the inky darkness, Lawrence turned to Holo. He wouldn't lose her, as even now he held her hand.

"What is it?"

"Do you not feel a stirring in the air?"

Lawrence wasn't sure where exactly in the city they were, but the scent of clean water in the air suggested that it was somewhere near the marketplace. He could at least tell that they were well away from the river that flowed alongside the city.

It was easy to imagine the countless people and horse-drawn carts passing above them. A bit of movement in the air was hardly surprising.

"Isn't it coming from above?" he asked.

"No . . ." said Holo. He could tell she was glancing this way and that. But they were in a tunnel — there were only two directions to go.

"If I had whiskers I would be able to tell . . ."

"Are you sure it's not your imagination?"

"No . . . there's a sound. I can hear it. Water? The sound of splashes —"

Lawrence's eyes widened at his instinctive thought — they were being pursued.

"It's from ahead. This won't do. We must retreat."

Before Holo could finish, Lawrence had turned on his heel and began running. Holo scrambled to follow him.

"There are no forks in this path, yes?"

"The path we were taking was direct. Going the other way, there's one branch. Take that, and it becomes a complicated labyrinth."

"I don't know that even I could keep from getting lost here . . . whoops!" said Holo as she stopped in her tracks again. Their hands came apart at the sudden stop, and Lawrence stumbled. As he hurried to turn around, it seemed like Holo was facing back the way they'd came.

"You, cover your ears."

"What? Why?"

"Even if we run, they'll catch us. They've loosed the hounds on us."

If they were being pursued down a straight path by well-trained hounds, it was hopeless. Holo could see quite well in the dark, but the dogs had their noses and ears. They had no weapons with which to fend the beasts off save the silver dagger Lawrence always carried.

They did have something rather houndlike, though — Holo the Wisewolf.

"Heh. So foolish-sounding, that baying," said Holo. Lawrence could now faintly hear the hound's cries.

It may have only been the overlapping echoes, but from the sound, Lawrence guessed there were at least two animals.

What was Holo planning?

194

"I'm not certain what I'll do if they're too stupid to understand this. Anyway, cover your ears!"

Lawrence did as he was told and plugged his ears. He'd figured it out — Holo was going to howl.

Holo took a long, deep breath. It lasted so long Lawrence began to wonder where all that air was going. There was a brief pause, and then she unleashed an earthshaking howl.

"Awooooooooooo!"

The force of the great noise was enough to send shivers down his hands and set the skin on his face trembling. It seemed as though the tunnel was about to collapse.

The wolf-howl was enough to strike fear into the heart of the strongest man. Lawrence forgot it was Holo howling and curled up into a ball.

The merchant remembered being chased across the plains by packs of wolves. They possessed overwhelming numbers, knowledge of the terrain, and physical strength no human could hope to match. They would bring all three to bear and attack — and the howl was the signal. That was why some villages, when stricken with plague, would imitate a wolf's howl to drive away the disease.

Holo coughed, jaggedly. "Ugh . . . my throat . . ." Lawrence heard her coughing once the howl had subsided and took his hands down from his ears. It wasn't surprising that such a great howl from such a small throat came with a price.

"An apple . . . I want an apple . . . *koff* —"

"You can have as many as you want once we're free. What of the hounds?"

"They turned tail and ran."

"Then we should do likewise. They'll know where we are now."

"Do you know the way?"

"More or less."

Before starting to run, Lawrence held his hand out to Holo, who gripped it firmly.

Ensuring that they wouldn't be separated, Lawrence ran. It was about then that he heard the voices of their pursuers.

"Still, how did they find us?" Holo asked.

"I doubt they knew exactly where we were. They probably came underground after being unable to find us above and then happened to run into us."

"Ah."

"If they knew exactly where we were, they would've cornered us by now. . . ."

"I see. You're quite right."

Directly ahead of them muffled voices could be distinguished, then a faint ray of light penetrated the dark tunnel. It was where they had first entered the passage.

Lawrence had never been so optimistic as to think that the Milone Company would come to their rescue.

He drew a sharp breath as the realization washed over him like a splash of cold water and quickened his pace.

Then a voice echoed down the passage.

"The Milone Company has betrayed you! There's no point in runnin'!"

As if to avoid the voices, they turned down the single branch, and from behind them came the same words. Lawrence ignored them and continued to run, but Holo was uneasy.

"Sounds like we've been sold out."

"And for a high price, no doubt. As long as you're here, the Milone Company will lose a branch, at the very least."

". . . I see. That's a high price, indeed."

If they were truly betrayed, Marheit would've been forced to put the entire branch on the line. If he'd really done so, he must've been planning to keep the branch's money and escape by himself to some far-off land. But it seemed unlikely that the huge Milone Company would let that happen, nor did he take Marheit for the kind of man to run.

Which meant their pursuers were simply lying on the spot — but to someone unused to such tactics, like Holo, it could be effective.

Holo nodded her head to indicate understanding, although her grip on his hand grew faintly tighter.

"Right, we turn right here."

"Wait —"

Lawrence stopped immediately after rounding the corner.

At the end of the slightly winding tunnel a lantern swayed. "There they are!" cried a voice.

Lawrence immediately took Holo's hand again and ran back along the path they'd first taken. Their pursuers broke into a run as well, but their footfalls did not reach Lawrence's ears.

"Do you know —"

"— the way? I do, it's all right," said Lawrence impatiently, but not because he was out of breath. The paths were strangely complicated, and all he could remember from what the Milone employees had told him were the paths that connected the entrance and exit.

It wasn't a lie to say he knew the way, but it wasn't the truth, either.

If which way to turn left or right, and after how many intersections, then it was true. If not, it was a lie.

His head filled with strange illusions that threatened to blank everything out — the sound of a column of mice running through the forest — tripping over the rubble of a crumbled stone wall. Traveling merchants had to remember complicated figures about how much they owed and how much they *were* owed, so they tended to have confidence in their memory. But

Lawrence's confidence lasted for only a moment after he asserted it.

The twisting tunnels were just too complicated.

"Another dead end?"

They'd gone a short distance after turning right at a T-junction before reaching the end. Lawrence kicked at the wall, breathing heavily. His actions made his worry clear, but Holo, her breathing also ragged, simply squeezed his hand tighter.

The Medio Company had apparently decided it was important to capture both of them — and they'd sent ample manpower to accomplish it.

Their footfalls and shouted voices echoed through the halls. They were so many that even Holo couldn't be sure of their number.

The companions' anxiety made them imagine a great swarm of men pursuing them, more numerous than ants.

"Damn. We'll have to head back. I don't remember anything else."

If they pushed ahead into unknown passages, there would be no going back.

Lawrence's memories were already quite shaky, but seeing Holo nod her assent, he didn't say so, not wanting her to feel any more uncertain.

"Can you still run?" he asked.

Lawrence was a hale and hardy traveling merchant, and despite his fatigue, he knew he could still run — but Holo could only nod her head in answer.

Perhaps her human body wasn't as capable as her wolf form.

"Just a bit," she said hastily as she gasped for air.

"Let's find a place to . . ." Lawrence began. He was going to say "rest," but he caught Holo's glance and the word never got out of his throat.

Her pupils glowed keenly in the darkness, every inch the forest predator scanning its surroundings.

Heartened to have someone like Holo as his companion, Lawrence quieted his breathing and listened carefully.

Crunch, crunch came the sound of their pursuer's cautious footsteps.

From where Lawrence was standing, it sounded as if they were coming from a passage that led off to the right some distance ahead.

The path they'd taken was now directly behind them. If they doubled back on it, many possible paths branched off of it. They hoped to guess the timing and run back, then escape down one of those paths

Crunch, crunch, came the sound as the footsteps grew closer. There was still a wall between them and the source of the noise, which was encouraging, but the footfalls were incessant — it was as though the Medio men were purposefully causing a commotion as they talked in some kind of incomprehensible code.

Lawrence felt as though they'd already fallen into the trap, and their pursuers needed only to toss a net out to capture them.

He gulped painfully, gauging the timing for their sprint.

He hoped to run as soon as there was another shout from the Medio Company people.

It was not a long wait.

"Ah, ah . . ."

Another sound came from the direction of the footsteps. A sneeze.

Lawrence took this as a blessing from the gods and grabbed Holo's hand tightly in preparation to run.

"Ah-choo!"

It sounded as though whoever sneezed realized his mistake and tried to muffle the sound with a hand.

But it was more than enough for the two to begin their flight. They turned left at the first junction.

Just then, something black crossed in front of their faces.

Lawrence realized it was no mere rat when Holo began to growl.

"Rrrrrr."

"Wha — shit! Here! They're here!"

A small, almost child-sized clump of darkness wove this way and that before Lawrence. He felt something hot on his left cheek. He realized it was a knife wound when he put his hand to it and felt the warm wetness there.

When he realized that Holo had abandoned escape and even now had her teeth in the arm of their knife-wielding attacker, Lawrence, too, lost control.

Strengthened by hauling loads heavier than themselves over mountains and across plains, traveling merchants had fists as hard as silver.

Lawrence put all his strength behind his right fist as he punched, hitting the man Holo was attacking square in the face at a slightly upward angle.

There was an awful squishing sound, as though a frog had just been stepped on, as Lawrence's fist connected.

With his other hand, Lawrence reached out for Holo and snagged the back of her shirt, pulling her back to him.

The shadow that the fist had struck tumbled slowly backward. There was no time to say anything — Lawrence took off running, trying to find a different path.

But he soon realized that the sneeze had been a ploy to flush them out.

As the body hit the ground with a *whump*, Lawrence felt a shock, as if the blood in his veins suddenly reversed direction.

The moment they tried to turn, a blade thrust directly into Lawrence.

"O holy God, forgive me my sins . . ."

Hearing his opponent's words, Lawrence realized this man intended to kill him.

There in the darkness, his assailant held his breath, surely thinking he had in fact slain his target.

But the gods had not yet abandoned Lawrence. The knife found purchase in his left arm, just above his wrist.

"Before you think about your sins," said Lawrence, raising his leg and delivering a vicious kick to the man's thigh, "regret your daily deeds!"

The man dropped soundlessly, and Lawrence grabbed Holo's sleeve with his right hand and sprinted past him.

The sounds of the Medio Company closing in echoed all around them.

They veered down a path to the left, then went immediately right — but not because of some plan or because Lawrence remembered the way.

They simply ran. Stopping was not an option. Lawrence's left arm felt heavy, as if it were sinking into a swamp, and it burned as though impaled on a piece of red-hot iron. His left hand was cold, perhaps from the blood that flowed freely from the wound in his arm.

He would not be able to run much farther. Lawrence had been wounded several times in his travels. He knew the limits of his own body.

It was hard to tell how far they'd come in the darkness. The confused echoes of their pursuers eroded his fading consciousness like rain over grasslands.

When even their pursuers started to sound distant, he had no energy left with which to worry about Holo. He didn't know how long he'd be able to keep going.

"Lawrence."

When he heard someone calling his name, he wondered if it was the Grim Reaper already.

"Lawrence, are you all right?"

He returned to himself with a start, realizing that he was leaning against the wall of the tunnel.

"What a relief. You weren't moving when I called to you."

". . . Ugh. I'm okay. Just a little sleepy," Lawrence said.

Lawrence wasn't sure if he succeeded in smiling. An irritated Holo hit him in the chest.

"Pull yourself together! We're almost there."

". . . We're almost where?"

"Did you not hear me? I said I can smell the warmth of the sun ahead. There must be a way to the surface close by."

Lawrence had no memory of hearing this at all, but he nodded, righting himself, and staggered forward. He realized his arm had been bandaged with cloth.

". . . This bandage?"

"I tore my sleeves off to patch you up. You didn't notice?"

"Uh, no, of course I noticed. I'm fine." Lawrence made sure to give a reassuring smile; Holo said nothing. When they continued walking, though, she led the way.

"Just a bit farther. We'll take this passage, then turn right . . ." she began, taking Lawrence's hand — but then stopped short. He could tell why.

More footsteps behind them.

"Hurry, hurry," said Holo hoarsely. Lawrence quickened his pace, feeling near the end of his strength.

Although their pursuers were getting closer, they were still some distance off. As long as they could climb to the surface, Lawrence imagined they would be able to convince the citizenry to help them, given his condition.

The Medio Company probably wouldn't want a scene in front of so many witnesses.

As long as she took the opportunity to contact the Milone Company, Holo's escape would be enough. The top priority now was to meet with the Milone people again and restrategize.

Lawrence mulled this over as he heaved his body forward, though it seemed to grow heavier by the second. At length, just as Holo said, he saw light ahead.

The light shone from the upper right down to the left. The footsteps behind them grew closer, but it looked as if they were going to make it.

Holo pulled harder on Lawrence's arm to hurry him forward; he tried his best to keep up.

At the end of the path, they turned right.

"It goes to the surface — just a little farther!"

Vitality had returned to Holo's voice, and Lawrence pressed forward, encouraged.

The prey had escaped the hunter by the slimmest of margins.

Of that much Lawrence was certain.

That is, until he heard Holo's voice on the verge of tears.

"N-no . . ." she said.

Lawrence looked up.

Even when he looked down, the light stung his eyes, which had adjusted to total darkness. It took him a few moments to focus, but once he did, he understood the reason for Holo's dismay.

Perhaps it was left over from when these tunnels supplied water. There was an unused well there with light stabbing down through a round opening in the ceiling.

But the hole in the ceiling was too high. Lawrence stretched and could just barely touch the ceiling, but the well opening was even higher than that.

Without a rope or a ladder, it was simply impossible for the two of them to escape.

Lawrence and Holo fell silent, despairing like loan sharks looking down the long path to heaven.

Then, as if to confirm that they were well and truly cornered, the source of the footsteps behind them rounded the corner.

"Found them!" a voice cried, at which point the pair finally looked back.

Holo looked up at Lawrence, who drew his dagger with his good right hand, and with a movement so slow it was as if he were underwater, blocked the path between her and their pursuers.

"Back up."

Lawrence planned to advance, but his legs had no more strength left in them. He was rooted to the spot, unable to take another step.

"You can't — you're through!" said Holo.

"Hardly. I can still move," Lawrence managed in a nonchalant tone. Turning to look at her over his shoulder would've been impossible, though.

"Fool, you don't need my ears to know that's a lie," snapped Holo. Lawrence ignored her and fixed his gaze straight ahead.

He saw five Medio men at a glance. Each wielded a knife or staff, and more footsteps signaled reinforcements on the way.

Despite their overwhelming advantage, the five men did not converge, choosing instead to stop at the corner and scrutinize the pair.

Lawrence imagined they were waiting for backup, though five men were more than sufficient to take both him and his companion. Lawrence was obviously in no shape for a fight, and Holo was just a girl.

But the men held fast, and at length more arrived. The first five looked back, then stepped aside.

"Ah —" Holo made a sound as a figure rounded the corner.

Lawrence, too, nearly spoke.

The man rounding the corner was none other than Yarei.

"I wondered, given the description we got," he said. "But to think it really *was* you, Lawrence."

Unlike the residents who lived within the city walls, or the dusty, sweaty merchants that traveled between them, Yarei wore the colors of the sun and the earth and looked almost sad as he spoke.

"I'm just as surprised," said Lawrence. "Most of Pasloe thinks only of sickle or hoe at the mention of metal — to think they'd be involved in such a grand silver scheme."

"There are few who understand this transaction," said Yarei, as if it wasn't his village at all, which was understandable given his attire. The depth of his connection with the Medio Company was self-evident in its color and texture.

A humble farmer would never be able to afford such finery.

"Let's catch up later, shall we? We've no time for it now."

"Come now, Yarei — I came all the way to your village and still wasn't able to see you."

"Ah, but you met someone else, didn't you?" Yarei glanced past Lawrence to Holo behind him. "I wouldn't have thought it possible, but she really is right out of the fairy tales. The wolf-spirit incarnate, responsible for harvests great and poor."

Lawrence felt Holo flinch but didn't turn to look at her.

"Hand her over," Yarei demanded. "We'll give her to the Church and put the old ways to rest forever!" He took a step forward.

"Lawrence, if we have her, we can destroy the Milone Company. Then once we've abolished the wheat tariff, the wheat of our village will be hugely profitable, and we who sell it rich men. Nothing is so profitable as an untaxed commodity."

Yarei was two paces from them when Holo grabbed Lawrence's shirt. Despite his dizziness, he could feel her hands trembling.

"Lawrence, our village still remembers that you bought wheat from us when we were suffering under heavy taxation. It would be no trouble to give you purchasing priority now. And we're friends, nay? Surely as a merchant you can figure gain and loss."

Yarei's words sank slowly into Lawrence's consciousness. Selling untaxed wheat would be like plucking gold from the stalks. If he took Yarei up on his offer, his fortunes would surely rise. When he'd saved enough, he could open a shop in Pazzio — and with those wheat options as his weapon, he'd continue to expand his business.

Yarei promised the fulfillment of his dreams.

"Oh, I can figure gain and loss all right," said Lawrence.

"Ho, Lawrence!" said Yarei brightly, his arms wide in welcome. Holo tightened her grip on Lawrence's shirt.

Lawrence used the last of his strength to turn back to Holo, who looked up at him.

Her amber eyes saddened as she looked at him; she soon closed them.

Lawrence slowly turned back around.

"However, a merchant must always honor his contracts," he said.

"Lawrence?" asked Yarei suspiciously.

Lawrence continued. "As fate would have it, this strange girl I've picked up wishes to return to the northlands. I have a contract to accompany her there. Breaking that contract is something I cannot do, Yarei."

"You —" a shocked Holo began as Lawrence stared down Yarei.

Yarei shook his head in disbelief, sighing deeply, then looked at Lawrence. "In that case, I have no choice but to fulfill *my* contract."

He raised his right hand, and the gathered Medio henchmen, who'd only watched until that point, took aggressive stances.

"I'm sorry our friendship was a short one, Lawrence."

"A traveling merchant is always saying good-bye," replied Lawrence.

"You can kill the man. Bring the girl alive." Yarei's voice was cold now, like a different person entirely. The Medio lackeys advanced.

Lawrence held the dagger fast in his right hand, but he was still unable to take a step either forward or back.

If he could somehow buy them just a bit more time, the Milone Company might yet come to their rescue. He clung to that hope as he waved the dagger about clumsily.

In that moment, Holo flung her arms around him.

"H-Holo, what are you —"

Her slender arms held him fast, then forced him to the ground.

He wondered where she'd gotten this sudden strength, but then realized it was probably because he had no power left to resist.

Holo couldn't actually support his weight, so Lawrence half-fell backward, landing on his rear. The impact dislodged the knife from his hand.

Lawrence reached for the dagger and tried to get up, but he couldn't manage it. Unable to support even his outstreched arm, he fell forward.

"Holo . . . the dagger . . ."

"That's enough."

"Holo?"

She gave no response save putting her hand to Lawrence's outstretched arm.

"This may hurt a bit. Please bear it."

"What —"

Lawrence failed to utter another word before Holo undid the bandage on his left arm and sniffed at the exposed wound.

Suddenly his memory returned. He recalled their conversation when they first met, when he made her prove she was truly a wolf.

He remembered her nonchalant reply.

To assume her wolf form, she needed either a bit of wheat or . . .

. . . *Fresh blood.*

"What are you doing! Hurry, take them!" Yarei shouted, and the Medio henchmen — whose advance had been stalled by Holo's strange actions — regained their senses and began to close in.

Holo closed her eyes, bared her fangs, and sank them into Lawrence's wound.

"Sh-she's drinking his blood!"

Holo opened her eyes slightly at the shout and glanced at Lawrence.

He couldn't have conjectured as to his own expression, but Holo seemed to smile sadly at him.

After all, only a demon would drink blood.

"Don't fall back! She's only a possessed girl! Get her!" Yarei's exhortations were no use; the men were frozen in their tracks.

Holo slowly pulled her mouth back from Lawrence's arm; her transformation had already begun.

"I'll always . . ." she began as her long hair began to stir, transforming into animal fur. Her arms, visible through her torn sleeves, took the form of wolf paws.

"I'll always remember that you chose me."

She cleaned the blood from the corner of her mouth with her bright red tongue rather than her hand, an image that lingered with Lawrence.

"Lawrence —" she said, standing and facing him. She had a small, sad smile on her face as she spoke her final words.

"Please don't look at me."

Her body grew up and out rapidly to the sound of tearing fabric, brown fur nearly exploding through it. Her wheat pouch fell to the ground among the tatters of clothing.

Lawrence automatically reached out for the wheat in which Holo lived. When he looked back up, a massive wolf stood before him.

Its paws were tipped with scythelike claws, and its teeth were so large that the shape of each fang was clearly visible. It looked capable of eating a man in a single bite.

The wolf was so massive that the very air around it felt heavy and hot — as if one might melt by mere proximity. In spite of that, its eyes were cool and calculating.

There was no escape.

Every man in the tunnel came to the same conclusion at once.

"Aaaaauuggh!" The single cry was the trigger. Most of the assailants dropped their weapons and ran. Two men hurled their weapons at the wolf, mostly out of terror.

The beast moved its muzzle adroitly, picking up each iron weapon in turn and crushing it between massive jaws.

This was a god.

In the northlands, the word "god" was used to describe anything beyond a human's ability to engage.

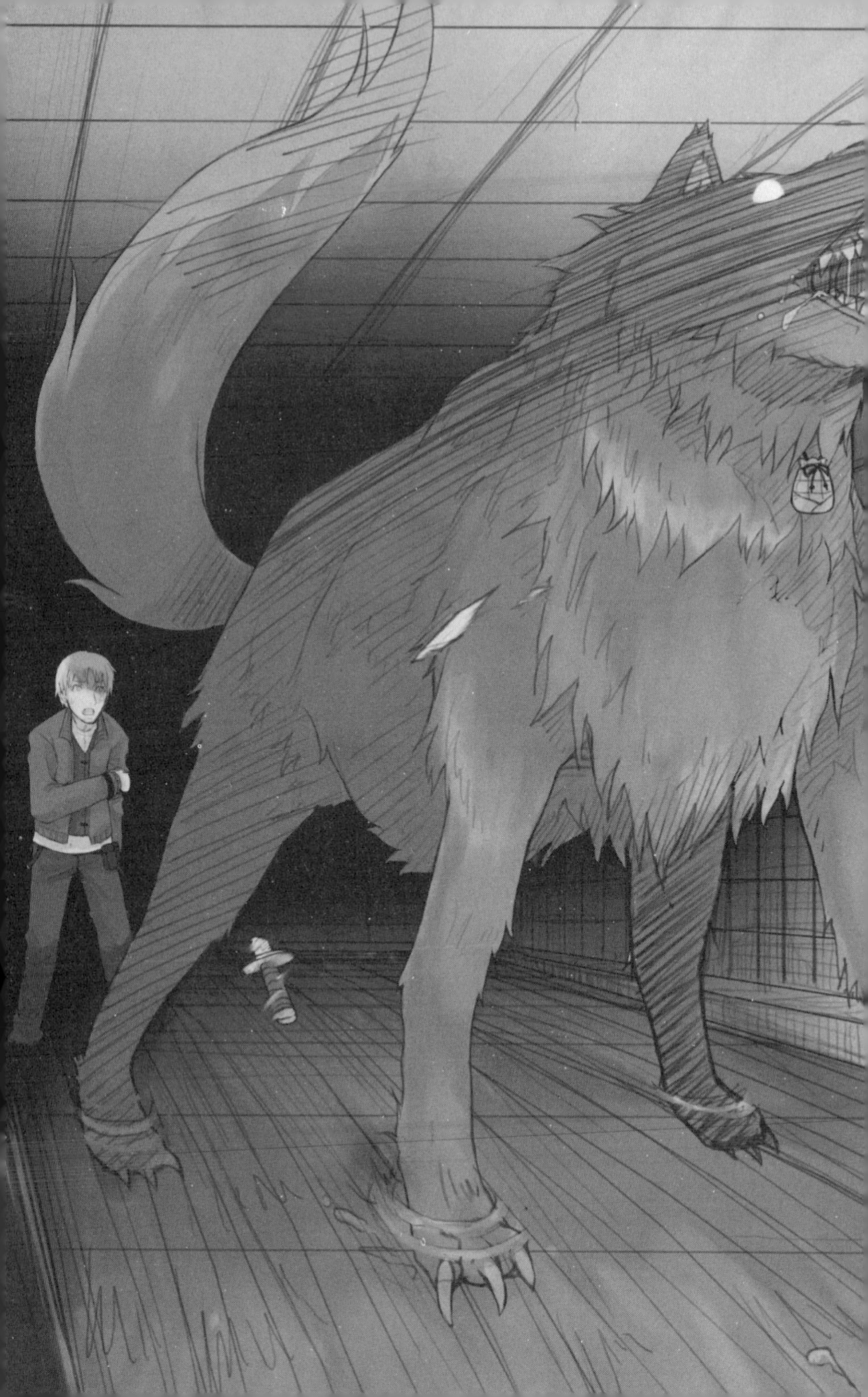

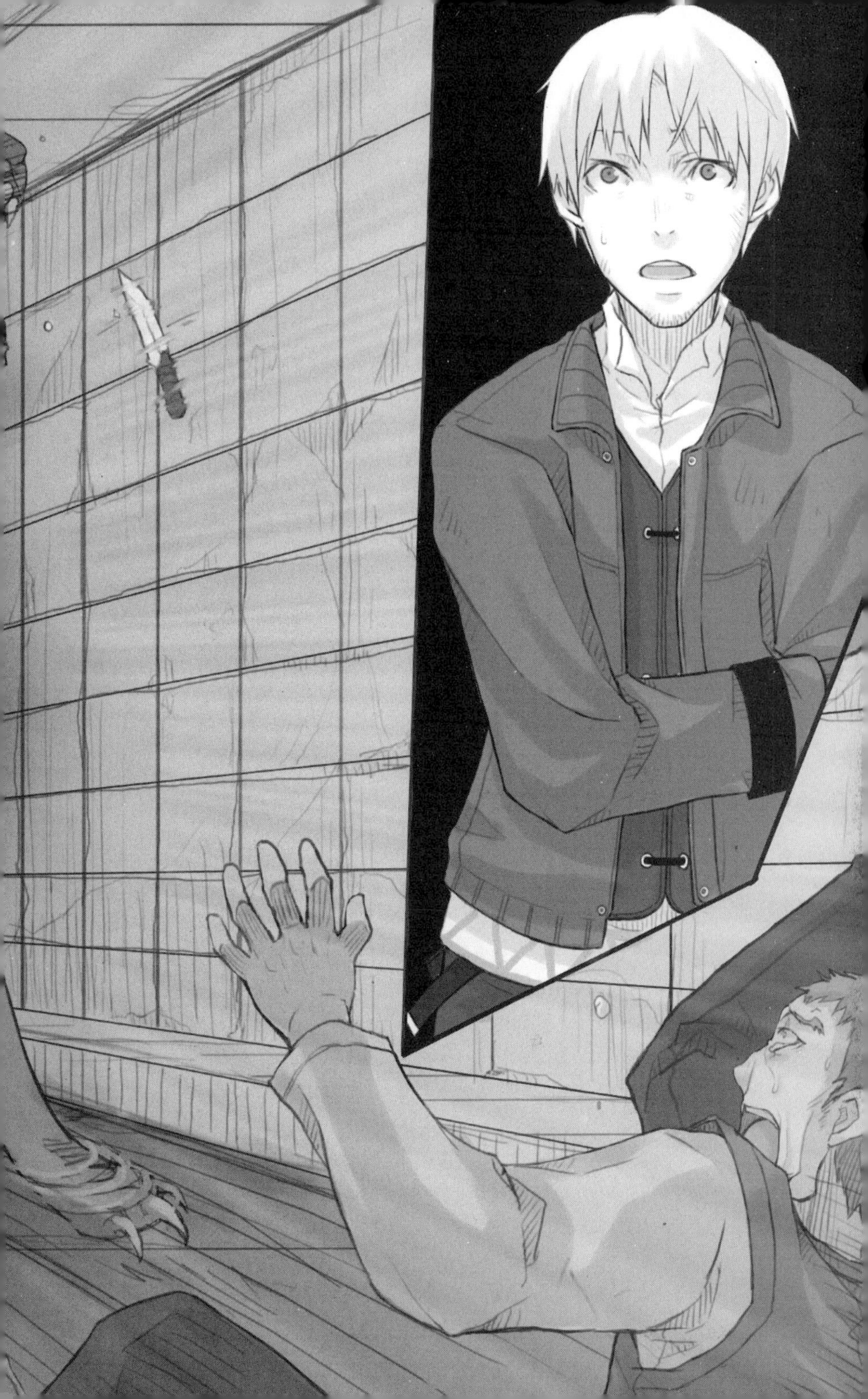

Lawrence had never understood that definition until now — and now he understood it all too well.

There was nothing anyone could do to this wolf. Nothing at all.

"Guh —"

"Wha —"

The two that threw their weapons made strangled exclamations that were barely worthy of the term.

The wolf swatted them aside with a massive paw, then ran forward, seeming almost to slide over the ground.

"None of you will leave here alive!" a low, bestial voice echoed. The sounds of claw striking iron mingled with the cries of the felled as Lawrence frantically tried to right himself.

But the massacre ended in an instant.

The wolf paused, and the voice of perhaps the last man left alive was audible.

"G-gods are always like that . . . always . . . unfair . . ." It was Yarei's voice.

There was no response but the sound of the colossal wolf opening its jaws. Lawrence cried out.

"Holo, no!"

There was a *snap*, surely those same jaws closing.

The image of Yarei's torso in Holo's fangs came unbidden to Lawrence's mind. It was unthinkable that Yarei could escape. He was a bird with no chance to avoid the hound's attack.

But after a few moments of silence, Holo turned around in the narrow passageway, and her teeth were not smeared with the blood Lawrence expected.

Instead, an unconscious Yarei dangled helplessly from her fangs.

"Holo . . ." Lawrence murmured her name in relief, but Holo merely dropped Yarei to the ground and did not look at him.

A low voice sounded.

"The wheat . . ."

The growl suited the great body, and Lawrence cringed to hear it.

He knew it was Holo, but he couldn't help himself. If she looked straight at him, he didn't know if he'd be able to stay composed.

The wolf demanded his awe.

"The wheat — bring it to me," repeated Holo. Lawrence nodded and held out the pouch of wheat in his hand. ,

Just then, Lawrence felt a heavy pressure, and his body recoiled from it.

When he saw Holo's lip curl over her fanged jaw, he realized he'd made a terrible mistake.

"That is your answer. Now, the wheat —"

Although he knew that Holo intended to take the wheat and leave, her words, as if by some strange magic, compelled his arm to reach out and hand it over.

But he lacked the strength to support the arm or even to hold the pouch.

First the pouch fell from his limp hand to the ground, then his arm collapsed against him.

He wouldn't be able to pick it up again.

Lawrence looked at the pouch in despair.

"I thank you for taking care of me," said Holo as she approached, deftly picking up the small bag in her massive jaws.

Those amber eyes never once glanced at Lawrence as she backed up one, two, three steps, then turned dextrously in the small tunnel and began to walk away.

The white-tipped tail that was Holo's pride and joy caught his eye. It was magnificent as it waved sadly and receded down the passage.

Lawrence shouted. His voice was so weak it could barely be considered a shout, but he sounded with all his remaining strength.

"W-wait!"

Holo kept walking.

Lawrence despised himself for recoiling at her approach earlier. How many times had she said that she hated when people regarded her with fear.

But his body had reacted instinctively. Humans couldn't help that they feared the unknown, and so he had cowered before Holo.

Still, Lawrence thought. Still, he called out her name.

"Holo!" shouted his hoarse voice.

It was useless, he realized — and just then, Holo stopped.

This was his chance. If he couldn't change her mind here, he would never see her again.

But what to say? Scenarios flitted in and out of his mind.

He couldn't convincingly claim he wasn't afraid of her. Her form still terrified him. But he wanted to stop her. He couldn't find the words to express the conflict he felt.

His mind worked frantically. No doubt Holo would've mocked him for being inarticulate as he tried to put together the words that would bring her back.

"How . . . how much do you think the clothes you destroyed cost?" was what he finally came up with. "I don't care if you're a god or not . . . I'll see you pay me back! You earned but seventy silver pieces — that's not nearly enough!"

He yelled at her, trying to sound angry — no, he was genuinely half-angry.

He knew that begging her not to go would be pointless. As he was still terrified of her form, he could only conjure this single reason to prevent her going.

The grudge a merchant will bear over money is deeper than a valley, and a merchant collecting a debt is more persistent than the moon in the night sky.

Lawrence put as much venom into his words as he could to convey that. He was not telling her that he didn't want her to leave. He was telling her that leaving would be pointless.

"How many years do you think it took me . . . to save up that much money? I'll follow you . . . I'll follow you all the way back to the northlands, if I have to!"

Lawrence's voice echoed through the underground tunnels for a while before finally fading.

Holo stood there awhile, then flicked her large tail.

Was she going to turn around?

Lawrence's strength finally failed him, and he collapsed to the ground even as his chest filled with a nervous impatience.

Holo began walking again.

Her paws pattered softly against the floor of the passage: *tupp, tupp*.

Lawrence felt his vision grow dim.

I'm not crying, the merchant told himself as his consciousness sank into eternity.

EPILOGUE

Lawrence stood in utter darkness. Where he was and what he was doing there he did not know.

Darkness hung in every direction, but strangely, he could see his own body.

He wondered where he was.

As he pondered it, he caught a flash of something out of the corner of his eye.

He turned to face it reflexively, but there was nothing. He rubbed his eyes, thinking it had been his imagination, when again the shape flitted across the corner of his vision.

Was it a flame?

He turned again to face it and this time managed a good view of the shape.

It was a chestnut-brown *something*, waving.

He stared at it, finally realizing that it was no flame.

It was fur. It was a long clump of brown fur that waved.

And it was tipped with a white tuft.

Lawrence's eyes widened and his breath caught. He sprinted toward it.

That tail — that white tuft —!

It was Holo. There was no mistaking Holo's tail.

It grew smaller as it waved, and Lawrence called out for it as he ran with all his might.

But no sound issued from his mouth, and the distance to Holo's tail never diminished.

His feet seemed to grow heavier, which frustrated him. He gritted his teeth and, even as he realized the futility of it, stretched out his right hand.

Holo's tail abruptly disappeared.

At that moment, Lawrence blinked and looked up at an unfamiliar ceiling.

"Ugh —"

He sat up with a start and pain immediately shot through his left arm. For a moment he was confused, but the pain brought his memories back in a rush.

The Medio Company pursuing him. His arm being stabbed. Being cornered.

And Holo leaving him.

Remembering her tail waving forlornly as she receded, Lawrence sighed.

Trapped in a body that could sit up only with effort, he wondered if there was anything else he could have said to her.

The question loomed in his mind, dwarfing the more immediate issue of where he was.

"Ah, so you're awake, are you?"

Lawrence turned to face the unexpected voice, and saw Marheit in the doorway.

"How are your injuries?" Marheit walked toward Lawrence, documents in hand, and opened the window beside the merchant's bed.

"Better . . . thanks to you."

A pleasant breeze blew in through the window, carrying sounds of hustle and bustle from which Lawrence inferred that he was in a room at the Milone Company.

Which meant they had come to his rescue after all.

"I must apologize for putting you in such danger through our ineptitude."

"No, no, my companion was the cause of all this originally."

Marheit nodded at Lawrence's words and paused, seeming to choose his next statement carefully.

"Fortunately you were never discovered by the Church, and the disturbance happened underground. If the Church had seen your companion's true form, well . . . it's quite possible the entire company would've been burned as heretics."

"You saw her true form?" Lawrence asked, stunned.

"Indeed. The people we sent to rescue you returned with a report that there was a giant wolf that said it wouldn't hand you over until I came personally."

There was no reason for Marheit to lie. Which meant that after Lawrence lost consciousness, Holo returned to him.

"What of Holo, then? Where is she?"

"She's gone on to the marketplace. She was quite impatient and said she needed traveling clothes," said Marheit lightly, not knowing the circumstances — but Lawrence guessed that Holo planned to set off on her own.

She was probably on her way to the northland even now.

The thought left a hole in Lawrence's heart but perversely also helped him feel that he could now make a clean break.

The days they had spent together had been nothing more than a strange coincidence.

Lawrence forced himself to consider it thus, bringing himself back to the mindset of a merchant.

Aside from Holo, there was another important implication in Marheit's words.

221

"You said Holo went to the marketplace. Does that mean negotiations with the Medio Company went well?"

"Yes. Our messenger returned from the Trenni castle this morning, concluding negotiations with the king. We've obtained the considerations that the Medio Company so desperately wanted, and they seem to have acknowledged their defeat. Everything has gone very smoothly," said Marheit, pride filling his voice.

"I see. That's good to hear. . . . So I've slept for a full day then, have I?"

"Hm? Oh, yes, yes you have. Would you care for some lunch? I was just in the kitchen, and I doubt they've turned off the stoves yet, so you could have something hot."

"No, that's quite all right. Could I perhaps hear the final results of our negotiation?"

"Yes, of course."

Lawrence found it slightly odd that someone from the south wasn't forcing food on him. Perhaps if he'd been from this area, Marheit would've been more insistent.

"The amount of silver we collected came to 307,212 pieces. The king plans to significantly cut the silver content of these coins, so he agreed to pay an amount equivalent to 350,000 pieces."

It was a staggering figure. Lawrence was not thinking about the absolute numbers, though — he was busy figuring his own approximate gain.

He was contractually entitled to five percent of the Milone Company's profit. Lawrence estimated it would come out to something in the neighborhood of two thousand silver pieces.

It would be enough for him to fulfill his dream, to open his own shop.

"According to our contract with you, Mr. Lawrence, we owe you five percent of our profit. Is that correct?"

Lawrence nodded, and Marheit nodded back.

Marheit then handed Lawrence a single sheet of paper. "Please confirm this," he said.

Lawrence didn't hear him.

An unbelievable figure was written on the paper.

"Wha . . . what's . . ."

"One hundred and twenty pieces — five percent of our profit," said Marheit coolly.

Yet Lawrence did not become angry. The paper made it clear what had happened to the gain they'd expected.

"The cost of transporting the coins, the transfer fee when the king paid us, the silver tax, and the cost of processing the contract. His advisers undoubtedly put him up to it. They knew they would have to give up those special privileges but wanted to limit their losses on the silver exchange as much as they could."

Looking at the details, he could see that the king had very cleverly exploited his position to get as much money back from the Milone Company as he could.

In addition to requiring that the company pay for the collection and transport of the coins, he made them remit the silver coins directly rather than using a note of exchange. The transportation had been hugely expensive, running into the tens of thousands of pieces after including horses, lockboxes for the money, and guards.

The king had even charged them an exorbitant amount for the drawing up of the contracts.

Though the signer on the Milone side was a wealthy merchant of noble descent from the south who operated his own branch of a large company, he was far from a king. There was no question of who held the upper hand. The Milone Company had to simply accept the charges.

"We calculate that our final profit was twenty-four hundred

pieces, five percent of which we're remitting to you as per our agreement."

Lawrence had schemed like a man possessed, been stabbed in the arm . . . for one hundred twenty silver coins.

When he considered that if he hadn't gotten involved in this business, Holo might not have left him, the only figures he saw in his mind were red. It simply hadn't been worth one hundred twenty coins.

But a contract was a contract. He had no choice but to accept it. Sometimes there were gains in life, and sometimes there were losses. It was a simple reality of being a merchant. He supposed that he should be happy not to have lost his life and to have come out one hundred twenty silver pieces ahead.

Lawrence slowly nodded.

"This was not something we expected. The outcome is regrettable," said Marheit.

"Unexpected outcomes are part and parcel of business," replied Lawrence.

"It is generous of you to say so. However," said Marheit, getting Lawrence's attention again — Marheit's tone had brightened for some reason. "Unexpected situations can also work out happily. Here."

Lawrence accepted a second sheet of paper from Marheit, his eyes flicking over its contents.

He immediately looked back up at Marheit in shock.

"The Medio Company badly wanted those special privileges, and they knew the silver they'd collected was going to depreciate rapidly soon, so it was like holding on to debt. They expected they'd be able to turn a profit with that tariff authority, and they would do anything to get it. They made us an offer almost immediately."

The document in Lawrence's hand stated that his share of the profit from this exchange was one thousand silver pieces.

"A thousand pieces . . . is this really acceptable?"

"It is a trifle," said Marheit with a smile. The Milone Company had no doubt made much more than that, but Lawrence was not so rude as to ask the exact figure. After all, being offered an extra-contractual amount like this was like picking up a bar of gold on the street.

Contracts were the core of commerce — monetary exchanges without them might as well have been nonexistent.

"Also, we've taken care of the fees for your convalescence, and we'll handle the care of your horse and wagon."

"Was my horse unhurt?"

"Yes — it seems even the Medio Company didn't find much worth in him as a hostage."

Lawrence couldn't help smiling at Marheit's hearty laugh.

This was all far better treatment than he had any right to expect.

"We'll discuss the payment details and so on another day, then, shall we?" said Marheit.

"That will be fine. Thank you so much, truly."

"Hardly; the pleasure is all ours. It is a small price to pay to remain in the good graces of a merchant of your ability, Mr. Lawrence."

Marheit looked at Lawrence with eyes that rarely missed a calculation, and he smiled his best merchant's smile — probably on purpose.

Still, the fact remained that Lawrence had received a thousand silver pieces from the branch supervisor of the huge company. They clearly thought of him as a person with whom a good relationship was important.

A mere traveling merchant like Lawrence should be pleased by that.

He nodded and thanked Marheit from his bed.

"Oh, I suppose I should ask," said Marheit, "do you wish payment to be in silver? If you would prefer a different commodity, that can be arranged."

A thousand coins would be heavy and would bring no particular benefit for the weight. Lawrence considered Marheit's proposal, thinking about the amount he'd been promised and the size of his wagon, and a single item came to mind.

"Have you any pepper? It's light and compact, and as winter falls, its price will surely rise as meat becomes more available."

"Pepper, you say?"

"Is there a problem?" asked Lawrence, seeing Marheit chuckle.

"No, not at all. I recently read a play we received from the south, and that reminded me of it."

"A play?"

"Indeed. A demon appears before a wealthy merchant and says, 'Bring me the most delicious, succulent human you can, or I'll devour you.' Not wanting to die, the merchant presents the demon with the youngest, most beautiful maids in his house, and the plumpest footmen. But the demon shakes his head in disapproval."

"I see."

"So the merchant scatters money throughout the city, searching for a suitable person. Finally he finds a handsome young monk who smells of milk and honey. He throws gold at the monastery to buy the lad and brings him before the demon. But the boy says, 'Oh ye demon who fights the gods, the most savory human in the land is not I.'"

Lawrence was completely absorbed in the tale. He nodded wordlessly.

" 'The most succulent human is before your very eyes — he has carried spices day in and day out in his quest for money, and his fattened soul is perfectly seasoned,' " continued Marheit cheerfully, gesturing expansively as he related the tale. In the end, he even imitated the wealthy merchant's terrified face before catching himself and grinning sheepishly.

"It's a religious play that the Church uses to preach moderation in commerce," he explained. "That's what I remembered. Pepper is surely appropriate for a merchant about to make his fortune, I think."

Lawrence couldn't help smiling at the amusing tale and Marheit's praise. "I hope I soon have a body suffused with spices myself!" he said.

"We'll look forward to that, and to many fruitful dealings in the future, Mr. Lawrence," said Marheit, and the two smiled at each other again.

"I'll see to your pepper. In the meantime, I have work to do . . ." Marheit backed toward the exit.

Just then, there was a knock at the door.

"Perhaps that's your companion," said Marheit, but Lawrence was confident that such a thing was impossible.

Marheit left the bedside to open the door, and Lawrence, his head on a pillow, looked out the window.

He could see the blue sky.

"Overseer, sir. We've received this bill —" Lawrence heard the door open and a reserved voice speaking to Marheit, along with the sound of a slip of paper being handed over.

It was undoubtedly some urgent business. Lawrence looked up at the small clouds in the sky and wondered when he would be able to have his own shop.

He soon heard Marheit speak.

"This is definitely addressed to our company, but . . ."

Lawrence looked back over at Marheit, who was looking at him.

"Mr. Lawrence, a bill's come for you."

The names of Lawrence's many trading partners and the debts he owed flashed through his mind.

He tried to think of which among them had an approaching settlement date, but in any case the amount of time he would remain in a given city was uncertain. Even if there'd been a settlement date yesterday, he couldn't think of anyone that would hold a traveling merchant to such a strict time frame.

And who would even know he was here?

"Could I see it, please?" he asked.

Marheit took the bill from his subordinate and brought it to Lawrence.

Lawrence took it and skipped past the standard contractual section, coming to the details at the end.

He thought that if he could see what the bill was for, it might tell him who it was from.

But the items on the bill did not ring any bells.

"Hmm . . ." Lawrence said, cocking his head curiously, but suddenly he sat bolt upright.

Marheit, shocked, tried to say something, but Lawrence ignored him and ran for the door, pushing it open and ignoring the pain in his left arm.

"Um, excuse me —"

"Let me by!" shouted Lawrence, and the shocked employee made way. Lawrence ignored the strange look he received and ran down the hallway before stopping.

"Where's the loading dock?" he demanded.

"Er, follow this hall to the end, turn left, and it'll be —"

"Thanks," said Lawrence shortly, dashing off.

The rather expensive bill crumpled in his hand as Lawrence ran as fast as his strength would allow.

It was the contents of that crumpled bill that had Lawrence in such a state.

The date on the bill was today, and it included items from a Pazzio textile merchant and a fruit seller.

There were two high-quality women's robes with silk sashes, a pair of traveling shoes, a tortoiseshell comb — and a large amount of apples.

In total it all came to a hundred and fifty silver pieces, and the apples in particular were far too numerous for one person to carry.

Despite that, there was no entry on the bill for the use of a horse or cart.

There was an obvious conclusion.

Lawrence arrived at the loading dock.

Mountains of products of every sort were lined up, with everything from goods brought from afar to exports about to leave. The dock overflowed with the horses and the shouts of people — the chaotic scene was just another day at the prosperous Milone Company.

Lawrence scanned the surroundings for what he knew must be there.

The large loading area was filled with horses and carts. Lawrence ran around, even slipping on a clump of scattered hay, before catching a glimpse of his own familiar horse and wagon and approaching it.

The other people working in the loading area looked at him strangely, but Lawrence took no notice of them, fixated on just one thing.

In front of a wagon bed piled high with apples, a small figure held a beautiful piece of fur in her hand, combing it with a tortoiseshell comb.

She wore an obviously expensive robe and a hood pulled low over her head. After a time, she ceased her combing and sighed.

Not turning toward Lawrence, the figure in the seat of the wagon spoke. "I wouldn't wish you to come to the northern forests simply to collect on a debt."

Lawrence couldn't help laughing at her sullen tone.

He approached the seat, and though Holo stubbornly refused to look at him, he extended his right hand.

Finally she glanced at him, and although she soon returned her gaze to the tail in her hands, she reached out to him.

Lawrence took her hand, and she finally relented to a smile.

"I'll return home only after I've paid my debt."

"But of course!"

Holo's hand gripped Lawrence's very, very tightly.

It seemed as though the travels of this strange pair would last a bit longer.

That is to say, the travels of the wolf and the spice.

AFTERWORD

Since I began entering writing contests with prize money involved, I've never been able to stop thinking about winning the grand prize.

Then, I think about using the prize money to buy stocks, increasing my investment, and pretty soon I'm daydreaming about ruling the world with my vast wealth.

Lately I've made enough money that I can order an extra-large bowl of soba from the soba stand without worrying about it.

My name is Isuna Hasekura.

Recently winning the silver medal of the 12th Dengeki Shosetsu Prize is an honor roughly equivalent to winning the moon in the sky. I couldn't believe it. I had three different dreams in which I got a phone call that they'd mixed me up with somebody else.

When I started editing the manuscript, I had two dreams that I'd missed the deadline.

I have no idea how many times I dreamed that I was wealthy enough to rule the world.

In fact, as I write this afterword, I'm wondering even now whether this is a dream or reality.

To the pre-readers, editors, and prize selection committee members that opened the door to this world of dreams, I give my most humble thanks. Also to the people at the prize-acceptance party who raised their voices in support; and most especially to Mitsutaka Yuki-sensei, who gave me a silver wolf accessory in connection with the *Spice and Wolf* title, I want to say thank you so much. The little silver wolf is even now enshrined by my computer.

I must also thank Ju Asakura-sensei for the gorgeous illustrations. They captured my characters perfectly. I hope my thanks are as great as my surprise at seeing them.

To all the people, things, and events responsible for putting me in the position I'm in today: Thank you so much.

It is my intention to put forth every effort to ensure that I never wake from this fleeting dream.

—Isuna Hasekura

THE JOURNEY CONTINUES IN THE MANGA
ADAPTATION OF THE HIT NOVEL SERIES

APRIL 2010

SPICE
&
WOLF

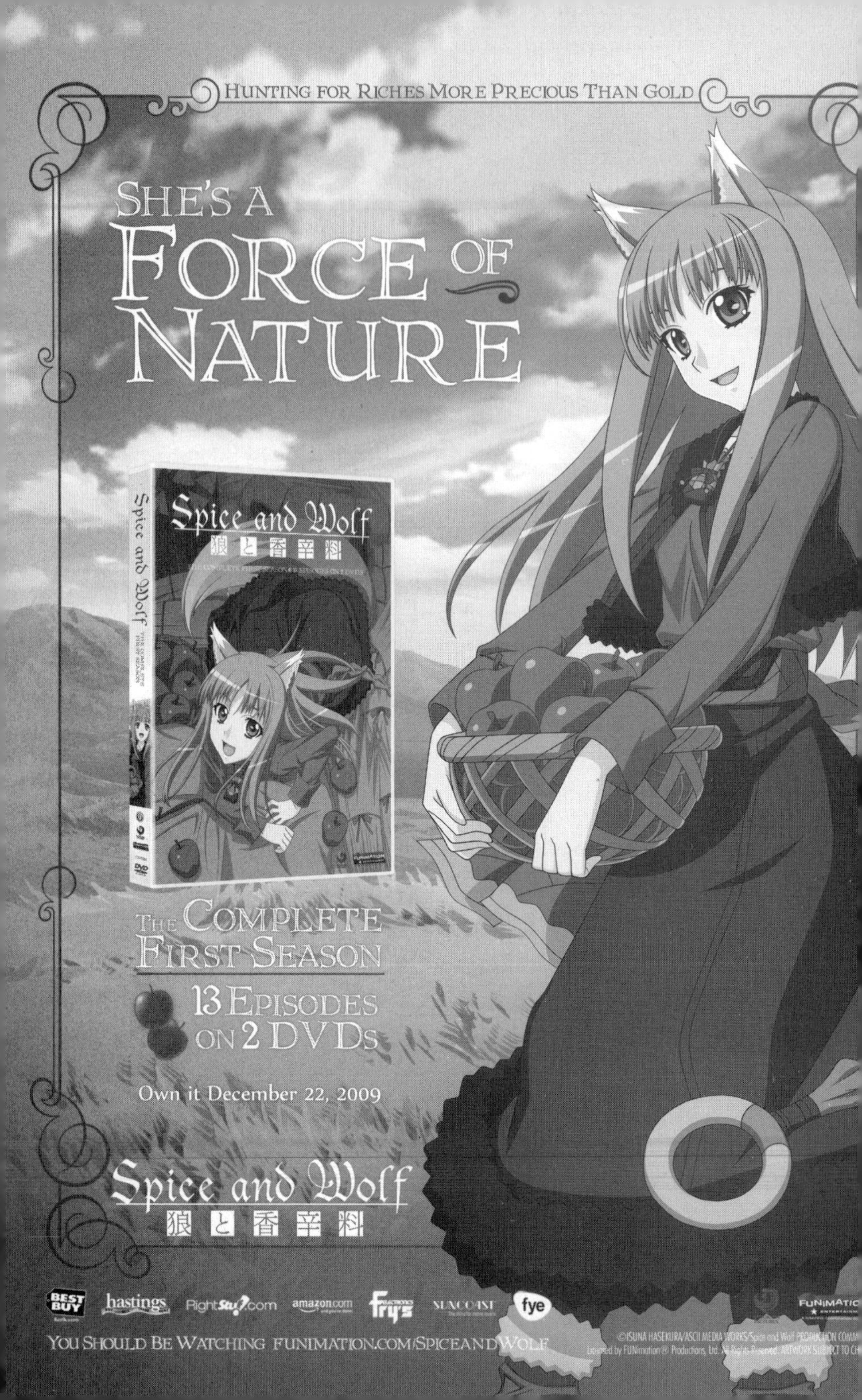
HUNTING FOR RICHES MORE PRECIOUS THAN GOLD
SHE'S A FORCE OF NATURE
Spice and Wolf
狼と香辛料
THE COMPLETE FIRST SEASON
13 EPISODES ON 2 DVDs
Own it December 22, 2009
Spice and Wolf
狼と香辛料
BEST BUY
hastings
RightStuf.com
amazon.com
Fry's
SUNCOAST
fye
FUNIMATION ENTERTAINMENT
YOU SHOULD BE WATCHING FUNIMATION.COM/SPICEANDWOLF
©ISUNA HASEKURA/ASCII MEDIA WORKS/Spice and Wolf PRODUCTION COMM
Licensed by FUNimation® Productions, Ltd. All Rights Reserved. ARTWORK SUBJECT TO CH